*For everyone who believes there are
no restrictions on who you can love.*

A SET OF *Three*

MELODY TYDEN

Chapter One

~**Kimber**~

The cool Vancouver rain dripped from the edges of my umbrella as I huddled beneath it with my cell phone pressed to my ear.

"Please tell me this is the day my life changes," I begged, only half-joking as I glanced around the back alley behind the coffee shop where I worked. My job could be fun at times and it paid the bills, but I definitely didn't intend to be doing it for the rest of my life.

My dreams had always been a lot bigger, just like everything else about me.

On the other end of the phone, my agent had the news I'd been waiting for, and if the decision went my way, my life really might be about to change. Last week, I had my third callback for the lead on a new TV series. The *lead*. I had worked as an extra more times than I could count, and more recently, I had even landed a few speaking roles, but they were always as the best friend, the funny, fat sidekick to the insecure yet beautiful - and stick-thin - heroine.

For this show, however, the director wanted someone with a more 'diverse' look to play the female lead, someone more of the viewers could relate to. Someone just like me, I hoped.

"The feedback is really positive," Shandal assured me, trying to boost my spirits as she always did. Unfortunately, because she always did, I heard the 'but' coming before she even said it. "But they've offered the role to someone else."

Oh, damn it. Damn it, damn it, damn it. The words hit me like a punch to the gut, robbing me of breath as all the hope I'd been carrying around for weeks evaporated into thin air, leaving my stomach feeling like a lead weight.

I really thought the big break I'd been working towards had finally arrived. Not getting the part wasn't the end of the world, but it stung anyway, like a kick in the teeth. Tears gathered in the corners of my eyes, but I quickly blinked them away.

"Oh well, next time!" I said out loud cheerily, pushing down my disappointment as I always did. People often told me that they liked how I always saw the bright side of things... or at least the actress in me always pretended I did, even when I felt the opposite inside.

Fake it till you make it: that was my motto. The world had enough bitterness already without me adding to it.

Shandal's sigh of relief echoed through the phone. Most actors took the news a lot more personally. "That's the spirit, Kim. The next one will be yours, for sure."

"For sure," I repeated, though I knew we were both fooling ourselves. Roles like this for someone who looked like me came around less often than Halley's Comet. Although I saw nothing wrong with the way I looked, TV producers generally had a different opinion. "Okay, well, I better get back to work. I'll talk to you later."

As soon as I hung up, I turned my phone camera on and put it in selfie mode to check my makeup, ensuring no evidence of my watery eyes remained before I headed back inside. Giving the wet umbrella one last shake out the back door, I headed back into the shop.

The scent of coffee and sugar assaulted my nose, as usual, and though I loved the smells, the idea that I'd be smelling them every day for a while longer didn't help matters.

"So?" the man behind the counter asked as I joined him again. Rocco owned the coffee shop and was a serious contender for the sweetest man alive. He had also declared himself my biggest fan, and he might be my only genuine one. "Are you going to be a star?"

"Of course I am," I replied and his eyes lit up. "Just... not quite yet."

"Ah, cazzo, I'm sorry, bella." He always swore in Italian, thinking it sounded less crude, and his big, strong arms wrapped around me for a moment before he took a step back and gave me a critical look. "Why are you messing with me like that? You know my heart can't take it."

Rocco always went on about his heart, though he hadn't even hit fifty yet. I figured his fixation stemmed from the fact that aside from working at the coffee shop, he spent most of his time looking after his aging, hypochondriac mother who spoke only Italian and had been on the verge of death for nearly 40 years, ever since Rocco's father had run off with someone. If she had always been as depressing to be around as she seemed to be now, I couldn't entirely blame the man for leaving.

"I'm sorry, Rocky," I apologized, using the nickname I'd given him when he accidentally socked me in the eye on one of my first days here, before we learned each other's rhythms. I'd gone to an audition that week with a black eye and, unsurprisingly, I didn't get that part either. "I was just joking."

"I like your jokes, but it's okay to be a bit sad too. I know you wanted this."

His kindness threatened to bring the tears back to my eyes. Rejection, I could deal with; compassion was harder to take. "Well, we can't always get everything we want, right?"

"Maybe," he agreed reluctantly, as if it pained him to admit it. "But speaking of things you want..."

He gestured with his head towards the front door where my favourite customer had just entered, and the butterflies in my stomach fluttered to life as they always did whenever I laid eyes on him.

If someone ever made a physical embodiment of my dream man, they couldn't do a lot better than Henry Zhang. Although I found him gorgeous, his good looks were just the tip of the iceberg. He worked as an environmental lawyer just down the street, which demonstrated an inspirational depth of compassion about the planet. Working as a lawyer also meant he dressed impeccably in a suit and tie most of the time, a look which, on him, made my knees weak. Most of the men around here with high-powered jobs preferred to go to the Starbucks across the street while Rocco's shop attracted more of the artist and free-spirit crowd. Henry bucked that trend by always coming to us instead. Since the first time he appeared, nearly six months ago, he hardly let a day go by without stopping in.

Rocco liked to tell me Henry came here for me, but I knew an exaggeration when I heard one. While Henry always had a smile and a kind word for me, seeming to enjoy our conversations, he'd never made any indication that he wanted anything more than the casual friendship we'd struck up.

Over our small talk whenever he came in, I'd learned a few things about him. He was 28, which made him a few years older than me. Born in China, he moved to Vancouver with his parents a few years later. Any accent he might have had originally had long since vanished. I also knew that he lived somewhere nearby, since he came in on his days off sometimes too, and that he spent a lot of time at the gym in his building.

Okay, he'd never actually told me that last part. I made the assumption based on the way his dress shirt stretched across his chest, but it certainly seemed likely. His obviously fit body only accented his jet-black hair, his chiselled cheekbones and his dark brown eyes.

Men who looked like him just didn't find women who looked like me attractive, not in the way I wanted him to, so despite Henry's warmth and friendliness, Rocco's attempts to build my hopes up fell on deaf ears. Keeping my expectations rooted in reality seemed safer, but even so, there was no harm in looking and getting a little turned on by the view.

"It's wet today, eh?" Henry asked as he came up to the counter, and for just a moment, I thought he somehow heard my thoughts and that his comment referred to the state of my underwear. My mouth flapped open uselessly until I remembered the rain outside. Of course.

"Oh. Yeah, sure is." I smiled a little too brightly as I tried to slow my pounding heart. "The usual for you today?"

"Yes, please."

Taking a deep breath to ground myself, I set about making his espresso which he always drank right there at the counter before heading to his office. Rocco had set up his coffee shop to resemble a traditional Italian bar as much as possible, where people often just stopped in for a quick shot of caffeine before going about their day.

"Something smells fantastic." Henry inhaled deeply, the sound making my stomach do somersaults all over again as I imagined him sniffing me that way. I could almost feel his breath against my neck in my imagination. "Did you bake anything special this morning, Kimber?"

Besides acting, baking was my next love and the main reason Rocco had hired me. Each morning, he and I took turns working in the kitchen to create the cookies and cakes that we sold alongside our coffee.

"It's a salted caramel pecan pie. Would you like some?"

Henry's hand went to his incredibly trim stomach. "God, I would love to, but Nick would kill me. He already caught me with chocolate on my face from the last time I snuck a treat."

Pride ran through me at the thought that my chocolate brownies had made that much of an impression. "Nick?" I repeated curiously as I put the espresso cup on a plate and brought it over to the counter. "Is that your boss?"

For some reason, that made him laugh. "He likes to think so, but no. He's my boyfriend."

The plate hit the counter hard as it slipped from my hand, the cup clattering noisily against its saucer. The liquid inside sloshed dangerously close to the rim of the cup, but thankfully stayed inside.

Henry instinctively reached out a hand to steady me. "Whoa, you okay?"

"Of course." I gave him my best sunny smile. "Butterfingers today, sorry. I can get you a new one."

"That's not necessary, this one's fine," he assured me. "Are you sure you're alright though? You look a little pale."

Of course I looked pale, but I called upon the actress in me as I turned up the wattage on my smile even more. "I'll tell you what. I'll give you two pieces of pie, on me, and you can take one home for Nick too. If he doesn't like it, I promise not to tempt you ever again."

Henry laughed, relaxing as he picked up his cup. "That sounds like a deal. I bet once he's had a taste, he'll be just as hooked as I am."

Luckily, someone else came to the counter, eliminating the need for any further small talk as I boxed up Henry's pie and went to take the newcomer's order instead. But even as I smiled and talked to the other customer, my thoughts were still with Henry.

Of *course* he was gay. Someone that good-looking but still kind and interested in talking to me? It made way more sense than any other scenario.

I had said I wouldn't get my hopes up, but the disappointment that filled my whole body, from head to toe, told me that, whether I realized it or not, I had been harbouring at least some small hope of something more with Henry.

It seemed life had decided to crush all my dreams today, one by one. Though it had barely begun, the end of the day could not come fast enough.

~Henry~

The smile remained on my face all the way to my desk. Talking to Kimber at the coffee shop always put me in a good mood and today was no exception. In fact, today might have even made me happier than usual because, after what happened when I mentioned Nick this morning, my theory that Kimber's interest in me extended beyond a simple customer/employee relationship now seemed a lot more plausible.

Getting from that point to where I hoped we might end up still seemed nearly impossible, but at least I'd crossed the starting line.

I never set out to keep my relationship status from her in the first place, it just never seemed to come up in conversation. I knew she didn't have a boyfriend only because Rocco, the owner of the coffee shop, had made a point of mentioning her single status in front of me a couple of times. His attempts at being subtle left a lot to be desired, and provided my first clue that Kimber might have some kind of feelings for me.

Up until then, I really hadn't been sure. Her friendly and open manner with me seemed pretty similar to how she treated everyone else. Several times, I stood at the counter, drinking my coffee and admiring the easy way she made small talk with each and every person who came in, always looking like she'd rather be having that conversation than doing anything else in the world.

Her warm smile and heartfelt laugh were infectious. Time after time, I watched people walk in with a scowl on their face and leave with a grin.

She was an actress, of course — I knew that about her too — but that didn't fully explain it. More than that, it felt like she genuinely liked other people and took an interest in them. She seemed to exist fully in the present, inhabiting each moment with a passion that exhilarated me. Whenever worry or stress or pressure overwhelmed me, just a few minutes in her company made me forget all about it.

Those qualities were almost the inverse of my own more cautious, introverted approach to life, and maybe that explained why I found her so appealing.

So today, I tested the waters a bit further by mentioning Nick as casually as possible. Would she look disappointed when she found out I had a partner already, or would it make no difference to her at all?

The fact that she nearly dropped my espresso seemed like a pretty good indication that it did mean something to her. Step one of my plan had been accomplished, but how we moved on to the next step, I had no idea.

I sent Nick a text as I sat down and got myself settled: *Picked you up some pie from Rocco's coffee shop.*

My phone chimed almost instantly with his reply. During business hours, his phone functioned as another appendage on his body. Because of the time difference between us on the west coast and the main stock markets in the east, he'd already been at work for three hours even though my day had just begun.

Did you pick up anything else?

I rolled my eyes even though he couldn't see it. *We can talk about it later.*

Putting my phone away, I got started on my inbox, but even as I worked, my mind kept wandering back to Kimber's pretty smile and the conversation Nick and I had over the weekend.

We'd been lying in bed in the dark, half-asleep when Nick rolled over and flipped his bedside lamp on. The sudden brightness made me wince and I turned my head away from him. "What are you doing?"

A moment's silence followed my question, which made me more curious. Catching Nick at a loss for words rarely happened.

"What is it?" I squinted my eyes open, trying to make out the expression on his face.

When he did finally speak, an uncharacteristic hesitation filled his voice. "Do you ever miss having sex with a woman?"

That woke me right up, my eyes popping fully open in surprise. "What?"

He shrugged as he pulled himself up to sitting and I quickly followed his lead. We were both still naked from earlier, and we usually slept naked in the big king-sized bed we shared ever since I moved into his downtown condo six months ago. His huge and beautiful home made an extremely welcome change from the house I had still been sharing with my parents until then.

"Are you unhappy with our sex life?" I asked, trying to figure out what brought this on. I had no complaints and I hadn't thought he did either. He certainly hadn't seemed to ten minutes ago.

"Of course not." He leaned forward and kissed me to reassure me, the rough stubble on his chin rubbing against my face. In the soft light of the lamp, his bright blue eyes looked darker and softer than usual as he smiled down at me, and the light around his short blond hair almost resembled a halo. "I love you, Henry. It's not about that."

"Then what is it about?" His words had thrown me off completely. He'd never said anything like this before.

"It's just... seeing Mark and Jillian earlier got me thinking, that's all." Mark and Jillian were newly married friends of ours who were also expecting their first baby. We'd had them over for dinner that night.

"You were thinking about Jillian?" With each sentence, this conversation grew more and more confusing, not to mention unnerving.

"No, not her specifically, but just how she's so soft and curvy, and her breasts are huge right now, how could you not look at them? And... fuck, this isn't coming out right."

He ran his hand down his face while I took a deep breath. Nick rarely tried to open up to me like that. Talking about his feelings went against his natural instincts, and me jumping to conclusions wouldn't encourage him to do it again, so I did my best to take a step back. "No, it's okay. You just took me by surprise, but I'm listening and I'm not upset. You miss being with a woman?"

We had both dated women before we got together. He had been with other men before me, but my experience had only been straight until we met. I guess that made us both bisexual, but we never really talked about it in those terms. We just loved who we loved, regardless of gender.

How to explain that concept to my very traditional Chinese parents, I hadn't quite figured out yet. When I told them Nick had invited me to move in with him, they assumed I meant as a roommate and I'd never bothered to correct them. Things were good between Nick and I but there had been no talk of any kind of permanent commitment yet. I figured once we got to that point, if we did, I would decide what to tell my parents then.

"It's just different," he tried to explain. "You're a lot of incredible things, Henry, but soft and curvy aren't on that list."

I poked him in his own firm abs. "You're one to talk."

He and I met while out jogging along the Stanley Park seawall last fall. We were running in opposite directions and stopped at the same spot to watch a couple of harbour seals that had swum close to the park. We both noticed each other and exchanged a few words, but nothing happened beyond that. He went his way and I went mine. He crossed my mind a few times over the course of the week: his intelligent blue eyes and his smile, but especially, to be completely honest, his broad shoulders and athletic body. I'd found men attractive in the past but had never acted on it before, and I'd never wanted to quite as badly as I did then.

What could I do about it though? I didn't even know his name, and even if I did, how could I know if he liked men at all, or me in particular? Luckily for me, the next Saturday, I went back at the same time, hoping I might run into him again, and to my delight, he had done the same. We chatted a bit more and when he found out I worked quite close to the building where he lived, he invited me to come over and use the gym on my lunch break. When I showed up, I found him already there working out too, and the rest fell into place from there.

"What are you suggesting?" I asked him now, pulling the blankets tighter against me. From what I knew of Nick, he wouldn't bring something like this up unless he had a plan.

"I don't want to do anything without you," he assured me. "It's not about replacing anything we have, just enhancing it a bit. I thought maybe we could try including a woman in bed sometime, if you're interested."

From the way my cock twitched beneath the blanket at the thought, I obviously had some interest, but I had some concerns too. "You know I don't like the idea of having sex with someone I don't know."

Sex was a very emotional thing for me. I had to feel a real connection with the person I slept with, which meant that my own experience had been a lot more limited than Nick's. My insistence on waiting to go to bed together when we first met had frustrated him, but when it finally happened, we agreed the wait had been worth it.

"Have you done this before?" I asked him. "A threesome, I mean?"

He nodded without hesitation. We were always completely honest with each other about things like this. "I have and the sex was really good. There are some things you can do as a threesome that we just can't on our own. And of course it would have to be someone you know and like, that's a given."

He really had given this some thought, so I asked the obvious follow-up question: "Do you have someone in mind?"

The name of one of our mutual friends rolled off his lips, and I immediately shook my head. "No, I don't think of her like that. It would be awkward."

He made a couple of other suggestions which I shot down almost as fast. Being difficult or negative on purpose wasn't my intention, but having another person with us would be strange enough in the first place. Anyone we approached would have to be someone I had complete trust in and comfort with.

"Well, who would you suggest?" he finally asked when he'd exhausted his list of options. "There has to be someone who's caught your eye since we've been together. I know you're not blind and I don't expect you to be."

One woman immediately sprang to mind, one who made me feel comfortable and happy since the first time I met her six months ago, but I had no idea if she thought about me in a physical way at all. And if she did, would something like this interest her? And if it did, would Nick find her attractive too? In my eyes, she was gorgeous, but I understood some people might find her weight a turn-off since society's standard definition of beauty tended to put a lot of focus on being thinner. How would Nick feel about it? There were a lot of variables involved.

"Who is it?" Apparently, my hesitation had given away the fact that I did, in fact, have someone in mind, and Nick pressed me for a reply.

I had to be honest with him, just like he'd been with me. "You remember me telling you about the sweet girl at the coffee shop? The incredible baker with the amazing smile?"

His own smile told me he did remember, which made sense. I had mentioned her more than once. "Do you think she'd be interested?"

Honestly, I had no idea. How on earth would you ask someone that?

Following that discussion, I came up with a plan to get my questions answered one-by-one. Step one, I had accomplished today: find out if Kimber had any interest in me, and thankfully, the answer to that seemed to be yes. I'd already laid the groundwork for step two at the same time by letting her know I had a boyfriend. Now I just needed to figure out how the hell to find out if the idea of sleeping with two men at the same time appealed to her at all.

Right now, I didn't have a clue where to start.

Chapter Two

~**Kimber**~

By the time 4:30 came that afternoon, the rain had only gotten worse. Rocco peered out the front window at the dreary, dark sky and shivered. "You should take a taxi home, bella."

Stretching my budget to cover taxi rides would be a challenge. "It's not that far," I said, though we both recognized my words as a lie.

I had lucked out with finding the tiny studio apartment close to Stanley Park. It belonged to a sweet woman in her 60s who had lived there as a young, single woman and had been renting it out ever since. As a result of the tenancy never changing hands, she kept the rent incredibly cheap for the area, but it would take me half an hour to walk there from the downtown coffee shop.

I tried to play off the distance now with a different excuse. "Besides, I'm trying to exercise more."

Rocco waved that comment away with a swish of his hand. "Don't let those casting directors get into your head, Kimber. You're perfect just as you are."

Honestly, most days I would agree with him. I'd long ago given up the idea that I would ever look like the size zero actresses I often ended up at auditions with, and most of the time being overweight took a backseat to the other worries in my life. I had no concerns about my health and I got a decent amount of exercise; I just liked to eat too. Maybe genetics were a factor since my parents were both overweight, but if I really wanted to lose weight, I knew how to do it. I just didn't see why I should have to in order to make other people happy.

My own happiness had little to do with my dress size. Being skinnier wouldn't have made Henry straight anyway.

"I can lend you the money if you need it."

Rocco's well-meaning offer made me wince. I already owed him enough. "I think it's letting up," I lied again as I looked out at the grey sky. "I'll see you tomorrow, Rocky."

Before he could protest any further, I headed out the door, popping my umbrella up as I joined the other people foolhardy or broke enough to be wandering around the drenched streets.

A city bus route made the trip down the street from the coffee shop to my apartment, but I only had enough to pay for one ride a day. Since the ride in the morning covered the uphill climb, and it had been raining this morning too, I'd already used my fare for today. At least the walk home would be downhill.

Just like my career path. That uncharacteristically morose thought spun around my head as I crossed the street at the lights.

Speaking of the bus, it came up behind me now, splashing through a large puddle just ahead of me and spraying water up onto the sidewalk. If I had been just a few feet further ahead, I would have been drenched.

Maybe my luck had finally turned, I thought as I continued to walk forward, but any temporary positive vibes I might have been feeling quickly disappeared as another car followed behind the bus, hitting the same puddle.

If someone had thrown a bucket of water on me, I couldn't have been any more drenched. Water dripped from my head to my toes, and since it came from the side, the umbrella offered no protection at all. Ice cold shock ran through me as I looked down at my sopping wet clothes.

Perfect. *Abso-fucking-lutely perfect.* Just what I needed today of all days.

Any other day I would have laughed about it. I must look ridiculous with my hair plastered to my head, my mascara running, and dirty water dripping off every inch of me.

But after today, after the disappointment of not getting the job and then finding out that Henry was already taken, heading back on foot to my apartment that I could barely afford, all by myself, no matter how hard I looked, I couldn't see the bright side.

All my disappointment and frustration and now the chill from the water too mixed together and built up inside me until I burst into tears right there in the middle of the street, in front of anyone who might happen to pass by.

Was this my rock bottom? It kind of felt that way. At this moment, this day couldn't get any worse.

"Kimber?"

Oh, no. No, no, no.

I just had to tempt fate, and now the universe answered me back: you want to see worse? Here's how it gets worse.

Slowly, I turned to see Henry standing beneath his umbrella, looking as handsome and put together as always while I stood there like some kind of drowned rat, my eyes watering and my nose runny.

That settled it: I had to quit my job and move. Another city, or maybe another country at this point. Anything was preferable to having to face him again after this.

He must have seen me get splashed and come over to help. A guy like him would do exactly that.

"Hey," I managed to say, my voice wobbling a little despite all my best efforts to keep it steady. The look of concern and dismay on his face threatened to break my last thread of composure, so I tried, as always, to lighten the mood. "I heard they might be doing a remake of Titanic, so I thought I'd practice getting in character."

He smiled, getting my joke, but worry still filled his eyes. "How far is your apartment? You can't walk home like that."

"I can't really get in a car either," I pointed out, my voice getting stronger as I called on all my years of acting training to bring the smile back to my face. "Unless you're secretly Superman and can fly me home, I think I'm going on foot. Have a good night."

I turned to go, but he immediately came up beside me. "Wait, hold on. My place is just around the corner. Why don't you come and get dry there?"

Any other day, I would have been over the moon at the idea of going to Henry's apartment, but after finding out about his boyfriend earlier, not to mention my physical state, I really just wanted to go home and sink into a warm bath and never, ever get out.

"That's really kind of you, but it's okay. It's not too far."

When I tried to move forward again, Henry stepped directly in front of me. "How far is 'not too far'?"

"Denman," I muttered truthfully under my breath, giving him the name of the closest major street to my apartment, and Henry immediately frowned.

"Kimber, that's too far. Please, come with me. I promise I'm not a psychopath. It's perfectly safe."

That hadn't even crossed my mind, and I gave him a suspicious look. "That's just what a psychopath would say."

Henry laughed, showing off his perfect teeth and the adorable dimple on one cheek that I may have noticed once or twice before. "It's not me you need to be worried about," he assured me, gently taking hold of my arm and steering me in the opposite direction. "Nick's the grumpy one, especially if you wake him from his nap."

"His nap?" I repeated. How old was this boyfriend of his?

"He calls it a power nap," he explained, trying to distract me as we turned the corner towards his building. "He has to get up really early for work so he's usually sleeping when I get home. But in another half-hour, he'll get his second wind and then we won't be able to keep up with him."

The easy, casual way he referred to me and him as 'we' sent a pang through my heart, weakening my resistance even further. It looked like we were heading to Henry and Nick's apartment now, whether I wanted to or not. Why not get a glimpse of life beyond my reach? This day seemed utterly determined to kick me while I was down.

Henry's building couldn't be further from the dated, slightly run-down one I lived in, and I felt awful as I dripped water across the pristine carpet from the front door to the elevator. Henry greeted the security guard casually, as though he returned home with a soaking wet, bedraggled, frumpy woman every day of the week. When the elevator arrived, he pressed the button for the 22nd floor, the top one, using his fingerprint to gain access.

"This is all pretty fancy," I remarked, partly to simply cover the sound of the dripping water on the elevator floor.

"I know," Henry agreed with a conspiratorial grin. "Trust me, I'm still getting used to it too, but there are some perks, like having a dryer in the apartment. We'll get you out of those wet things and I'll have them dry for you in no time."

A shiver went through me at the thought of Henry getting me out of my clothes that had nothing to do with the damp or cold, and I had to shake my head at myself. Obviously, he didn't mean that the way it sounded.

He quickly clarified exactly what he meant as we arrived at his floor and he let me into the gorgeous, huge condo that took up half the floor. I'd never seen an apartment this big and I couldn't begin to imagine what it cost.

"Come on, the bathroom's through here," Henry directed me, still not seeming bothered as I dripped along the hardwood floors leading down the hall to the beautiful bathroom with a massive bathtub and walk-in shower. Once inside, he opened one of the many cupboards and pulled out an empty rubber basket. "Put your clothes in here once you've got them off and leave them outside the door. I'll throw them in the dryer while you have a shower or a bath and get warmed up."

Everything he did radiated kindness and thoughtfulness, to the point that my eyes started to water again. I couldn't remember the last time I'd been so close to tears so many times in one day.

"I'll just shower quickly and get out of your hair," I suggested, frowning as I took a look at all the dials and levers in the shower. That might be easier said than done.

"There's no rush," Henry assured me. "The dryer's going to take about half an hour, so you might as well relax. We all need a breather sometimes and you're not in the way at all. I've got no other plans."

In that case, a bath did sound heavenly, especially in the huge tub in front of me. "Thanks, Henry. I really appreciate this."

"Anytime." He gave me a warm smile before leaving me alone to get undressed.

Well, it might not be the way I hoped it would happen, but as I peeled my clothes off, I realized that, if nothing else, I would soon be naked in Henry Zhang's apartment.

If someone had told me this morning that my day would bring me here, I would never have believed them.

~Henry~

My heart thumped as I carried the bucket with Kimber's soaked clothes to the laundry room. This had to be some kind of sign. I had been on my way home from work, debating whether I should stop back in at the coffee shop to try to talk to Kimber again, when I saw the car splash into the puddle and drench the person standing on the sidewalk.

Naturally, I hurried over to see if I could help, but only when I reached her did I realize that the person in question was the very woman I had just been thinking about.

Or at least, she looked a lot like her. When Kimber turned to face me, the light had gone from her eyes, missing that liveliness that always drew me to her, like the water had somehow extinguished it when it washed over her. Her expression held a sadness and a vulnerability that I'd never seen there before, and I felt an almost overwhelming urge to do whatever I could to make things better for her.

So I invited her back here. I would have done it for anyone. No one deserved to be left outside, wet and cold like that.

At least, I tried to tell myself that as I squeezed the water out of her things and placed them into the dryer. But when I got to her bra, bright and colourful just like her, my heart beat even faster and I had to be honest with myself and acknowledge my mixed motivations.

Perhaps with her here, a natural opportunity would arise whereby I could find out what she felt about the proposition that Nick and I had for her. It seemed far more likely to come up casually here in my apartment than with her behind the counter of the coffee shop.

"You know, if you're thinking about trying drag, that's really not the right size for you."

Nick's voice made me jump as he appeared in the doorway of the laundry room, dressed only in his pajama pants, his hair still tousled from his nap. The sight of him set my heart racing, as always, and from his teasing tone, I could tell he was in a good mood.

"It's not for me," I quickly explained, tossing the bra into the dryer with the rest of Kimber's clothes. "We've got a guest."

Nick's eyebrows raised in surprise. "A naked guest? Who fits this?" He reached in and pulled the bra back out, grabbing hold of the tag and reading the size out loud: "44DD."

He whistled as I snatched it back from him defensively. "She's a little on the bigger side."

"Apparently." He said the word matter-of-factly, still curious rather than derisive.

I went to put the bra back in the dryer once more, but Nick took it from me again, shaking his head.

"You don't put a bra in a dryer. I thought you dated women before." He didn't seem to be kidding as he took it and hung it from the drying rack instead.

"I dated them, but I never did their laundry." Although I tried to play the whole thing off, Nick knew me better than that.

"So why are you doing it now? And why is there a river in the entry-way?"

I shut the dryer door and turned it on before stepping out of the room. "Sorry about that. I'll mop it up now."

"Wait, Henry." Nick followed after me as I went to the supply closet and grabbed the cleaning supplies. "Why are you so flustered? What's going on? Whose bra is that?"

Taking a deep breath, I stopped and turned to face him. I might as well tell him everything since he would find out sometime within the next half hour anyway. "It belongs to Kimber, the woman from the coffee shop."

This time his eyebrows nearly shot through the roof. "She's here? Naked?"

He quickly looked around as if she might be hiding just out of sight, and I had to try not to laugh at his enthusiasm. "Yes to both, but not for the reason you're hoping. She got sprayed by a car in the rain and I brought her here to dry off. She's having a bath now while I dry her clothes."

With the basic explanation out of the way, I turned my attention to the trail of water between the front door and the bathroom.

"So you still haven't talked to her about us," Nick guessed, leaning against the wall as he watched me work.

I shook my head. "No, not yet, but maybe this is better. We could ask her to stay for dinner and just get to know her without making it sexual right away."

"It sounds like a date," he pointed out, sounding a little amused at the idea.

"Kind of," I admitted. "But people do usually date before they sleep together. And if you don't like her, there's no point in pursuing anything. I think it makes sense all around."

No disagreement came from Nick, but he did watch me closely as I finished wiping up the water from the floor. "It sounds like you're thinking about more than just one night."

I honestly had no idea what I thought. I'd never done anything like this before, but now that he'd said it, I had to admit it made sense. "Well, if we all like it, why not? It's a lot of work to get someone on board just for one night."

I wrung the mop out into the bucket and carried it into the kitchen where I had already put my bag down earlier. Nick headed straight for my bag now, rooting around in it while I emptied the bucket.

"What are you looking for?" I asked curiously.

"You said you had pie," he reminded me, and I had to laugh. I hadn't expected him to remember that, especially with everything else going on.

"Right. It's already in the fridge."

By the time I put all the cleaning supplies away and checked on the dryer, Nick had the two pieces of pie out on the kitchen island, with only one fork in his hand.

"Are you planning on eating them both?" I teased him. He knew I didn't mean it since he rarely indulged in desserts. One or two bites were his limit.

"I thought we could feed each other," he teased me right back, sinking the fork into the sinful-looking pie. "Open up."

I loved when these rare playful moods of his came around, so I did as he requested, standing in front of him with my mouth open. As soon as the salty caramel topping and the buttery pastry hit my tongue, I couldn't help groaning in pleasure. "Damn, that's good."

Nick's lips twitched as he tried to figure out if my reaction was an exaggeration. "Let me try."

He handed me the fork, expecting me to feed him now, and I grinned as I cut off a particularly big piece. "Here you go."

His eyes widened as his lips closed around the fork. "Holy shit."

"I told you," I reminded him with a laugh as his eyes rolled back in his head dramatically. "It's that good."

"Inviting this woman into our lives is a bad idea then," he said as he took the fork back and put another piece of the pie into his own mouth.

"Hey, leave some for me!"

We were both laughing as I reached for the fork. It had been a while since we'd been silly like this together. It made a nice change. Nick kept hold of the fork, but he conceded defeat anyway. "Alright, I can share. Here."

He fed me another piece, watching appreciatively as I savoured it.

"We should put this away for now," he suggested, and I had to agree. Tonight would already be a test of nerves for me and Nick had an abundance of energy too, for whatever reason. A ton of sugar wouldn't help matters.

Nick put the pie back in the fridge before coming back over to me, still smiling as he looked me up and down.

"What?" I knew that look, and it meant the best kind of trouble.

"You've got some caramel on your face," he said, gesturing towards my mouth.

"Where?" I wiped my mouth quickly with the back of my hand. "Did I get it?"

"Nope." His smile widened as he stepped closer. "Right here."

His tongue swept across my lips before I realized what he meant to do, and a shot of desire ran through me, my body reacting to him like it always did. His hand held the back of my head tight as he kissed me harder, his touch firm and demanding.

"Henry? Could I get... oh!"

I sprang back from Nick at the sound of Kimber's voice, but not fast enough. From the look on her face when I turned to see her standing in the kitchen door, she'd obviously seen us.

She had on one of the bathrobes from the bathroom, a towel wrapped around her long, dark hair. Though it covered her top half completely, the robe only came to the middle of her thighs, giving us both a good look at her bare legs.

"I'm sorry, I wanted... I just...where are my clothes?"

With perfect timing, the dryer beeped loudly, signalling the end of its cycle.

"Let me go and grab them," Nick offered, walking over towards her. "I'm Nick. It's nice to meet you, Kimber."

Kimber's eyes darted between me and the man in front of her as she shook his outstretched hand. "Nice to meet you too. I'm sorry for showing up uninvited. Your apartment is beautiful."

"You weren't uninvited," he disagreed. "Henry invited you. What's mine is his, and vice versa."

As he left the room, he shot me a wink behind Kimber's back, and I had to struggle to refrain from rolling my eyes again. Nick had very little filter at the best of times, and suddenly, asking Kimber to stay for dinner seemed like a potential minefield. However, as I noticed the blush on her cheeks, my hope began to rise. I'd already established her interest in me, so if she found Nick attractive too, that would be another step in the right direction.

Maybe this had a chance of working out after all.

~Kimber~

My heart had never beat so fast in my entire life. In the bathtub, I had actually managed to relax a little bit, to the point that I could almost forget what a crappy day it had been. The huge soaker tub resembled a swimming pool more than it did the tiny tub in my apartment that I could barely fit into.

Just as I leaned back with my eyes closed, I heard voices out in the hallway and my eyes immediately popped open again. One of the voices belonged to Henry, I would recognize it anywhere, and another one answered him, one even deeper than Henry's voice. The door muffled the sound too much for me to hear what they were saying, but just the timbre of their voices as they spoke to each other was soothing and more than a little sexy.

I must really be starved for male companionship for some reason. My last date hadn't been *that* long ago. Just a couple of weeks... maybe a month... wait, how long had it been since Valentine's Day? I groaned out loud as I did the calculation in my head and realized just how long it had been. This might be the longest dry spell of my life, and if I measured by the last time I had sex, the numbers were even higher. No wonder distorted voices through a bathroom door were turning me on.

Shaking my head at myself, I got out of the tub and dried off with one of the huge, fluffy towels from the closet. It hadn't quite been half an hour yet, but I opened the door and peered outside anyway. My clothes were nowhere in sight, and neither were Henry or Nick. Closing the door again, I looked around, trying to decide what to do next. A couple of robes hung on the back of the door which I hoped would be okay for me to use. On most people, the robe probably went to their knees, but since it needed to stretch across my body more than most, the bottom rode up on me, all the way up to the middle of my thigh when I pulled the belt tight. Wrapping my hair up in the towel, I went in search of Henry and my clothing.

Getting lost in the huge apartment would have been easy, but I thought I heard voices coming from a room to the left of the entrance, so I headed that way and arrived just in time to see Henry and the man who must be Nick with their lips locked together in a kiss that looked far more passionate than any I had *ever* taken part in.

My initial vision of Nick as an old man couldn't have been more wrong. Young and toned, his chest bare and his hand holding the back of Henry's head firmly as their bodies pressed together, watching them together sent a shot of pure desire and longing through me.

Seeing these two breathtakingly handsome men showing their attraction to each other so unabashedly might have been the sexiest thing I had ever seen.

Unfortunately, my big mouth ruined it because I had started talking before I saw them, so as soon as they heard me, they broke apart. Henry looked a little embarrassed, his cheeks turning adorably pink, but Nick, on the other hand, appeared completely unbothered as he shot me a smile.

He came right over to me, wearing only a thin pair of cotton pants, and I swallowed hard as I tried to maintain my composure. Normally, I preferred men who were a little less sure of themselves, having been around far too many arrogant actors in my time who thought they were God's gift to the world, but as Nick stared down at me, his gaze firm but not condescending, my body reacted against my will. I couldn't help imagining what it would be like for him to kiss me the way he'd just kissed Henry, a little roughly, a little dominating, but with real affection too.

Of course, those thoughts wouldn't be anywhere in his head, not with me standing here with my hair wrapped in a towel and no makeup on my face. I could hardly have made a worse first impression.

He went to get my clothes and I turned back to Henry, hoping I didn't look nearly as flustered as I felt. Uncertainty clouded his expression, though whether it stemmed from me catching them making out or my current state of undress, I couldn't be sure.

And as much as I liked the idea of Nick kissing me, I still liked the idea of kissing Henry too. Part of me wanted to go over to him right now and ease his discomfort by kissing him softly and sweetly.

What the hell? I had never been this desperate before, so needy that I blatantly fantasized about two different men who were clearly into each other and not me.

"Your bathtub is amazing," I blurted out, seizing on the first thing that came into my head that bore no relation to our current situation. "If that remake of Titanic ever gets off the ground, they could film it in there."

Henry's shoulders relaxed as he followed my lead in changing the subject. "I don't know if we'd fit a whole film crew in there, but it's pretty big. There's a hot tub down in the gym too. If you'd like to use it sometime, I could get you a guest pass."

So he *did* spend time in his building's gym. I knew it. "How long have you lived here?"

"Six months," he replied. "It's Nick's place, he's been here a few years. I moved in back in November."

I gave an impressed whistle as I took in the fully fitted out kitchen for the first time, its gleaming countertops and stainless steel appliances making it better equipped than the kitchen in Rocco's shop. I could create some real baking masterpieces in here. "He lived here on his own? How loaded is this guy?"

"Very." Nick himself answered my question, returning with my laundry just in time to hear me ask it, and I kicked myself internally. *Nice, Kimber.* Really nice. He'd put a shirt of his own on, so I no longer had to worry about staring at his chest, even though I missed the view. "Here are your clothes. Why don't you get dressed and then we can figure out what we're doing for dinner? Do you like Vietnamese?"

Although he seemed to be looking right at me as he asked the question, I still had to check. "Are you asking me?"

Nick smiled in amusement as Henry cleared his throat. "Ah, sorry, I haven't had a chance to ask you yet. We'd like you to join us for dinner, if you don't have any other plans tonight."

Join them? Seriously? I looked back over at Nick and for the first time registered that in his arms were my clothes, including my very large, very bright bra right on top.

Oh, God. Were there any ways left for me to humiliate myself today? I quickly snatched the clothes from him, tucking them under my arm. "Vietnamese is great," I replied, starting back towards the bathroom. "Dinner would be great. Bun cha for me, thanks."

I had the bathroom door closed behind me before they had a chance to reply.

~Nick~

As Kimber disappeared back into the bathroom, I turned to Henry curiously. "So that's your type, eh?"

He shrugged, pulling up the food delivery app on his phone so that he wouldn't have to look at me. He used that trick often. "I don't know if I have a type, but she's sweet and really funny, and yeah, I think she's beautiful. What do you think?"

What *did* I think? I'd been surprised when I first saw her, I had to admit. In all the times he'd mentioned her, Henry had never told me what Kimber looked like, but coming from him, that made sense. Appearances weren't the most important thing to Henry and I loved that about him. He took care of himself but simply to be healthy, not because of the way it made him look, and I knew deep down that he loved me for me and not the way I looked either. The same couldn't be said for a lot of people I'd dated in the past.

The big question, really, centred around whether I found Kimber attractive, and Henry's opinion on that had already influenced me a little. If he liked her as much as he did, she must have good qualities, so he'd already predisposed me to like her even before I laid eyes on her.

The robe and towel weren't particularly flattering, but her bright blue eyes were intriguing, and I found the way she reacted to me very interesting too. Unlike Henry, she held my gaze when I took a more assertive tone. If anything, it seemed like she relished a challenge.

To be quite frank, I'd never slept with anyone her size before, but the idea didn't turn me off. If Henry wanted us all to get to know each other a little better, I would go along with it and see how things went from there.

"I said I wanted soft and curvy," I reminded Henry. "She definitely fits that bill."

He looked up at me tentatively, his expression too blank for me to know whether my answer pleased him or not. "So you still want to pursue this?"

"Yeah, I do. Let's see how it goes."

We placed our order with our favourite Vietnamese restaurant and I poured some wine for all of us as we waited for Kimber to return. A little alcohol never hurt to help everyone relax a little.

When Kimber reappeared, I finally got my first proper look at her, and I quite enjoyed the view. She'd used the hairdryer in the bathroom and her long, dark hair looked soft and inviting as it curled over her shoulders. She must have had some makeup in her bag since she had a little bit on now, some eyeliner and mascara that brought out her eyes even more.

As for curves, well, she had a ton of them. She easily filled that bra I'd handed her a few minutes ago and truth be told, she could probably go a size bigger. My mind wandered to what those breasts might feel like in my hands or in my mouth, and the thought definitely held some appeal.

I offered her a glass of wine as we all moved to the living room with its view over the white sails of Canada Place and the North Shore mountains. Although the windows were rain-streaked today and the sky grey, Kimber's jaw still dropped as she walked up to the floor-to-ceiling window.

"This is gorgeous," she breathed in appreciation. "It must look amazing in the sunshine."

She looked out a moment longer, taking a drink of her wine as she admired the view, before turning to me.

"So, how'd you get so rich?"

Her bluntness made me laugh. I could guess that she hadn't meant for me to overhear when she called me 'loaded' earlier, but rather than pretending she hadn't said it, she chose to lean into it.

I liked that, and I matched her honesty in return. "My parents are well off, and they figured a trust fund made up for the attention they didn't give me growing up. That's what paid for the condo in the first place, but I make a lot of money at work too."

"What do you do?" Her eyes stayed on me as we all took a seat, and though the question might be a typical one, the way she asked it made me feel like she really cared about the answer. It felt deeper than simple small talk thanks to the warm, inviting look in her eyes.

"I'm an investment banker. People give me their money and I make them more money. It's pretty simple."

"He's being modest," Henry jumped in, though nobody else would ever use that word for me. "It's a lot more complicated than that and Nick is great at it."

"He must be," Kimber agreed, looking from Henry to me. "Do your parents live here in the city too?"

My parents were a bit of a sore spot, but I wouldn't allow them to ruin my good mood today. "No. I'm not sure where they are at the moment."

That reply seemed to surprise her, but I turned the question back on her before she could follow up.

"What about you? Did you grow up here?"

Kimber shook her head, taking another drink from her wine glass. "No, I'm from the prairies. I grew up on a farm in the middle of nowhere. My family's all there still, but there isn't a lot of work for a TV actress in Saskatoon so I decided to try my luck here instead."

"TV actress?" I repeated in surprise. Henry hadn't mentioned that. "What would I have seen you in?"

A self-deprecating laugh bubbled from Kimber's lips. "Nothing, unless you were paying a lot of attention to the background as the actors walked by."

We talked a bit more about her work, and then about Henry's, the conversation flowing easily, and I began to really see why Henry liked her. Everything about her felt warm and genuine and I had her full attention every time she spoke to me. Not to mention that the way Henry looked at her, a look of appreciation and interest, made me feel even warmer. Jealousy played no part since Kimber and I weren't in competition. What she could offer him differed entirely from what I brought to the table.

I could see the three of us having a lot of fun together.

When the food arrived, we moved back to the kitchen, setting ourselves up at the circular kitchen table. Henry and I ate off each other's plates as usual, sharing everything between us, while Kimber watched in amusement.

"How long have you guys been seeing each other?" she asked, and Henry and I exchanged loaded glances. We'd been waiting for just that opening, a chance to talk about our relationship and how she might fit into it.

Time to test the waters to see how she felt, since Henry had already made his decision and now, I had too.

Chapter Three

~**Kimber**~

Having dinner with Henry and Nick felt surprisingly natural. By the time I had my clothes back on and had touched up my hair and make-up as well as I could, my mood had significantly improved. When I left work, my plans for the evening consisted of pot noodles and a binge-watching session of whatever caught my eye on Netflix; now, I had an invitation to stay for dinner with two handsome, successful, charming men, and I intended to make the most of it. It might not be a date, but I could still have a good time and get to know the men who were both being so kind to me.

The food? Excellent. The wine? Amazing. And the company? Even better. They were so comfortable and casual with each other that it made me feel right at home too. I couldn't help smiling as they stole things off each other's plates over dinner, seeming to have exactly the kind of relationship I'd always wanted, and experiencing it, even vicariously, for a little while made for a nice change.

Curious how long it had taken them to get to this level of comfort with each other, I asked how long they'd been together, and I noticed the glances they exchanged when I did. Shouldn't I have asked that? There definitely seemed to be some kind of silent communication going on between them.

Nick answered me, putting his fork down and placing his hand over Henry's. "It's been just over six months."

That made sense. Henry had told me he moved in here about six months ago and that matched up with when he started coming to the coffee shop too. They must have moved in together pretty quickly after they started dating.

As if he'd heard my thoughts, Henry confirmed it. "He kind of swept me off my feet," he said, smiling over at Nick with that dimpled smile that always made my stomach flutter, even when directed at someone else. "Those first few weeks were a bit of a whirlwind, especially since I'd never dated a man before."

I nearly choked on the piece of pork I had just put in my mouth, and grabbed my wine glass to wash it down as quickly as I could.

Both men started to stand up to help me if I needed it, but I waved them off. "I'm fine," I managed to say. "Just went down the wrong way."

Nick's twitching lips made it clear my explanation hadn't fooled him, but he didn't call me out on it. They both stayed silent instead, waiting for me to say something else as I tried to figure out what the hell I ought to say now.

I finally settled on something I thought should be relatively harmless as I turned to Henry. "So, what were you doing before then? Were you a monk? A priest? Did Nick lure you from your calling?"

Nick grinned, looking pleased about the idea of being the one leading Henry into temptation, while Henry laughed, that adorable dimple making another appearance. "No, nothing like that. I dated before, but only women. Nick is my first boyfriend."

So he *used* to date women? Just my luck to meet him now and not then.

"I've dated women too," Nick added, his eyes on me over the rim of his glass as he took a drink. "We're both bisexual."

Oh. *Oh.*

As soon as the word left his lips, the fire that had been simmering in my stomach ever since I saw them kissing roared back to life again.

Okay, calm down, Kimber. As interesting as that might be, it had nothing to do with me personally. Just because they had both been attracted to women in the past, it didn't change the fact that they were currently in a relationship with each other.

But why, exactly, were they telling me this? It really wasn't any of my business.

"Well, you obviously make a great couple," I told them both, trying to sound a lot cooler and more in control than I felt. "On behalf of the female gender, I can say that your mutual gain is definitely our collective loss."

That made them both smile, and once again, they exchanged looks with each other, sharing some secret communication that went over my head.

And again, Nick took the lead after their silent exchange. "Well, it doesn't have to be *your* loss. Not personally, anyway."

"Excuse me?" The words came out as a squeak, but the fact that they came out at all impressed me given how out of control my body felt. What did he mean by that? It couldn't be what it sounded like. My imagination needed to slow down.

"Nick," Henry chided his boyfriend. "You're making her uncomfortable."

"No, he's not," I lied. Uncomfortable definitely described my current situation, what with the heat running through my body and the butterflies in my stomach, but this particular kind of discomfort, I could live with. "I just don't understand."

"Well, let's make it clearer then," Nick suggested, looking at Henry, not me, almost as if he were asking for permission. With a slight grimace, Henry inclined his head, giving his blessing, so Nick turned to me. "We like you, Kimber. Both of us."

Once again my body and my brain had completely opposite reactions: my thighs clenched together as my mind tried to remind me this couldn't possibly be what it sounded like. I had been on my own far too long and my imagination had gone off the deep end.

"I like you both too," I replied with a smile, glancing between the two gorgeous men looking back at me, trying to appear far more calm than I felt. He must be talking about liking me as a friend, nothing more.

"That's a good start," Nick said, flashing a smile back before adopting a more serious expression. "But I'm going to be completely frank with you here. And before I am, I just want you to know that if you're not interested, that's not a problem. We can still be friends if you'd like to. It doesn't change anything, and we're certainly not going to force you into something you're not comfortable with."

I spoke too soon earlier when I said that my heart had never beat faster. Now, it set a whole new record. My stomach fluttered in both exhilaration and terror as I waited to find out exactly what he meant. "Interested in what?"

"In being with us. Both of us. Sexually."

I waited a few seconds, waiting for them to laugh. He had to be joking, right? The odds of the two of them thinking about me like that were infinitesimal.

But the seconds ticked by, one by one, and no one laughed. Nick held my gaze, cool and confident, and when my eyes went to Henry, his red cheeks and downturned gaze finally made it sink in, far more than Nick's assurance.

They were serious.

They actually wanted to have sex with me. Both of them? *Together?*

If it were possible to drop dead of shock, there would have been a Kimber-shaped corpse on the floor right there and then. But since that didn't happen in real life, all I could do was swallow and blink as my brain tried to remember how to make words come out of my mouth.

"I... uh... I... are you sure?"

The Oscar-worthy speech I managed to come out with made Nick smile again, this time at my lack of eloquence. "I'm pretty sure, yeah. We've already talked about it."

Once more I looked at Henry, searching for confirmation. "When did you talk about it?"

Did they come to this decision while I got dressed in the bathroom? It seemed like a pretty big thing to decide in such a short amount of time.

This time Henry did look up at me, answering my question though his cheeks still flamed red. "A few days ago, but it's not why I asked you here today. Or not the only reason, at least. I really did just want to help, but since you were already here, it seemed like a good time to ask you if you might be... uh, interested."

He seemed to be almost as flustered as I felt, even though he had a lot more warning than I did about this conversation.

I looked back at Nick, still trying to wrap my head around the turn that this evening had taken. "But you just met me."

He nodded good-naturedly. "I did, but Henry has been singing your praises, and I trust his judgement. Now that I've met you myself, I trust him even more."

My eyes swivelled back to Henry. "You talked about me?"

Although my words were still coming out in short bursts, overall, I thought I was doing an admirable job of acting like this kind of thing happened to me all the time, being propositioned by two of the most gorgeous men I'd ever seen.

"I've really enjoyed getting to know you, Kimber," Henry said, offering me a small smile at last. "So when Nick suggested having a woman join us, you immediately came to mind."

How could I not be flattered by that? I honestly had no idea he had ever thought about me that way. He'd done a very good job of hiding it.

"You don't need to decide right now," Nick interjected. "We're not expecting anything to happen tonight. I just wanted to get the idea out there, in the open, and you can think it over. Will you do that, Kimber?"

The sound of my name from his lips sent a shiver of longing through me, a shiver which did not go unnoticed by the man in question. He gave me a sexy, confident smirk as I gave my agreement, at least to taking it under consideration. "I'll think about it."

Somehow, we managed to move on to talking about other things, the conversation flowing smoothly once more, but my mind refused to move on. As they spoke, I couldn't stop looking at their hands, imagining how they would feel on me, or watching their lips forming each word. When Nick reached over to wipe off some sauce from the corner of Henry's mouth, my whole body tingled again. As much as I liked the idea of being with them, the idea of being with them while they were with each other excited me almost as much.

These were things I had never thought about before, never imagined, since I'd never had any reason to. Now, I could think of nothing else.

They both took me home after dinner in Nick's stylish car, Henry sitting in the back while I rode shotgun to direct Nick to my apartment. Even though they parked right in front of the building, they both got out of the car to walk me to my door like the gentlemen they were.

"Here's my card," Nick said, handing me a professional looking business card with black and gold lettering. "You can reach me at any time."

"I'll be at the coffee shop tomorrow as usual," Henry promised, giving me a smile.

The words they weren't saying lingered in the air between us just as much as the ones they did; they were waiting for my answer, but they weren't going to push me for it.

And as I watched them walk back to the car, Nick's hand grazing Henry's ass, I knew what I wanted my answer to be, even if I couldn't bring myself to say it out loud just yet.

Offers like this came around once in a lifetime, and if I let this one pass me by, I would regret it for the rest of my life.

~Henry~

My whole body slumped in relief as I got in the front seat of the car next to Nick. That went a lot better than I expected it to. At least we hadn't scared Kimber off entirely, which I had been afraid we would. I couldn't even bear to look at her when Nick told her bluntly what we were interested in from her. How he had the nerve to say something like that without any hesitation, I would never understand.

In my job, I had no trouble holding my ground or speaking my mind, but the circumstances were different. Confident in my prepared words and sure of my position, I could make an eloquent argument to convince others of my cause.

This situation had no such structure or rules. Were we doing the right thing here? Was there even such a thing as right or wrong when it came to what we were talking about? As long as all involved consented to it and no one got hurt, it sounded perfect, but if it changed the way that Kimber felt about me, I would truly regret having brought it up at all. Her smile and friendly conversation brightened my days and I would truly miss her if she disappeared from my life.

If it were up to me, I would have waited longer, spent more time together with her as a set of three before we broached the subject, easing into it more gradually, but Nick operated on a different level. When he wanted something, he went for it. For someone like me who had always been more cautious, being around someone like him could be exhilarating, but sometimes it felt dangerous too, and never more so than tonight.

Still, so far, it hadn't backfired too badly. Kimber had said she would think about it, and we left it at that, returning to the pleasant, easy conversation already in progress. She didn't seem freaked out or turned off by the idea, and I couldn't hope for much more than that.

"So, that went pretty well," I said out loud, voicing my thoughts to Nick as he pulled out back into the street. He had given up trying to get me to drive his car. It cost a lot more than I made in a year, and even though he had insurance, the guilt would kill me if something happened to it.

Nick had no such reservations about his methods of persuasion with Kimber as he sped down West Georgia Street, heading back to our condo. "It went perfectly," he assured me, keeping his eyes on the wet road. "She'll agree. No question."

"How can you be so sure?" I hadn't seen anything to indicate that level of commitment on her part.

He shot me a heart-meltingly cheeky grin. "Have you seen us? How could she resist?"

My eyes rolled so hard I almost gave myself a headache while Nick laughed.

"Seriously though, if she had no interest, she would have said so already. She doesn't seem like the type to beat around the bush. And now that it's in her head, she'll be thinking about it day and night, just like we are."

He had a point. I'd been unable to stop thinking about it ever since he first raised the idea, and when we got back to the condo and into bed together, Nick brought it up again.

"I bet Kimber is lying in bed right now thinking about us. Maybe she's even touching herself while she does."

That thought turned me on just as much as it clearly did for him, and as Nick and I made love, though neither of us mentioned her name again, I would have sworn we were both thinking about what it would be like to have Kimber there with us.

God, I hoped Nick's hunch turned out to be right. Now that he'd put the idea in my head, it didn't want to go away, and I suspected it wouldn't until our mutual fantasies became a reality.

~Nick~

The next morning, I woke up feeling almost like I had a hangover, and I immediately recognized the warning signs. Yesterday, I had been on such a high for a lot of reasons: it had been a great day at work, Henry and I were getting along perfectly, and we had our dinner with Kimber and the potential of a lot more with her. Life felt light and full of promise, and my mood matched perfectly.

But these highs were always accompanied by a low for me, they always had been, a trait I seemed to have inherited from my mother. Her mood swings defined my childhood in so many ways, but unlike her, I always tried my best to shield those I loved from the effects of it.

Henry shouldn't feel like he had to walk on eggshells around me, the way I always had around my mother, never knowing what mood she'd be in or which version of her I would find when I got home from school.

So when I felt it coming on that morning, I did what I always did: I made a plan to beat it. Pushing myself out of bed, I headed for the gym first, working my frustration and negativity out on the machines there. I worked myself until my muscles screamed in protest and sweat poured down my back, but it made no difference.

At work, my spotless office with its floor-to-ceiling windows and sleek, modern furniture usually brought me at least a small feeling of satisfaction, but today it all faded into the background as I tried my best to focus simply on not lashing out. I told my assistant, Erin, that I had some files to catch up on and shouldn't be disturbed. Snapping at her wouldn't be fair either.

Finally, I sent Henry a text to let him know I might have to work late tonight. That would buy me some time to make sure I felt more like myself before I went home.

He didn't need to know how out of control I felt at times like this. No one needed to know. My problems were my own, and I could deal with them through sheer force of will. Nick Lewis, the golden child, would always come out on top. A little determination and hard work would fix everything.

"Nick?" Erin's voice, usually pleasant and sweet, sounded like nails on a chalkboard to me right now.

"What?"

She shrank back from my surly tone but answered me nonetheless. "Mr Montgomery is here, he'd like to see you if you have a few minutes?"

Mr Montgomery sat on the board for the company I worked for, making him a key person I needed to impress if I wanted to move up the management ladder. Which I intended to. An opportunity to speak to him privately would have been welcome at any other time, but at the moment, I only felt annoyed. I forced myself to answer in the affirmative anyway. "Fine. Where is he?"

"He's right here."

The man in question walked in behind Erin, answering me himself, and I quickly got to my feet, forcing a smile onto my face that felt strained and fake. At times like this, I couldn't remember what a smile ought to feel like. We shook hands as Erin closed the door behind her and I invited him to take a seat. His expensive watch glistened in the sunlight through my window as he rested his hands on the arms of the comfortable chair I kept for clients.

"I've been hearing good things about you," he began, looking around my office. His eyes rested for a second on the picture of me and Henry on my desk. Taken a couple of months ago when we took a trip to Salt Spring Island, we were both grinning in the sunshine. Looking at it, I could smell the salt tang of the sea air and remember the taste of it on Henry's lips as I kissed him. I never hid my relationship from anyone, since there was no reason to. I had no reason to be ashamed. "That investment you made last week has made a lot of our biggest customers very happy."

It should have. They'd made millions, thanks to me.

"Everyone should have seen the opportunity," I told him bluntly. "It couldn't have been more obvious."

His brow furrowed and I winced internally, trying to adopt a friendlier tone as I offered another stiff smile.

"But it's easy to say that in hindsight, isn't it?"

That seemed to help as his brow cleared again. "Quite right. But you're the one who saw it first, and you've got people talking. This is your boyfriend, isn't it?"

He gestured to the photo he'd just been looking at, and my nostrils flared as I tried to guess what might be coming next. I had no idea what his particular views were, so I limited myself to a terse one-word answer: "Yes."

Mr Montgomery nodded. "Good. The board has been talking about needing to diversify our upper management. It's a bit of an old boys' club."

No kidding. Our senior executives were practically carbon copies of each other, each with greying hair, matronly wives and 2.4 children, give or take.

"I'd like to put you forward for one of the roles that will be opening up when Murphy and Giller leave in a couple of months," he told me, and my eyebrows raised. I hadn't known they were leaving, and from the way he chuckled at my reaction, he obviously knew that. "It's still under wraps, but I trust you to keep it to yourself. Personally, I'd like to see you and Jennifer Cartwright in those roles to shake things up a bit."

My brow furrowed now, mirroring his own reaction a moment ago. I knew the woman being referred to, and her performance hadn't impressed me in any way. "Jennifer isn't one of the top performing brokers."

He simply smiled. "No, but she's a woman. As I said, we could use a bit of a shakeup."

Indignation shot through me as I recognized the true purpose behind him showing up here today. Someone, somewhere, had decided the company's image needed to improve, at least when it came to diversity, so he intended to nominate a woman and a gay man in an attempt to pander to the people who cared about such things.

"So who I'm sleeping with is more important than how well I do my job?" I asked, a healthy dose of bitterness laced into the question.

Mr Montgomery's eyes narrowed, his good mood clearly diminishing in the face of my insolence. "Watch your tone, Lewis. You might think you're all that, but there are a dozen other guys out there who make good deals every day. What sets you apart is your lifestyle. Not all that long ago, you people were being discriminated against, and now it's working in your favour. Take advantage of it."

A dozen more responses rushed to the tip of my tongue, but I didn't trust myself to say any of them right now. Pushing all my feelings down, I kept my tone as neutral as possible. "Thank you for your support, sir."

After a few more strained pleasantries, he left my office and I told Erin to cancel the rest of my appointments for the day. Getting any work done seemed impossible. What I really needed right now was a drink.

~Kimber~

The rain clouds had completely disappeared overnight, and when I headed out in the early morning to Rocco's coffee shop, the bright sun on my skin, blue sky above me and fresh air in my lungs made me feel like anything was possible.

After last night, how could I really doubt it?

Maybe I hadn't got the role I wanted for the TV show, but my life had suddenly got a lot more interesting all on its own. Who needed to live vicariously through a character when there were two amazing men interested in the *real* me instead? I could still hardly believe that conversation had taken place, but I lacked the imagination to invent it, which meant it must be the truth.

Rocco immediately noticed the change in my attitude as I got to work baking some chocolate chip monster cookies in the coffee shop kitchen, the air sweet with sugar. "You seem to have swallowed some sunshine today, Kimber."

"I'm always in a good mood," I protested, humming a little as I measured out the flour.

He shook his head. "No, you always *act* like you're in a good mood. Today, you are."

Sometimes, he knew me too well. "Apparently, I need to work on my acting skills if you can tell the difference."

That drew a chuckle from him, the corners of his eyes crinkling as he laughed. "No, you just need to be happy more often. Whatever you did last night, keep doing it."

My cheeks flushed red at the thought of doing the things I had only talked about doing last night. If I felt this good just thinking about the two of them, what would it be like if we actually went ahead with what they'd suggested?

I stayed in the back while Rocco opened up, but as it got closer to the time that Henry usually came in, I made my way out front to help with the morning crowd, placing the freshly baked cookies in the centre of our display.

"Did you make those yourself, dear?" a sweet-looking older lady on the other side of the counterasked. She had two teenagers with her, possibly her granddaughters and I gave them all a warm smile. .

"I sure did, and you're in luck. They're fresh out of the oven. Would you like to try one?"

The teenagers tittered behind her. "I'm surprised there's any left," one of them said to the other, attempting to whisper but missing the mark by quite a ways.

Their grandmother looked confused, but I knew exactly what she meant, implying I'd been eating the cookies while baking them, because of course every overweight person couldn't control themselves around food. As far as fat jokes went, I'd rate it as weak.

"You can have one too," I offered to the girl, looking her straight in the eye. "Chocolate makes people happier, and happier people are usually nicer and funnier. You might want to give it a try."

She simply rolled her eyes at me, unimpressed, but I kept the smile on my face as I got them their order.

"Is that your secret?" Henry's voice took me by surprise as I spun around to see him already standing at the corner with his espresso cup. I had no idea how I'd missed him when I came out, but his lips twitched nervously as he watched me, unsure how I would behave with him today after everything that happened last night.

"My secret to what?" I asked, giving him a far more genuine smile than the one I'd just given the bitchy teenager.

As soon as he saw my smile, he visibly relaxed. "Your secret to being nice and funny. Is it the chocolate?"

So he'd heard all that, had he? "Chocolate definitely helps. The better the quality, the nicer I'll be."

"I'll remember that." Something in the way he said it made me think he really would. "For now, can I have one of those cookies?"

"Of course." I put one in a small take-out bag and handed it over to him. "Just the one?"

He smiled almost shyly, his cheek dimpling. "Nick and I can share."

My pulse instantly kicked up a notch as his words sank in. They could, apparently. They *would*.

"I've got to get going," he apologized before I could formulate a response to that. "But I'll see you tomorrow, if not before. Have a great day, Kimber."

"You too." I watched him go as his words repeated in my head. *If not before...*

If I needed any further invitation, he'd just provided it.

The rest of the morning rush kept me distracted, but as the customers dwindled, my mind wandered again. Could I really go through with this? If I said yes, if I got in touch with either Nick or Henry today, I had a very good chance of being in their bed tonight. They'd both made that abundantly clear.

But even so, it still seemed impossible. Surely they could have their pick of women to do this kind of thing with. Why me? It didn't make any sense. I felt out of my depth, as though an important piece of the puzzle had gone missing and I had no idea where to look to find it.

"I think the machine is clean now," Rocco said over my shoulder, bringing my attention to the fact that I'd been wiping down the same coffee machine for the last five minutes. "Are you okay?"

"Of course." I gave him my usual bright, fake smile. "Just distracted, sorry."

"Why don't you take off early?" Rocco suggested. "It's quiet now and Shelley is due to start in half an hour."

I only worked until noon today, my one half-day of the week. Usually, I used the afternoon off to run errands and do things that could only be done during business hours, but today I had nothing pressing to do. I had idea what to do with myself other than continuing to stew over my current situation.

"I don't mind staying until she gets here," I told him. "It might get busy."

He shook his head at me. "It won't. But if you really want to put in your hours, you can run a delivery over to Bar None for me."

A popular nearby venue, Bar None had recently started ordering Rocco's special coffee blend to serve to their customers. It looked good for them to support a local business, and the coffee tasted damn good too.

"I can definitely do that," I agreed. Going to the back room, I took off my apron and grabbed my spring jacket instead. As soon as Rocco brought me the delivery bags, I headed out to walk the few blocks in the sunshine.

I'd never been anywhere that could compare to Vancouver when the sun shone. As I looked over to the North Shore mountains beneath the bright blue sky, I couldn't imagine how anyone could be in a bad mood on a day like today.

A gentle buzz of conversation greeted me when I arrived at Bar None. Although evenings were their busiest time, naturally, they did serve a light lunch too, so there were a few groups eating and a few people seated around the large wrap-around bar, having a liquid lunch. The employee at the bar took the packages from me and gave me a receipt as we chatted for a couple of minutes. Just before I headed back out the door, I spotted a familiar-looking blond head at the end of the bar.

"Nick?" For a moment, I couldn't be certain I had the right guy. Gone was the confident, teasing smile of last night. His face looked drawn and tired instead, but when he looked up at me, his eyes registered recognition.

In his crisp white shirt and tie, with his suit jacket slung over the back of his chair, he looked like someone taking a break from work, but what brought him to a bar in the middle of the day, I couldn't begin to guess.

He quickly rubbed a hand down his face, blinking as he tried to put on a smile. I recognized that move, the fake face a person showed to the world when they wanted to hide their true feelings.

"Hey, Kimber. This is a surprise, running into you here." The flat tone of his voice hardly sounded like the same man I'd met yesterday either.

"You normally wouldn't," I agreed, taking a seat next to him even though he hadn't invited me to join him. He really looked like he could use a friend. Whenever I felt down, it helped to have someone else there. "I just had to drop something off for work, and now I'm finished for the day. What are you drinking?"

He looked down at the drink in his hand like he couldn't quite remember. "Bourbon, I think."

Even though I had no money to spare, I ordered the same.

Nick grimaced as the bartender walked away. "I really don't want to be rude, Kimber, especially since we don't know each other very well, but I kind of came here to be alone."

I always said things like that too, but then when the person left, I felt guilty for pushing them away. Though I couldn't be certain Nick would respond the same way, I decided to take a chance and stay anyway.

"That's okay. I could use some alone time too. You don't have to talk or entertain me. We can be alone together."

The bartender brought over my drink and, as I promised, we both drank in silence. I watched the other people in the bar, trying to guess what they were talking about, making up backstories for them all, like they were characters in a TV show. It helped to keep my mind off my own dilemma, especially since one of the men involved in it sat right next to me.

It could have been uncomfortable to be there with Nick, but it actually felt rather natural. He seemed to relax once he realized I had no intention of forcing a conversation on him, and we sat in companionable silence, not quite strangers but not quite friends.

When I'd emptied my glass, I got to my feet. I really couldn't afford another one, and I had probably overstayed my welcome anyway. "Well, enjoy the rest of your day, Nick. I'll see you later."

I started to walk away, not expecting a reply, but he called out after me. "Kimber?"

I turned back to find him watching me with just a hint of a spark in his eyes. Not as much as there had been yesterday, but more than when I walked in. "Yeah?"

"Thanks."

I really hadn't done anything, but I'd be glad if it made him feel even a little better. "Anytime."

I had just started to turn to go again when Nick got to his feet too, grabbing his suit jacket off the back of his chair. "Where are you heading now?"

"Home," I replied truthfully. "Though it's such a nice day, I might go and sit in the park for a while."

"Can I join you?"

I gave him a completely real smile, not the fake kind at all. "I would love that."

Chapter Four

~**Nick**~

The dark cloud over me had started to lift a little bit, at least enough that I felt I could control myself again.

At first, when Kimber sat down next to me, it took everything I had not to snap at her and tell her to go away and leave me alone. When I felt like this, my reactions weren't always in my control and I didn't want her to see me this way. I didn't want anyone to see me this way.

I managed to say, politely enough, that I wasn't looking for company, but she insisted on staying anyway, which honestly kind of pissed me off at first. Not trusting myself to be as polite a second time, I held my tongue and kept focused on my drink, my third one since I sat down at the bar. The alcohol slowly started to numb me, the bourbon losing its bite with each mouthful, and as the minutes passed, I realized that Kimber's presence actually felt kind of comforting in an unexpected way.

She gave no indication that she thought me strange for sitting here on my own in the middle of the day and being a little short with her. She acted as though it were completely normal for us both to be sitting and drinking and not talking to each other, thinking things over, and her acting that way made me feel a little more normal too.

So when she got up to leave, I got up too. I wanted to hang on to this feeling of normality, this calmness that she'd brought to my day, so I asked to go with her. I'd already cancelled my appointments in the office; what did it matter if I took the rest of the day off? And when we got out into the sunshine and began to walk towards Stanley Park with the sun shining and the air fresh from yesterday's rain, the whole world started to feel a bit brighter too.

Thankfully, my low seemed to be passing. Some days it went on a lot longer than that. Sometimes, it lasted more than a day at a time, so I would count this as a blessing. With each step, I felt more like myself, and though Kimber seemed happy to continue in silence as we had been in the bar, eventually, I found myself wanting to talk.

"Did you see Henry this morning?" It seemed safe to stick to the one thing I knew for sure we had in common.

As she smiled, her eyes lighting up softly, I knew the answer before she said a word. "He came in for his coffee, as usual, and to try my cookies."

My eyebrows shot up. "Excuse me?"

Kimber laughed, her cheeks turning a rather adorable shade of pink. "Actual, literal cookies. I made some cookies at the shop."

"A likely story," I teased her, starting to smile too, a smile which felt a lot less strained than when I had done it this morning. The way she smiled at the mention of Henry's name had me curious. "You like Henry, don't you?"

Her cheeks turned even pinker. "Of course I do. He's a likable guy."

"That's not what I mean." This might be putting her on the spot, but she'd already kind of forced her way into my day, and I felt like it would be useful to get it out in the open. "Do you have feelings for him?"

Kimber's lips pursed as she looked away from me, debating her answer, but when she turned back, her expression held only resignation instead of embarrassment. "He never mentioned he had a boyfriend, so yeah, I've had a little crush on him. I guess I still do, since it doesn't just go away, but I totally accept that you guys are a couple and you're happy together, so if we were to do anything like... well, like what you said last night... I know it wouldn't change that. If you're worried about me getting too attached or trying to sabotage what you have..."

"Whoa, slow down." I held up my hands to stop her, since she'd read way too much into the question. "I don't think you're a homewrecker trying to break up my relationship, I didn't mean to imply that."

"Oh." She exhaled in relief, looking sheepish. "Then why were you asking?"

"Because he likes you too," I told her bluntly. "And for Henry, an emotional connection is important in a sexual relationship."

"So you *want* me to have feelings for your boyfriend?"

Well, when she put it that way, it sounded a little strange, but also accurate. "Yeah, I do. If we're going to go ahead with what we talked about last night, then I think it's important that you care about him too on some level since he likes you. I don't want him to get hurt."

Kimber took a deep breath as she thought that over. "You said it's important for *him* to feel an emotional connection during sex," she reminded me. "But not for you?"

I had to laugh at her perceptiveness. "It's better, of course, but not necessary. I'm more of a manwhore than he is."

Kimber joined in my laughter, and the cloud over me got even fainter as this morning's bad mood faded further away.

"Well, at least you're owning it," she teased me. "You might be a whore, but you're an honest one."

Talking about all of this so openly convinced me even more that we'd made the right choice in her. A lot of women would be put off. "What about you, Kimber?"

This time, her eyebrows raised. "What *about* me? Am I a whore, do you mean?"

Her tone made it clear she took it in good humour, so I grinned at her. "I would have put it a little more delicately than that, but basically, yeah. Are you more like Henry or more like me?"

Her smile faded as she considered her answer. "Well, I don't have an awful lot of experience to know for sure."

My brow furrowed as I tried to figure out what she meant. "You're not a virgin, are you?" That would certainly put our proposal to her last night in a whole new light.

Kimber laughed once more. "You look a little nauseated, Nick. I'm tempted to say yes just to see your reaction, but no, I'm not a virgin. However, I haven't been with a lot of men either, and definitely not two at the same time."

That didn't really answer my question. I wanted to know if she required some kind of deeper connection. "Were you in love with the men you have been with?"

She shook her head hesitantly. "No, I wouldn't say that. I liked them, they weren't strangers, but I don't know if I've *ever* been in love before. And I'm sure no one's ever been in love with me."

I found that hard to believe, but saying so might sound patronizing. In even the brief time we'd spent together, I got the impression she never fished for compliments, and if she wasn't looking for pity, it must honestly be what she felt.

"Well, until Mr Right comes along, our invitation still stands," I said instead, and her cheeks coloured once more.

Luckily for her, we had arrived at the park and she changed the subject, asking me where I wanted to go. I suggested we simply walk around Lost Lagoon where we could find a bench and sit in the sunshine for a while. The warmth on my skin soothed me even further, as did talking to Kimber, and I quickly lost track of time until my phone buzzed with a text from Henry.

His message said he'd left the office, which he always texted to tell me, and asked if I would be home in time for supper. As my eyes moved from his text up to the clock on my phone, I could hardly believe the time. How did it get to be so late?

"I should get going," I told Kimber, stretching out and getting to my feet. "I'm sorry if I kept you from anything."

"I had no plans," she assured me. "I enjoyed getting to know you better, Nick."

"Ditto."

For a moment, we simply looked at each other, neither of us quite sure what to do next. I didn't really want her to go, and I got the feeling she'd rather not go either.

"What are you doing for supper tonight?" I asked as we started walking back towards the park entrance, and sure enough, interest sparked in her eyes.

"I don't have any particular plans."

"Do you want to eat with us again?" She still hadn't said a word about whether or not she wanted to accept our *other* invitation, but perhaps our condo would be a better place to have that discussion anyway. "Now that the weather's improved, we can eat out on the balcony. The view's incredible."

"I'm sure it is." Her expression suggested she meant more than just the mountains, and it made me smile. Her finding me and Henry attractive would only help. "I don't want to intrude though."

"I wouldn't ask if I thought you would."

She seemed to accept that logic. "In that case, I'd love to. Do you mind if we swing by my apartment first, though? I'd like to change out of my work clothes."

"Sure." I couldn't wait to see what she planned to put on.

Only when we left the park and headed towards Kimber's building did I realize my bad mood had completely dissipated. In its place was a sense of contentment and a strong feeling of anticipation. Once we were all back together in the privacy of our apartment, who knew what the night might bring?

~Henry~

Nick's reply came right as I unlocked the door of our condo. It told me he would be home in about half an hour and would be bringing someone with him for dinner. Kicking my shoes, I sighed in frustration. Not because of Nick coming home; of course that made me happy, but I would have preferred him to be alone. I needed to talk to him about something, and spending the evening with one of Nick's work colleagues, whom I assumed the guest must be, would make that pretty much impossible.

I'd already had one other disappointment today. I had stopped at Rocco's coffee shop on the way home, hoping for another friendly smile from Kimber to tide me over, but someone else stood behind the counter in her place. Though I never mentioned her name, Rocco told me that she only worked a half-day today when he caught me looking around. Apparently, I needed to work on my subtlety.

To keep my mind occupied until Nick arrived, I began prepping vegetables to make a stir-fry for supper, hoping to distract myself. However, even as I got into a rhythm chopping everything into bite-sized pieces, the phone call I'd received earlier stayed at the front of my mind.

It had been my father who called, unusually. Typically, my mother phoned, when anyone phoned at all. We had our weekly Monday evening dinners together, but outside of that, my parents lived their lives and I lived mine. To outsiders, it might not seem like we liked each other much, but I liked them fine; we just didn't have much in common. They were reserved, private people, and they had raised me to be the same. Conversation typically centred on three topics: work, the weather, and gardening. Their small garden provided an unending source of fascination, at least for them.

So, when my dad called today to say that they planned to host a party next weekend to celebrate my mom's 60th birthday, my mouth fell open in surprise. They had booked out a room in the Chinese Cultural Centre, not far from the small store my father ran in Chinatown, and all their friends had been invited. Of course I said I would be delighted to go, though the whole idea stunned me. My mom usually shied away from the spotlight.

It confused me until my father mentioned that several of their friends would be bringing their unmarried daughters, and I began to get an idea of their true intentions. My mom had been making more and more offhand comments about her advancing age and how she had no grandchildren, and how she wanted to see me happily married before she died. Not that she would be dying anytime soon; her health probably put mine to shame. She just wanted to make the point that I should be getting settled down.

Of course, I already had a committed relationship, they just weren't aware of it. So many times, I'd been close to bringing it up when the three of us sat around their small kitchen table on a Monday evening. But each time I thought I might say something, they would bring up one of their friends' children who had recently got married or had a child, and what a happy occasion it must be for the family.

We never talked about gay couples. If they knew any, they never mentioned it to me. As far as I knew, the whole concept resided completely outside their realm of experience.

And so, each time I thought I *might* tell them, I ended up chickening out. I could make excuses, but really, it came down to fear. Avoiding the conversation meant no chance of disappointing them.

But now, they intended to parade me in front of a who's who of women whose own parents were getting desperate too. The time had definitely come to tell them about my relationship, but after all this time, breaking the news would be even more difficult.

The worst part of it was that Nick had no idea about any of this. He knew I had my weekly dinners with my parents, which he took as a sign that we were close, given how absent his own parents were. He thought they knew about him. He had asked me once, early on, if I told my parents about moving in with him, and I said I had. They knew I lived with Nick; they just didn't know I slept with him too.

I told him, truthfully, that they were private people who spoke mediocre English. Whenever we were together, we spoke Mandarin. My father's shop served almost exclusively Chinese clientele and my mother had a group of friends who had all emigrated around the same time she had. They could speak enough to get by, living in a primarily English-speaking city, but in their day-to-day lives, English took a backseat.

Faced with my explanation, Nick dropped the subject, not pressing me to introduce him, and I never offered.

My guilt had been growing each week as Nick and I got more serious and settled, and this party put the nail in the coffin. I had to come clean to both Nick and my parents, and I would have to start with Nick.

I'd been hoping to talk to him about it tonight, but now, it would have to wait.

Just as I finished getting everything ready for dinner, the front door opened and Nick's voice called out, "We're here!"

Just the sound of his voice made me feel better, and he sounded upbeat too. Often, when he had to work late, he came home subdued and quiet. I would ask him if anything was wrong, but he always told me no. Thankfully, today, he sounded more like himself.

"In the kitchen," I called back, and a moment later he appeared in the doorway, still dressed for work with his suit jacket over his arm. As always, the sight of him took my breath away, especially when he smiled like he did now. As desire stirred in my groin, I once again bemoaned the fact that we had company.

"Sorry for the short notice," he apologized. "But I figured you wouldn't mind having this guest tonight."

He gestured for the other person with him to come in, and to my surprise, Kimber stepped through the door.

At the coffee shop, she always wore dark clothes, usually black pants and dark-coloured shirts, covered by her work apron. I hadn't even seen her without the apron on before last night, and now, she looked completely different.

She wore a white top with green polka dots and a matching green high-waisted skirt that came to her knees. Her legs were bare beneath, and so were her feet. She must have worn sandals over here and left them at the door.

With her long, dark hair pulled back into a loose bun and her shining blue eyes, the whole look exuded warmth and brightness, just like her, and my body immediately reacted to it, building on the arousal I'd already felt at the sight of Nick.

"Kimber. Hi." I quickly washed my hands and went over to give her a kiss on the cheek before giving Nick a dirty look. "You could have told me who you were bringing."

He grinned, enjoying my reaction. "I could have, but that would have ruined the surprise. I'm just going to go get changed and I'll be right back to help with supper."

He left us alone as Kimber wandered over to the counter, taking a look at my preparations. "This is impressive. Do you cook a lot?"

"Quite a lot, yeah. My mother taught me." I had no siblings, so my parents had wanted to pass all their combined knowledge down to me, overwhelming me at times. "How did you... I mean, why are you... did you call Nick?"

I wanted to know what her being here meant. Had she agreed to our proposal from last night? My heart already beat faster at the idea.

Kimber gave me a warm smile. "No, we just ran into each other and he invited me over. I hope that's okay?"

Okay was an understatement, and, not wanting to rock the boat, I didn't press her for any further information about where or how she and Nick had run into each other. I just felt grateful they had. "It's great. I actually stopped back at Rocco's this afternoon, but you had already gone."

"Were you back for more cookies?" she teased. "I told you you'd want more than one."

"Not at all. I went to see you."

I hadn't meant to tell her that so bluntly, it just came out, but once it did, the slight blush on her cheeks made me glad I'd said it. I *had* been thinking about her, so why pretend I hadn't? Before the phone call from my dad, most of my thoughts throughout the day had centred around what it would be like to kiss her.

Kimber's big blue eyes looked up at me as I stepped closer to her. A strand of hair had come loose from her bun, and I couldn't stop myself from reaching out to tuck it back behind her ear. As my fingers brushed her cheek, her eyes closed for a second, her chest rising as she inhaled, and I knew, as surely as I knew the colour of the sky, that she felt the same way I did. She'd been thinking about it too.

"You guys aren't starting without me, are you?" Nick's cheery voice forced me to take a step back, reluctantly, reminding me that nothing had been agreed yet.

"Wh-what?" Kimber stuttered, looking over at the doorway as he came in, her eyes wide. "We haven't started... nothing happened... what?"

Her flustered state made Nick grin. "Supper," he clarified, pointing to the counter as he looked between us with a slight smirk. "I said I'd help. You didn't start without me, did you?"

That smirk told me he definitely meant more than just the meal, so I answered him honestly. "You're just in time."

Nick came to stand on the other side of Kimber, just as close to her as I stood. "Well then, what are we waiting for?"

~Kimber~

Okay, wearing a skirt was a bad idea.

When Nick and I went back to my apartment, I couldn't help cringing as he looked around the tiny space, which he could do by simply standing in the middle of the room and turning around. My bed stood against the wall in the corner, and thankfully I had made it this morning. Some days I simply left it, since usually no one came over to see it. The whole apartment could have easily fit inside his huge kitchen.

Leaving him sitting on my couch, I went into my large walk-in closet, which also served as the only storage area in the apartment, and tried to decide what to wear. I needed to strike a compromise between not trying too hard, but, in case anything did happen tonight, not looking like a total slob either.

Finally settling on the blouse and skirt, I also grabbed a new set of underwear. Sexy underwear sat at the top of my very small list of indulgences, next to chocolate. They were the only things I really splurged on. Most of the time, I had to wear drab colours to work, but knowing that I had something bright and colourful and sexy on underneath made me feel better.

Just like my apartment, though, most of the time, no one came over to see it.

Today, the set I chose had a black base, with multi-coloured embroidered hearts stitched over it on both the bra and panties. I found it sexy, and hopefully Nick and Henry would too.

Oh God, did I really intend to go through with this? I quickly tried to think about something else before I needed to change my panties again.

Putting my shirt and skirt on over top, I examined myself in the mirror and the final result passed my satisfaction test. The high waist of the skirt helped to smooth down my stomach and accentuated what existed of my waist. I had worn something similar for a part in one of the few TV shows I'd actually been cast in, and when I saw myself on screen, I appreciated the flattering style and went out to buy myself something similar.

Normally, when I wore skirts, I would wear shorts underneath them too to stop my bare thighs rubbing together and chafing, but if we did actually get to a point tonight where my skirt came off, the shorts might require an explanation. Therefore, I left them off. Nick had offered to get us a cab back to his place, and though he hadn't said anything about bringing me home, I had a feeling he would drive me or pay for a taxi back home for me too. He seemed like that kind of guy.

As long as I didn't have to walk too far, my thighs should survive.

But now, standing here in their kitchen, Henry on one side of me and Nick on the other, I regretted the skirt for a completely different reason. The fire in my body had already started thanks to their proximity and the inherent sexiness, and my panties were growing damp from the heat. Unless I got myself back under control, that slickness would start running down my legs with nothing to stop it.

"So, what are we making?" I asked brightly, trying to turn the focus back to dinner. With running into Nick earlier, I hadn't eaten lunch, and my stomach had already protested a couple of times. If it growled out loud in front of my two gorgeous companions, I might have to run away.

Henry looked down at the counter where he'd laid the food out, and I took a moment to admire him. Damn, he looked good today. He still wore his work clothes, but he had removed his suit jacket and his tie, leaving him in grey pants and a white button-down shirt. The top two buttons had been undone and he had rolled the sleeves up in order to do the cooking, I imagined. His strong biceps strained against the remaining fabric as he reached out to point things out to me.

"It's just a simple stir-fry. The sauce is my mom's recipe. Everything's ready to go, so we just need to heat up the wok and throw it all in. Would you like to help me, Kimber?"

How did he make something as mundane as cooking supper sound like an adventure?

Nick chuckled on the other side of me. "Just be warned, Kimber, it's a gas stove and Henry likes it hot. Are you ready to play with fire?"

Did he try to make everything sound ridiculously sexy, or did it come naturally? Nick had changed out of his suit when he left us, and now looked much more casual in jeans and a light blue shirt that made his blue eyes even brighter. His arm brushed against mine as he reached over and grabbed one of the chopped sugar snap peas, popping it into his mouth as both men turned to look at me, waiting for my response.

Pushing down my nerves, I gave them both a smile. "I can handle a little fire," I promised, helping myself to one of the peas too. "Lead the way."

With a grin, Henry guided me over to the huge stove on the counter and turned on one of the burners, the blue flames roaring to life while he pulled out a heavy, sturdy wok. Nick held back, watching us both with enjoyment.

"First, some oil," Henry told me, handing me a bottle of oil with Chinese lettering on it. "As soon as the wok is smoking, pour some in."

"How much?" I asked, not wanting to mess this up. Though I knew my way around cakes and pies, I had more limited experience with cooking.

"You can choose," Henry told me, smiling over at me as he lined up the rest of the ingredients, ready to go. "I like quite a lot and Nick prefers a little. We're used to compromising."

They certainly seemed to be able to come to agreements between them. Everything they said sounded like a double entendre, unless my mind created the filthy connections on its own.

Once the wok had begun to steam, I poured a swirl of oil into it, which soon began to shimmer from the heat. Henry passed me some chopped garlic which I tossed in next, stirring it to keep it from burning, and then quickly added some of the vegetables he'd already prepared.

Nick came over to stand on my other side, watching me. "Keep stirring," he advised. "You don't want anything to stick. It needs your full attention."

Easier said than done in this kitchen.

Once the vegetables were ready, Henry expertly slid them onto a plate, returning the wok to the heat and adding a bit more oil before handing me some chicken to cook next. When it had cooked through, he instructed me to push the meat up the sides of the wok, leaving a hole in the centre.

"Now we need to fill that hole," Nick said, his low, sexy voice giving the words an entirely different meaning. "Are you ready for Henry's sauce?"

He *had* to be doing that on purpose. Fuck. I tried to keep my legs steady as my knees tried to buckle. So much for getting through dinner without my hormones raging.

Henry handed me the small bowl of sauce and I added it to the wok, letting it bubble for a moment before stirring the meat and vegetables back in. It smelled divine as Henry switched off the heat and Nick grabbed some bowls from the cupboard, adding some rice to them from a rice-maker which sat on the counter. Henry added the stir-fry to the bowls, throwing on some toasted almonds to finish it off. Now it looked just as amazing as it smelled.

"Time to dig in," he announced, and my thighs clenched again.

Thankfully, once we sat down at the table, the conversation became less sexually charged, or at least I stopped reading things into everything they said. The meal tasted as good as it looked and smelled, completing the trifecta, and Nick brought out some more very good quality wine. As our bowls emptied, they asked about my acting work again and what I had coming up.

I told them the honest truth: "I think I'm pretty good, though I'm sure I could improve with experience. It's just hard to get experience when everyone wants the same kind of look."

"What's wrong with your look?" Henry asked, sounding genuinely perplexed as he pushed his empty bowl to the side and picked up his glass of wine.

He couldn't be that naïve. "Well, though a lot of women in real life wear the same dress size as me, not very many women on TV do."

"That's bullshit," Nick observed, leaning back in his chair. "It should be about how well you do the job."

I had to laugh. "That might be true in a lot of professions, but acting isn't one of them. Most show creators have a very specific idea of what they want their characters to look like, and usually, it's not like this."

I gestured down at my body and the eyes of both men went straight to my chest, sending another wave of heat through me.

Okay, that one was my fault.

"I think you look great," Henry said, his eyes lingering on my breasts a moment longer before he looked back up at me. "I would watch anything you were in."

"Thanks, Henry." He couldn't be any sweeter. Those mornings in the coffee shop had been just the tip of the iceberg.

"So how do you change their minds?" Nick asked analytically.

I shrugged. "I'm still trying to figure that out. I nearly got a role earlier this week, since they were actually looking for someone 'diverse' to play it, but they chose someone else."

Nick frowned again. "Diversity for the sake of diversity is bullshit too."

His objections sounded quite personal. "It's okay," I assured him. "It's the way the industry works. I'm used to it. I think I look perfectly fine, and I'm not going to let anyone else tell me otherwise."

They both looked pleased with that response, and Henry took another sip of his wine. It seemed to be helping him relax, and he looked far less nervous than he had last night.

"Can you show us something you've been in?" he asked.

"I've got some clips from my audition reel on my phone, but they're not great," I demurred, though it flattered me that he cared enough to ask. "I've been meaning to update them. I'm much better in person."

"How about a live performance, then?" Nick suggested, his earlier gruffness fading away as his teasing smile came back. "Maybe something a little bit sexy?"

I raised my eyebrows at him. "What kind of shows do you think I'm in?"

"You tell me," he teased good-naturedly.

As I looked between them, their eager, interested expressions made it clear they really did want to see something. They weren't just humouring me, so I thought back over the scenes I had auditioned with for the role I'd just tried out for, until I settled on one which might work.

"I need you both to stand up then," I said, getting to my feet. "You don't need to say anything, I just need your bodies."

I groaned internally as soon as I realized what that sounded like, and both men grinned at me, clearly hearing it too. "Where do you want us?" Nick asked.

Setting up a stool in the middle of the kitchen, I instructed Henry to sit on it before placing Nick to the side in front of him. When the positioning felt right, I set the scene for them: I played a young woman whose parents had died, leaving her in charge of her two teenage brothers, and she had just caught them getting high at a party. The emotional, impassioned speech my character served to stop them from making mistakes she had made and deal with their grief properly.

In the high-class kitchen, I threw myself fully into the scene just as much as I had at the audition. Pretending to be someone else had always come easy to me, when the words I had to say were already planned out in advance.

If only real life were that easy, where everyone had the same script and stuck to it.

Henry and Nick stayed quiet, reacting to me now and then when I spoke to their characters, but mostly staying still and watching. When the scene finished, a long silence filled the air.

Immediately, the confidence I'd had in my performance began to waver. Did they find it amateurish? Over the top? Why weren't they saying anything?

Unless... maybe they simply thought I hadn't finished yet?

"That's it," I said, giving them both a shrug. "The end."

Instantly, they both leapt to their feet, applauding loudly, and I shook my head, smiling at the overcompensation.

"Kimber, that was incredible." Henry came over to me, his eyes shining. "Honestly, I've never seen anything like it in real life. You were a completely different person."

"I agree," Nick added as he stepped closer too. "You're very talented."

"Thanks." My cheeks flushed again, but it could have been either the compliments or how close they were standing, both to each other and to me. "Maybe someday a casting director will agree."

Nick ignored my attempt at deflection. "Have you ever kissed someone on camera?"

Just the word 'kiss' from him made my eyes drop to his mouth, but I quickly raised them back up, babbling out a reply. "Uh, no, not yet. That's usually reserved for the lead characters. I have done it in auditions, though."

"Tell me about it," he commanded.

I took a shaky breath, trying to stay in control. "Well, I tried out for this one show where my character had two guys fighting over her. I had to kiss them both to see if we had any chemistry."

"And did you?" Henry asked the question, but they both leaned forward in eager anticipation of my reply, dangerously close to me.

I grimaced at the memory. "I guess not. The casting director said no one would ever buy that I had two men interested in me."

My eyes went wide as I realized what I had just said, and Henry and Nick smiled at each other for a second before turning back to me.

"Apparently, he didn't have a very good imagination, then," Nick said, just before he leaned in and kissed me.

Chapter Five

~**Nick**~

Up until now, I had been admirably restrained.

Way back in the park this afternoon, I already thought about kissing Kimber. It felt like she wanted me to, like she wouldn't have complained if I did, but I held back for two reasons: first, because she still hadn't technically agreed to anything, and second, because we were missing Henry.

We were supposed to be doing this together, and even though we were all clear on the situation, it would be better not to confuse the issue by moving forward without him.

When we went to her apartment afterwards and she came out of the bathroom looking both sweet and tempting in her pretty skirt, I nearly kissed her then too, but I stopped myself again for the same reasons.

Then, once we got to our apartment, I walked into the kitchen to find Kimber and Henry face-to-face, only inches apart, and I knew he found it a struggle to hold himself back too.

What made Kimber so appealing? I couldn't quite put my finger on it. She was pretty, yes, but so were a lot of other women and I could always control myself around them. She had some of my favourite qualities in a friend and a lover, being blunt and funny and yet still easy to tease, which helped to explain it more. But the biggest turn-on for me seemed to be the idea that Henry liked her too. We often had pretty divergent tastes on a lot of things, but on the subject of Kimber, we were in complete agreement, and it felt good to have a mutual interest and a mutual goal.

Would I still find her attractive without Henry? Sure. Would I want her quite as much as I did right now? Probably not. Separating one thing from the other seemed impossible, and at that moment, I simply knew that I wanted her, and I would willingly push the issue just a little to see if we could all get closer to what we wanted.

Especially since I knew she wanted it too. She'd had plenty of opportunity to say otherwise if she didn't, but instead, she got dressed up, came over here, flirted with us and performed for us, all while knowing exactly what we wanted from her. If that wasn't a green light to take things a little further, I must be colour-blind.

So when my lips finally connected with hers, I couldn't have been more ready for it. Or so I thought, but her kiss still managed to take me by surprise. Given how unsure she'd been last night when I first brought up the idea, I expected a little hesitation, but instead, I found only desire.

I could taste the wine she just drank along with the fruity flavour of her lip gloss as her soft, pink lips moved against mine. Her light, floral perfume added to the array of sensations stoking the fire inside me, and so did Henry's hand on my shoulder, warm and supportive. It obviously pleased him that I'd made a move. He wanted me to.

Still, I shouldn't be greedy, so after a minute, I pulled back, looking into Kimber's blue eyes with a warm smile before moving to the side. Henry immediately took the cue, stepping into the space I'd just vacated, and with his hand on her face, he kissed her too.

No hint of jealousy or resentment existed as I watched their kiss, my hand on Henry's arm as his had been on mine. In fact, this might just be one of the hottest things I'd ever seen: two people who I found attractive, who both found *me* attractive but were also attracted to each other, enjoying their first kiss while fully aware of my presence.

My arousal, which had been growing all day, got even stronger as I watched their lips, knowing how it felt to kiss them both myself. My jeans grew uncomfortably tight as my cock swelled within them.

Henry broke the kiss, smiling at Kimber just as I had, and when he turned to look at me, his eyes bright with excitement, I couldn't help it: I leaned forward and kissed him too. I wanted him to know how much I had enjoyed watching them and how excited I felt to share this moment with him. As much as this involved Kimber, our relationship still came first. That had been the impetus for the whole idea in the first place. In his kiss, I could feel his excitement too, making me more confident than ever that we were on the same page.

When we parted, I immediately looked at Kimber, wondering what her reaction would be, and what I saw in her eyes made me even harder than before. She had enjoyed watching us just as much as I enjoyed watching her and Henry.

Despite my certainty that we were all on the same page, I still wanted her to say it. I wanted to hear the words, so I asked her the question now: "We haven't given you the full tour of the apartment yet, Kimber. Would you like to come and see our bedroom?"

She swallowed, her eyes darting back and forth between me and Henry, our arms still around each other, and, to my great relief and elation, she nodded.

"Yes. I'd like to see it all."

~Kimber~

This was insane. I couldn't believe I had agreed to it, and yet, I had. Nick asked me and I said yes. I knew exactly what going to their bedroom meant and I said yes anyway.

I could blame the wine, but that would be a cop-out. The truth? I wanted them, both of them. Just like that casting director had said, I had never imagined myself as the kind of woman who would have two men interested in her at the same time, but now I had even gone one step further. I had two men who wanted me who also wanted each other. Their kisses were both amazing, different but equally exciting, and when they kissed each other afterwards, the aching between my legs only got worse.

I hadn't known something like this would turn me on, but it definitely did. And though I didn't know exactly how things would play out with all three of us together, they made me feel comfortable and desired enough that I wanted to find out.

Nick took my hand while Henry put his arm around my back and the three of us walked together out of the kitchen and down the hall into an absolutely massive master bedroom suite, dominated by a huge King-sized bed with black and grey bedding. The whole room felt masculine and strong with no hint of a woman's touch. It made me feel like a bit of an intruder, and yet, the room's occupants could hardly have made it more clear that they wanted me here.

As soon as we were in the middle of the room, Nick kissed me again, his lips warm and firm against mine as his hands cupped my breasts, pressing against them with just the right amount of strength. My nipples were straining against the fabric of my bra, my vagina throbbed with need, and my panties were drenched.

It only got worse... or better... as Henry came up behind me. His body pressed against me, sandwiching me between him and Nick, with his stiff cock hard against my ass. I moaned into Nick's mouth as Henry kissed my neck, his hands circling around to my chest.

With four hands on me and two mouths, I already felt closer to orgasm than I had in months.

In my lustful haze, it took a moment for me to remember that I had hands too and there were things I could be doing with them. The first thing on my list involved getting Nick's shirt off since he stood right in front of me. My fingers went to his buttons, fumbling as I tried to undo them with my trembling hands. Luckily, he took pity on me and as soon as I had a couple of them open, he stepped back, reached over his shoulder, grabbed the back of his shirt and pulled it over his head.

Holy hell. How could one simple action be so hot? Almost as hot as the sight of him standing there shirtless, the defined muscles of his chest and abs begging to be touched.

I knew just how shallow those thoughts were, especially since my own body left a lot to be desired compared to the accepted ideal, but I couldn't help it: I wanted to lick every damn inch of him.

The rustle of fabric behind me told me that Henry's shirt would soon be on the floor too, and Nick grinned at me. "Your turn, Kimber."

For a woman of my size, I had far fewer body image issues than most, but I'd also never been in a situation quite like this, with both of them staring at me as Henry moved around in front of me, his chest bare too as they waited for me to make the next move.

Well, fuck it. If they were going to be turned off by my body, it would have happened already, so I might as well just go for it. Reaching behind me, I unzipped my skirt so I could pull my shirt out, then lifted it up over my head, revealing my heart-embellished bra for them both to see.

The heat-filled look they exchanged let me know they definitely approved. "Take the skirt off too, Kimber," Henry requested, his voice thicker than usual. "Please."

Nick wouldn't have said 'please', I knew that much already. There were many differences between them, and I honestly couldn't say which I preferred. I liked Henry's sweetness and politeness, and I liked Nick's confidence and dominance. The fact that I could have both at the same time still felt like a dream come true.

As he'd asked so nicely, I pulled my skirt down too, letting it fall to the floor, leaving me standing there in just my underwear while two of the sexiest men I'd ever seen looked me over, their eyes roaming across my body shamelessly.

If they were going to change their minds, it would happen now, and I held my breath as they took their time, examining me from head to toe.

"You know what, Henry?" Nick asked, looking over at his boyfriend again once he'd sized me up completely. "I'm suddenly in the mood for a little dessert."

A jolt of pleasure and anticipation ran through me. I might have been reading too much into his statements in the kitchen earlier, but this time his meaning seemed pretty clear.

Henry grinned at him in response. "Only if you're willing to share." "Of course."

They both turned back to me, hunger in their eyes, and my knees nearly buckled as Nick took a step towards me. He kissed me again, harder this time, and I had to hold onto him just to stay upright. The force of his desire left me breathless, as did the anticipation of what came next.

The kiss served as a distraction while the two of them went to work removing my few remaining scraps of clothing. Nick's tongue slid into my mouth as Henry ran his hands over my ass, pulling my panties down as he went. Nick's hands released the clasp on my bra as he kept kissing me, and Henry picked up where he left off, sliding the straps over my shoulders. I had never been so overwhelmed with sensation, or felt so special with these two incredible men focused entirely on me.

Gently, Henry pulled me back, out of Nick's embrace, and my bra fell away too, leaving me completely naked. There were only a handful of people who had ever seen me naked before, and yet I had never felt as comfortable in my own skin as I did right now. The looks they were both giving me were full of appreciation, with no hint of disappointment.

"Why don't you lie down on the bed?" Henry whispered in my ear from behind me. "We can't wait to get a look at you, Kimber."

They were already seeing it all, I thought, until I remembered exactly what he meant: *their dessert.*

Thankfully they were both ready to help me over to the bed as I didn't know if I could even walk on my own, my body so weak with need and anticipation. Henry placed a pillow in the middle of the bed as Nick lowered me down and then, as if they'd agreed it in advance, they both moved to my breasts, each of them latching onto one of my nipples, their faces right beside each other.

"Oh, God." Desire and pleasure rushed through me as their mouths went to work. Nick took things a little rougher, his teeth scraping over one pink peak, while Henry kissed the other, his tongue swirling around it. With my head propped up on the pillow, I could see the top of their heads, their dark and light hair forming a perfect contrast to each other. A moment later, Nick looked up at me, gave me a wink, and started to move lower.

My legs trembled as he got down between them, his big, warm hands running down my hips and over my thighs before insistently pushing them apart. My fingers threaded through Henry's hair as he continued to take his time with my aching, sensitive nipple.

"Fuck!" The word slipped out of my mouth before I could stop it as Nick's tongue made contact with me, and he groaned in satisfaction.

Henry raised his head, giving me an almost shy smile before turning to face Nick. "Is it that good?" he asked eagerly.

Nick grinned up at him. "You know that pie you brought home the other day?" Henry nodded. "Even sweeter."

His words and the way they were both talking about me in general, like something precious and desirable, had me almost writhing with need. When Nick went back for another taste, with Henry watching this time, I let out a desperate whimper. Fuck, I couldn't believe how close I was already.

"You really need to try it," Nick said, still talking to Henry as if I couldn't hear them. "Here."

He reached up and grabbed the back of Henry's head as their mouths connected. I could see their tongues tangling, sharing my own taste between them, and I whimpered once more.

"Please." They both turned to look at me as I moaned the word. "I'm almost there, please."

Nick gave me a satisfied smile before turning to Henry. "Do you want the honours?"

Henry bit his lip in anticipation as they traded places, him taking the spot between my legs as Nick moved up the bed towards me.

"Kiss me, Kimber," he commanded, his breath hot against my skin. "Henry already had a taste, and you can too, while he makes you come."

His mouth claimed mine before I could protest, not that I had any intention of doing so. I could indeed taste my own essence on him, and my senses went further into overdrive, especially as Henry's tongue connected with my clit.

This time they kept going, both of them, hands and mouths claiming every part of me, until I completely fell apart, falling into my orgasm and into the blissful delights of being wanted and desired by these two amazing men.

My brain was clear of all thoughts as wave after wave of pleasure ran through me, but when it finally started to work again, one thought stood out above all others: yesterday might have been the worst day of life, but today looked set to be the best.

~Henry~

Kimber tasted incredible, whether on Nick's tongue or straight from the source. It had been a long time since I'd done this on any woman, but it all came back to me as soon as I got up close to her pretty pink pussy which matched the colour of her lip gloss almost exactly, my mouth watering.

As I dipped my tongue into her and heard her moan in response, pride and excitement ran through me. I really liked Kimber, and I loved the idea of making her feel good. It wouldn't have been the same with anyone else. It being Kimber made it this good.

And Nick being there too, clearly enjoying himself, just added to my enjoyment. He lay next to Kimber on the bed, kissing her as I worked my tongue around her centre, meaning his groin sat eye level with me, making it impossible to miss the growing bulge in his pants that matched my own. The mutual arousal in the room was undeniable.

Kimber gave us warning of her imminent orgasm and she meant it. Her body trembled against my face as it hit her, sending a wave of pleasure through me too with the knowledge that we had done that to her. Greedily, I lapped up every drop of sweetness that her pleasure produced, savouring the taste and scent of her and the way she felt against my mouth, so different from Nick and just as good.

When I raised my head, Kimber's eyes were closed, her lips parted, and Nick smiled down at me. His eyes dropped to my mouth and I knew exactly what he wanted: to share her taste, just like he'd done with me, and I had no objections.

I crawled up the bed on the other side of Kimber and leaned across her to kiss my boyfriend, hard and deep. He groaned as his tongue swept across mine, the taste and the feel of it combining into an intensely sensual experience for us both. It felt forbidden, a little taboo, but perfectly natural at the same time.

When we broke apart, panting from the force of the kiss, we both looked down at Kimber who had her eyes open now, watching us, and she gave us a captivating smile, somehow shy and seductive at the same time. "I don't know why it's so hot to see you guys kiss, but it really is."

Nick and I both grinned. I loved her honesty, and I wanted to be honest with her too. "I loved watching you and Nick kiss too," I admitted. "I haven't done anything like this before with three people. I didn't know if I would like it, but I think you can see that I do."

I gestured down to my straining pants, and Kimber raised her head to get a better look, inhaling as she did.

Her eyes returned to my face, still with that same look, hesitant and bold at the same time. "Can I see you?" She turned to Nick, not wanting to leave him out. "And you, too?"

"I thought you'd never ask," Nick teased, pulling Kimber gently up to a sitting position before he and I crawled back off the bed.

Knowing for sure now that she enjoyed watching us, he grabbed hold of the waist of my pants, pulling me close to him as he kissed me once again. My body pressed against his, our cocks rubbing against each other through the fabric of our remaining clothes as his mouth moved against mine. My hands went to his zipper at the same time that his went to mine, both of us undressing each other as our appreciative audience of one eagerly took in the show.

Nick had the advantage since my work pants were looser than his jeans, so he got my cock out first, his big, warm hand wrapping around it and giving it a firm squeeze as I groaned into his kiss. Nothing compared to that first touch of skin on skin, sending the blood straight to my cock and making it even harder. Finally, I got his out too, returning the favour, and then we broke apart to quickly remove our own pants, leaving us both standing there just as naked as Kimber herself.

As we both turned to face her, her gaze didn't waver from the two equally hard shafts in front of her, and I tried to guess what she might be thinking. Nick's cock was certainly impressive, thick and strong. I could still remember being slightly intimidated by it the first time I saw it, wondering how he would ever fit inside me.

It wouldn't be too much of a spoiler to say we eventually figured it out.

Mine had a different shape, not quite as wide as his but a bit longer. He had measured it once, just for fun, when one of his particularly playful moods came on.

Kimber raised her hand tentatively, reaching towards me before stopping and looking up at me. "Can I?"

I gave a slightly strangled laugh. I wouldn't be standing here like this unless I wanted her to, but I appreciated that she asked anyway. "Please," I invited.

As her soft, gentle hand took hold of me, my eyes closed and I exhaled in pleasure. The feel of her hand differed significantly from Nick's hand on me, but both were exquisite. Thankfully, nobody wanted me to choose a favourite between the two sensations, since it would be almost impossible.

"It's a great cock, isn't it?" Nick asked, and I opened my eyes to find the two of them sharing a smile. "It feels even better inside you, trust me."

His words and Kimber's touch combined to make my cock jump, blood rushing to it once more. I wouldn't be able to take a lot more of this.

Nick's bluntness would have made me blush, but it seemed to have the opposite effect on Kimber. She smiled up at him, still holding onto me. "Yours isn't bad either."

He raised his eyebrows in mock offense. "Not bad? Are those the words you'd use, Henry?"

Invited into the conversation, I tried to play along, to make him feel as good as his words made me feel. "It's amazing. Touch him, Kimber. I bet you can't even get your hand all the way around it."

That seemed to be the right thing to say as they both smiled. Kimber willingly followed my instruction, taking hold of him too, and Nick inhaled sharply as she squeezed, trying to make her fingers touch. "You're right," she told me with a laugh. "Not quite."

Still smiling, she began to stroke us both at the same time, me with her left hand and Nick with her right, as Nick leaned over and kissed me again. My body flared with desire, alight with a hundred different sensations. I never knew it could be like this.

"Although I hate to interrupt this," Nick said as he pulled away from me, "we need to discuss a few things before we go any further."

Kimber stopped her movements but didn't let go of us, still holding us both firmly by the cock. "Like what?"

"Condoms," Nick replied bluntly. "Yes or no? Henry and I are both clean, we got tested when we got together and we haven't been with anyone else since."

Her gaze dropped to her hands and the shafts she held onto, biting her lip as if she might be imagining them inside her. "I'm clean too," she told us. "And I'm on the pill, though it's hardly been necessary lately."

Her truthfulness made me smile. "Hopefully we can make up for that."

Her eyes returned to my face, warm and teasing. "I'm sure you can."

"So that's a no on condoms?" Nick clarified, obviously wanting to move things along. When she nodded in confirmation, he asked his next question: "Anything you don't like?"

Kimber shrugged sheepishly. "I don't think I've tried enough things to know for sure."

That didn't bother Nick. "Okay, we'll figure it out as we go then. If you're not enjoying something, just say so and we'll do something else."

"It sounds like you've got something in mind," I pointed out. This type of focus usually meant he was building up to something.

He grinned over at me. "I do, and I'm pretty sure you're going to like it. Kimber, shuffle back onto the bed."

She quickly complied, letting us go and moving backwards until she lay completely on the bed.

Nick gave me my instructions next: "Henry, you're going to fuck her, missionary-style."

My cock jumped again as I looked over Kimber, naked in all her soft, curvy glory. As happy as that idea made me, I couldn't see one piece of the puzzle. "What about you?" I asked Nick.

His grin grew even wider. "I'm going to fuck *you*."

Just the idea of it sent a thrill through me. I had certainly never done anything like that before, and I glanced over at Kimber to see what she thought.

The excitement in her eyes gave me her answer even before she could. "That sounds amazing."

I thought so too, so I gave Nick one more kiss. "I love you," I whispered to him, and he pressed his lips against mine harder, returning the sentiment with his actions even if the words weren'st said.

As he went to the bedside table to grab the lube, I crawled up onto the bed between Kimber's legs. When we were face-to-face, that beguiling shyness returned to her eyes. "I've imagined this a few times," she admitted to me, whimpering as my hand went between her legs, making sure she needed no further preparation. "Before I knew about Nick, I mean."

Just when I thought I couldn't get any harder, I kept getting proven wrong. "I thought about you too," I told her honestly. "About how if I were single, you were just the kind of woman I would like. I can't believe you're really here."

"Neither can I," she agreed. "But if this is a dream, don't wake me up yet."

She could always make me laugh. "I don't think it is. But let's see for sure..."

I let my word trail off as I lined my aching cock up against her slick entrance, where my face had been just a few minutes before, and as I slid into her, we both exhaled in satisfaction.

There really was nothing quite like a vagina.

I loved making love to Nick, but it felt different. The way her snug, naturally wet walls expanded around me satisfied me completely, like sinking into a warm, welcoming pool of pure pleasure. Having her breasts beneath me only enhanced the experience, as did the look of desire and satisfaction in her beautiful blue eyes.

Fuck, I owed Nick big-time for suggesting this.

I thrust into her a few times, slow and languid, getting used to the feel of her as she got used to me, lost in the mutual pleasure we were feeling until the bed sank down beside us and I looked over to see Nick watching us, his blue eyes full of satisfaction too, the shade of them similar to Kimber's but not the same.

"You two look so incredible," he told us both. "I almost hate to intrude."

Kimber smiled over at him. "I'm the one intruding," she claimed. "Come and join us."

I nodded my agreement. "I want you, Nick."

Heat filled his eyes as he rubbed his hard cock, covered with lube now. "I want you too, Henry. Fuck, I want you so bad."

My cock jumped hard inside Kimber, making her moan, and I leaned forward over her to give Nick better access. His lubed fingers pressed into me, getting me ready for him, and his cock quickly followed as I took a deep breath, relaxing to let him in.

"How does that feel?" he whispered to me from behind, and I could hardly find the words.

"Amazing," I managed to stutter truthfully. Having him inside me while I rested inside Kimber was the most intense pleasure I'd ever experienced. I had never felt so fulfilled.

And then, he began to move. He pulled almost all the way out of me, his hands on my hips as he drew me back too, and then he thrust into me hard, pushing me back into Kimber in a chain reaction, him controlling us both, and Kimber's moans of satisfaction mingled with mine as I surrendered to it completely.

In and out, forward and back, receiving and giving, it all mixed together into a great kaleidoscope of pleasure until I no longer knew where I began and he ended, or I ended and she began. And when Kimber came again, her walls tightening around me, I let myself go too, calling out both their names in a breathless moment of glory. It only took a few more thrusts before Nick finished too, his cum warm inside me.

All three of us were silent afterwards, taking a moment to process what had just happened, still joined together in our chain. Nick had told me it would be good, but I never imagined it would be *this* good. I only hoped they both enjoyed it as much as I did, because I definitely wanted to do that again.

Chapter Six

~**Nick**~

As the intensity of my orgasm faded, a deep feeling of satisfaction remained. Although my expectations had been high for this evening, they'd just been exceeded.

I had done this before, a threesome with another man and a woman, and I had enjoyed it then but not nearly as much as I did tonight. Maybe Henry had a point about sex being better with people you cared for. I loved Henry, of course, and it turned me on to see him enjoying himself so much, which played a big part in my overall satisfaction. I also really liked Kimber too. Her sweet sounds coming from beneath Henry enhanced the whole experience for me, even though I hadn't touched her directly. Knowing that all three of us were equally engaged and equally stimulated elevated all of it to another level.

As we gradually disentangled ourselves, me flopping down onto the bed on one side of Kimber and Henry on the other, she looked between the two of us with a satisfied smile. "Well, I'm never going to forget that."

Henry and I both smiled back, exchanging pleased glances with each other. We definitely wouldn't either.

"Do you need anything?" Henry asked her, his naturally caring nature shining through as usual. "How are you feeling?"

"Honestly, I feel incredible," she told us, and from the smile on her face, I believed it. "I never imagined doing anything like this, and nervous doesn't begin to cover how I felt coming over here tonight, but you've made it wonderful, both of you. Thank you."

I appreciated the confirmation that she enjoyed it too, even though I would have bet any money on that fact based on her reaction in the moment. But now, she took us both by surprise by sitting up and getting to her feet.

"If it's not too much trouble, could one of you give me a ride home?"

Henry's brow immediately furrowed and mine did too as Kimber began to gather up her clothes. "There's no rush," he protested. "It's still early."

"You can even stay here tonight if you'd like," I offered. "I could drop you off at home in the morning before work."

She would need to change for work, naturally, but we could find a way to work around it.

Kimber's smile stayed on her face, but it had turned slightly strained. "That's really kind, but I don't want to make things weird. Let's not ruin this great experience."

Without giving either of us a chance to say anything further, she took her clothes into our ensuite bathroom, closing and locking the door behind her.

Henry looked over at me with concern and dismay written across his handsome face. "What brought that on?"

At first, I had no idea, but as I reviewed both tonight and last night in my head, I began to form a theory. "You remember I asked you last night if you wanted this to be more than a one-time thing?"

He nodded, his forehead still creased in worry.

"I don't think we told *her* that."

That must be it, and from Henry's pained expression, he obviously agreed. Kimber thought we'd gotten what we wanted from her, end of story, but nothing could be further from the truth. Countless other possibilities existed for the three of us, if she had the interest, both in and out of the bedroom. I liked the dynamic the three of us had together, not just sexually but in conversation too. No one could say how long it would last, but we might as well enjoy it for as long as it did. Life could be hard enough on its own without passing up a good thing when it came along.

So, we needed to tell her that, and I thought she might feel more comfortable having that conversation with our clothes on, so I grabbed my pants and Henry's too, tossing them over to him. We had both just finished zipping up when Kimber came out of the bathroom, dressed back in her cute skirt in record time.

She averted her eyes, her cheeks colouring at the sight of us both standing there with our chests bare, which seemed rather ridiculous since we had just been a lot more naked a moment ago. Now that the heat of the moment had passed, she appeared to be a little uncomfortable, but hopefully the frank conversation I had in mind would fix that.

"Do you have time for another drink before you go?" I asked Kimber as I threw Henry his shirt and pulled mine back over my head.

Confusion flickered across her face. "Why?"

That seemed to confirm my theory. She thought we had nothing left to discuss, and I quickly set the record straight: "Because there's something we'd like to talk to you about."

Without waiting for a response, I headed back to the kitchen, topping up her wine glass and Henry's and handing them over before leading the way to the living room where we could be a bit more informal. I left my glass behind since I'd had enough to drink at the bar earlier, plus I still needed to drive Kimber home after we finished talking.

She took a seat in one of the chairs, making it impossible for anyone to sit next to her, while Henry and I sat down beside each other on the couch. While she took a long sip of her wine, I decided to dive right in. "Kimber, I think there may have been a misunderstanding here."

Her pretty blue eyes went wide with worry. "Did I do something wrong?"

"Not at all," Henry quickly assured her. "I think maybe we did."

Kimber's expression shifted from anxious to confused. "I don't understand."

I jumped in again, leaning forward to look her straight in the eye. "When I told you last night that we wanted to have sex with you, I didn't mean to imply we *only* wanted sex from you. Tonight ticked every one of our boxes and if you would like to repeat it again sometime, we definitely would too. But if you don't, that doesn't mean we have nothing else to talk about. We'd still like to keep getting to know you, even if it's just as friends."

"Really?" Her reaction made it clear that I had hit the nail on the head. She really had thought we were done with her. Shit.

I tried to clarify further. "If I left you with the impression that we just wanted you for your body, I'm sorry. That's not the case at all."

At last, her brow cleared and she gave a soft laugh. "Nobody has ever only wanted me for my body before. Trust me, it hasn't crossed my mind."

"Then what is it?" I prompted. "Why are you so anxious to get out of here?"

"I don't know," she admitted, sighing as she leaned back. At least she looked a bit more comfortable now, not quite so much on edge. "I guess I kind of feel like a third wheel. And I know, you invited me here and what we just did ... I have no words. Incredible. Unreal. But this is *your* relationship. I don't want to get carried away and I don't want to make anything weird for you guys. You're such a great couple."

Henry and I exchanged another quick smile. We certainly thought so too. "Nick and I are on the same page about this," Henry promised her. "And that page involves spending more time with you, in whatever capacity you'd like."

Kimber smiled too, but hesitancy lingered in her eyes. We hadn't fully convinced her just yet. "Well, I think for now I really just need a bit of time to process all of this. So I would still like to go home, but it doesn't mean I'm upset or that I regret any of this, because I really don't. I had a great time."

Since her mind appeared to be made up, we took her home, as she requested, both of us walking her to her front door and giving her a kiss on the cheek before saying goodnight. When we got back in the car, Henry turned to me curiously. "So, you were right last night when you said she'd agree to sleep with us. What does your gut tell you now?"

I had been trying to figure out the same thing, and I'd already settled on an answer. "I think we'll hear from her soon. Very soon."

Maybe that was wishful thinking, but I hoped not. Now that we'd all seen what it could be like with the three of us together, it would be hard to let it go.

~**Kimber**~

I had a fitful sleep that night. No matter how hard I tried to turn my brain off, it kept returning to the large bed, the two gorgeous men, and the things that had happened with them there. Even when I finally fell asleep, my dreams were filled with hands touching me and mouths on every part of me, so that when I woke up, my body throbbed almost painfully in need. With a groan, I reached over to my bedside table and grabbed my rose sex toy which, before last night, had been the only thing to get near my clit in months.

The dream had taken me so far down the road already that by the time the toy began sucking on my clit, I came in about ten seconds flat. *Fuck.*

It did help to take the edge off but I still couldn't relax, not with so many different thoughts flying around my head.

It wouldn't be an exaggeration to say that having sex with Henry and Nick easily constituted the most erotic experience of my life. Not that there were many contenders for that title, but even so, what happened tonight set a bar that would be almost impossible to clear.

So why did I run? *That* was the real question that kept me from being able to rest.

When Henry and Nick laid down on the bed beside me, both spent from their activity, and I looked between them, I felt a surge of emotion far stronger than simply lust. Lust played a role, certainly, but something deeper stood behind it, and it scared me.

They were both so wonderful in their own way, it wouldn't take much for me to fall for either of them, or even both, and that road only led to danger. They were already committed to each other and, as I told them, they made a great couple. Compared to the strength of their relationship, my presence served as a temporary distraction, something to liven up their lives until they moved on, and though it could certainly be a hell of a lot of fun for all of us, in the long run, I worried it could only end in disappointment for me. If I could keep it simply about sex, like they were, then there would be no problem, but that didn't seem entirely realistic.

Though I had never been in love before, this felt like the verge of it, standing on the edge looking at two people whose hearts were already claimed. I might not be the smartest person in the world when it came to relationships but I liked to think I had *some* sense. Neither of them would leave the other to be with me instead, and I wouldn't want them to, not when they were so good together. Breaking them up would be a crime.

The only way this could end was with my heartbreak, and yet, their offer to extend our little ménage tempted me anyway. I had never felt as truly desired as I did with them. Last night had been incredibly hot, and based on what Nick said, it had only been the tip of the iceberg. What else could the three of us do together?

By the time I got to work the next morning, my resolve still flipped back and forth indecisively, no closer to making a decision than I had been in the middle of the night, and as the clock ticked nearer to when Henry usually came in, I got more and more nervous. How strange would it be to see him in the light of day knowing what we did together last night?

The coffee shop got busy, thankfully, helping to keep my mind off my own worries, and only when the rush started to die down did I realize Henry hadn't come in at all, leaving me with a whole new thing to worry about. Why would he be avoiding me? Did he and Nick talk about me last night and decide they'd rather not continue? A million different scenarios played out in my overactive imagination until I told Rocco I would go into the kitchen to work on the menu for next week in an attempt to distract myself.

No more than ten minutes passed before he appeared at the door, a big smile on his face. "Kimber, there is someone here to see you."

To see me? I glanced up at the clock where the hour hand had just passed ten. Henry and Nick would both be at work, and I couldn't think of anyone else who would be looking for me. Baffled, I followed Rocco back out to the counter to see for myself.

Despite the hour, Henry's handsome face greeted me, looking almost as shy and nervous as I felt. As pleased as I was to see him, I didn't understand what brought him here now, and why hadn't he come in earlier.

"Did you sleep in this morning?" I joked, trying to get an answer to my questions without coming right out and asking him.

He smiled too, my tone seeming to set him at ease. "No. I missed my coffee this morning, but I wanted to wait until the florist opened to come and see you."

Florist? The word confused me until he held up a beautiful bouquet of flowers I hadn't even noticed in his hands. I'd been completely distracted by his face, as usual.

"These are for me?" I hardly knew what to say as he handed the flowers over. No one *ever* bought me flowers. That only happened to other girls. "Why?"

"They're not for last night," he said, before blushing a little. "I mean, they are, because I had a wonderful time, but they're for more than that. They're just for you because you make me smile."

He winced as the words came out of his mouth.

"Okay, that's cheesy, but I mean…"

"I love them," I interrupted, giving him a warm smile. His flustered babbling only made him more adorable, and knowing he shared my feelings of being out of my depth in this situation made me feel a million times better, not to mention that the flowers were absolutely beautiful. A quick glance around the shop told me that some of the other women who saw the exchange clearly thought so too. More than a few envious looks were being tossed in my direction, though they might be because of Henry himself rather than the flowers.

If they only knew.

"Oh, and these are for you too," he added, stretching out his other hand with a box of Purdy's chocolates. "You don't need to be any nicer or funnier, but I thought you might like them anyway."

The fact that he remembered what I'd said yesterday to the judge-mental teenager and had gone out of his way to get the chocolates for me touched me even more than the flowers did.

"Most people would say I don't need to eat more chocolate," I pointed out, my hand trembling as I took the box from him. None of the men I'd dated before had ever treated me this well. He couldn't be sweeter.

"I think you should do whatever makes you happy," he replied, and the slightly wistful look in his eyes suggested he hoped he might be one of those things. "But in the meantime, I wonder if you have plans for next Saturday?"

"Saturday?" I repeated, still trying to wrap my head around this whole conversation.

Henry nodded. "Not tomorrow, but a week from tomorrow. My par-ents are having a party, and I want to take Nick but it might get a little awkward, and you're so good with people, I just thought, if you wanted to, it might help if you're there, and it shouldn't be that bad, overall. There will be good food, at least."

He lost me part way through that but I got the gist: he wanted me to go to a party with his family, and him and Nick. That seemed like kind of a big deal for someone he had only really just started to get to know, but it truly flattered me. It also supported what he and Nick had said last night about wanting to be friends aside from anything sexual that might happen between us.

"It sounds interesting," I replied, and his eyes lit up hopefully. "I'm supposed to be working, but I can ask for the day off."

"You can have the day off," Rocco called out from behind me, clearly listening to every word we exchanged, and Henry laughed as I rolled my eyes.

"That's great, thank you," Henry said, smiling at Rocco before turning back to me. "We can talk about it more later, I'll give you all the details then. I've got to get back to work, I just ducked out to get the flowers, but there's a card in there too with my number in it. I know you've got Nick's already, but if you ever want to talk or just text or whatever, you can reach me too. Have a good day, Kimber."

"You too." I watched him go until I couldn't see him anymore out the window, still standing at the counter holding onto my flowers and chocolates and smiling like an idiot.

"Is there something you want to tell me, Kimber?" Rocco asked from behind me, and when I turned back, he gave me a pointed look.

I hated to lie to him, but how could I explain everything that had happened in the last couple of days when I barely understood it myself? "He's just being friendly," I explained weakly. "He helped me out the other day, and we spent a bit of time together. He's really sweet."

Rocco clearly didn't believe me, but he also took pity on me. "Go put those in some water," he instructed, gesturing to the flowers in my hands. "There's a jug in the kitchen you can use for now."

Grateful to him for dropping the matter, I returned to the kitchen and found a jug, filling it with water and placing the flowers inside. Just as I bent over to take a deep sniff of their sweet floral scent, my phone rang. My agent's number flashed across the screen as I pulled it out, taking me by surprise.

"Hello?" I've heard back for all the roles I'd auditioned for lately, but maybe she had something new to put me up for.

"Hi, Kim, it's Shandal," she replied, as if I wouldn't know. "Are you sitting down?"

"No. Why?"

"Because I have amazing news. One of the casting agents that saw you in the callbacks for the show last week called today to ask if you wanted to come in to meet with the producers for a different show, as one of the leads."

When she named the show, my knees nearly buckled. She hadn't been kidding about needing to sit down.

"I thought Amanda Sills had that role?" I stayed up to date on casting news in the city, and that had been big news a few weeks ago.

"She did have it," Shandal told me. "But then they found some... let's say, less than fully clothed productions she took part in. This is a big network show, they want a more wholesome image for their star."

Amanda had done porn? Colour me surprised, and I felt bad for her that it had ruined her shot at this show. But none of that was my fault, and I couldn't pass up an opportunity this huge, almost as big as the part I had missed out on earlier this week.

"I told him he couldn't get any more wholesome than you," Shandal continued breezily. "So they'd like to see you next week."

"Thank you!" I didn't know what else to say, but it seemed to be enough and she promised to email all the details to me later that afternoon.

As we hung up, I couldn't believe the turnaround in my fortune in just a few days, but as my eyes fell on Henry's flowers, my elation began to dull. What I had done last night could hardly be considered wholesome by anyone's standards. 'No one ever has to find out about that', I argued with myself. 'Amanda probably thought the same thing', my brain argued back. 'But she had to know about the camera,' interjected my vagina. 'It doesn't mean *we* should suffer.'

I couldn't make all the parts of me agree, but I knew one thing for certain: my decision about Henry and Nick had just gotten even more complicated. Two days ago, my career prospects had stalled, not to mention my sex life. Now, both were kicking into another gear, but I also might need to choose one over the other.

Life could never be simple, could it?

~Henry~

As always, talking to Kimber brightened my mood. Though Nick seemed convinced that she would be back for more, I felt more uncertain. When we were all dressed again last night, after what could only be described as the most incredible sex of my life, she kept saying how much she had enjoyed it but her body language suggested otherwise. Her shoulders were tense, her smile tight, and doubt and uncertainty clouded her usually bright eyes.

She claimed to be worried about coming between me and Nick, but I honestly couldn't imagine how that could happen. She obviously respected our relationship and wasn't the kind of person who wanted to cause drama. On top of all of that, I had never felt closer to him than I did right now.

I had a sneaking suspicion that Kimber's hesitation stemmed from something else, though I couldn't imagine what, and I hated the idea of causing her any kind of distress. I thought the flowers and chocolates might be a way to demonstrate that sex made up just a small part of what we wanted and what we liked about her. Perhaps she would find the gesture clichéd, but I hoped she would recognize that it came from the heart.

And when she smiled at me – her real smile, not the fake one I'd noticed her give other, ruder customers – everything seemed lighter again. Maybe Nick had it right. Maybe she simply needed a little time and everything would be okay.

I felt so good while speaking to her that I went ahead and invited her to my parents' party though I still hadn't even told Nick about it. My confession to him was long overdue, and I knew he would be upset to learn that my parents didn't know about him, but I *did* intend to tell them at the party. I figured they wouldn't make a scene with a bunch of other people around; my parents were not that kind of people. But more than that, I hoped that if they saw us together, they would see just how right we were for each other. Kimber could see it right away after meeting Nick; why should my parents be any different?

It came to me earlier this morning that having Kimber there might help to smooth things over when I made the revelation to my parents. She always made things better and easier, and this should be no exception. If she backed me up that Nick and I were made for each other, it seemed more likely that they would also believe it. And when she agreed to come to the party, I immediately felt better, and braver too.

Brave enough to finally tell Nick the truth.

Nick and I always had lunch together on Fridays. The rest of the week, our disparate work schedules kept us apart, but we made time on Fridays without fail. Putting each other first helped build and maintain the relationship we had, and unfortunately, by not telling him the truth before now, I'd failed at it. I hoped he could forgive me.

When I walked into the café where we usually met, he sat at our regular table and my chest warmed at the sight of him, like it did every single time.

I was such a lucky guy.

"Hey," I greeted him as I walked up to the table, leaning down to give him a quick peck on the lips. "How's your day?"

"The office is going crazy," he replied. "Management announced that two of the vice-presidents will be leaving at the end of the summer."

A wide smile spread across my face as I realized what that must mean. "So you're getting promoted?"

Nick had been wanting to move up in his company for as long as I'd known him. Though I still struggled to understand exactly what he did, I knew just how well he did it, and I had no doubt he deserved to be recognized. I couldn't be more proud of him.

But to my surprise, he grimaced before shrugging. "Nothing's official yet, but I'm definitely in the running."

The waitress came over to take our order, interrupting our conversation, and I had to let a couple of minutes go by before I could ask him to explain further.

"So what's the problem? You don't look as thrilled about it as I thought you'd be."

With a sigh, he told me about the conversation he had with the board member yesterday. "Basically, I'm being considered, but not for the right reasons. When the news came out today, people immediately started speculating on who would get the positions, and my name came up quite a lot."

Although I tried to follow his train of thought, the issue remained fuzzy to me. "That's great! So even if there's some reverse discrimination going on, people know you deserve it anyway."

"The problem is that nobody mentioned Jennifer Cartwright, the woman the board is pushing. If they choose the two of us, as Mr Montgomery told me they were considering, people will wonder why. It won't take much for them to put things together and assume they chose both of us for optics rather than because we deserved it."

At last, I thought I got it. "So your promotion would be tainted by association, even though you do deserve it."

He nodded grimly. "It would put a big target on my back in the office, and Jennifer's too. Everyone would be waiting for us to fail so they could crow about how we didn't deserve it in the first place. It's not fair to either of us."

I couldn't argue with that, and though I wished I could help, it had nothing to do with me. I could only be supportive. "So what are you going to do?"

Nick grimaced once again. "I haven't decided yet. I just wanted to talk it out with you. I would have told you last night, but... you know. We had other things on our minds."

That also explained why I hadn't shared my own news with him, and he couldn't have given me a better opening to do it now. Taking a deep breath, I dove in. "Actually, I wanted to talk to you about something last night too. I heard from my dad yesterday. My parents are throwing a party for my mom's birthday next weekend."

I rarely mentioned my parents, so Nick's curiosity immediately piqued. "Are we going?"

"Well, that's what I want to talk to you about. I want us to go, and to introduce you to them."

His warm smile made it clear the invitation touched him, which only made the rest of what I had to tell him even harder. Still, I had to come clean. I had let this go on long enough already.

"They, uh, they don't know about you yet. I mean, they know you exist, but they don't know that we're together. They don't know you're my boyfriend."

Nick's smile faded, replaced by a look of confusion. "What do you mean? You see them all the time."

"I do. And they know I'm living with you, just not... in that way."

Understanding dawned across his face now, accompanied by disbelief. "So they don't know you're gay?"

His tone, no matter how justified, made me wince. "No, they don't."

"What the hell, Henry? Are you ashamed of it? Of me?" Hurt laced his voice, which had gone dangerously quiet. Rather than shouting when something bothered him, Nick withdrew instead, and I tried to clear things up before that could happen.

"Of course not. I love you, Nick. Everyone at work knows about you and all my friends do too." He knew that. He had been to my office before, had come to work functions where I'd introduced him to everyone as my boyfriend. He couldn't truly think he embarrassed me in any way. "It's just different with my parents. They're very traditional and I didn't see the point in upsetting them if..."

I trailed off as I realized how the words in my head would sound if I finished that sentence out loud, but I didn't catch it in time. Nick had already figured it out. "If you changed your mind?"

His face had darkened, and again, I couldn't blame him. He had every right to feel upset. It would hurt me too if I realized Nick had been keeping an escape clause, and whether I meant it that way or not, I couldn't argue with how it looked.

I screwed up, and denying it would be pointless. The best way forward would be to apologize and try to do better.

"I'm sorry, Nick. I was being a coward and it's not fair to you. I want to make it right. Please, come with me to the party and let me introduce you to them there. I figure once they see us together, they'll see just how right we are for each other and they won't be able to complain."

His lips were still tight as he scanned my face, but after a moment, he shook his head. "Shit, Henry. How am I supposed to stay mad at you when you look at me like that?"

I would have to try to remember that for the next time I messed up. "So you'll come?" I pleaded.

He sighed, clearly not happy about the whole thing but not looking for a fight either. "I guess. But don't you think it'd be better to tell them ahead of time rather than springing it on them at the party?"

I had thought it over, and I really thought telling them at the party made the most sense. No matter how much I wanted to get it out in the open, I simply couldn't imagine telling them while the three of us sat around my parent's kitchen table. That explained why I hadn't done it yet. "The party will provide a good distraction and give them time to think it over. And I've asked Kimber to come and smooth things over in case it doesn't go the way I expect it to. I've seen her deal with people at her work, she's great at calming people down."

Surprise flashed in Nick's eyes. "You invited Kimber?"

Did he have a problem with that? It hadn't occurred to me that he might. "As a friend. Is that okay?"

He blinked a couple of times, thinking it over. "Sure, I suppose. And she said yes?"

"I think so?" As I thought back over the conversation, I realized that she hadn't actually said the words. She just said she'd need the time off, then Rocco said she could have it, and I had taken that as an agreement. But she had never actually said yes, or no either for that matter.

Nick smiled, almost despite himself. "You *think* so? When will you know for sure?"

"Shut up," I mumbled. He always teased me about not being forceful enough, not bold enough about what I wanted. Like with my parents, I supposed.

"Well, I think the fact that she is even thinking about it is a good sign," Nick said, and I breathed a sigh of relief as we moved on from my mistake. I might not be totally forgiven yet, but Nick always tried to see my side even when he would have handled things differently. I really loved and admired that about him.

"I think so too," I agreed, following his change of topic to discuss Kimber instead. "I'm hoping we might hear from her soon.."

I hadn't even finished my thought when my phone and Nick's both pinged at exactly the same time. He got his out of his pocket a fraction of a second before me.

"Speak of the devil." Nick grinned over at me, and my heart beat a bit faster as I opened up Kimber's text, sent to both of us.

There's something I'd like to talk to you both about when you've got time.

Short and to the point, I had no idea what it might be that she wanted to say. When I looked up again, Nick had his eyebrows raised at me. "Should we invite her over tonight?"

Just the thought of Kimber back in our apartment had all kinds of dirty thoughts running through my head. "Sure," I agreed, trying to sound nonchalant, though I knew he wouldn't be fooled. "She can come straight over after work if she likes."

Nick quickly texted her back as our food arrived and we dug into our lunch. The weight on my chest had eased now that I'd told Nick the truth, and as a bonus, I might have a visit from Kimber to look forward to. The rest of the work day could not go fast enough.

Chapter Seven

~Kimber~

Nick replied so quickly that I couldn't help feeling flattered. He had a lot going on in his life; being in touch with me didn't have to be a priority and yet he made it one.

I'm with Henry right now, we'd both love to see you tonight. Come over when you're finished at work. I might be in bed but I'll leave a key for you with security.

The thought of Nick in bed sent a rush of excitement through me and I had to shake my head at myself. Henry had told me he often had a nap when he got home from work. I shouldn't read anything more into it than that.

Rereading his response, I chewed my lip, filled with indecision. Was going to their apartment really such a good idea? What I wanted right now involved simply talking to them about the call I'd received and asking for their honest advice. Going to their place seemed like an invitation for a lot more than that to happen.

On the other hand, what alternatives did I have? I couldn't invite them to my place. With three people in there, there would hardly be room to move.

'Not to mention it would be a little cramped on that twin bed,' my libido piped up in the back of my head.

Not helpful, I told myself firmly. First and foremost, we needed to talk, and if my apartment wouldn't work, that only left going out somewhere in public for what would essentially be a very private conversation, and that felt like a bad idea too.

So their apartment made the most sense, though it felt like walking into the lion's den where a very big part of me *wanted* the lions to eat me.

Seriously, Kimber! Stop that, I admonished myself.

I texted them back before my thoughts could get any more outlandish. *Sounds good. See you later.*

No flirting, nothing suggestive. I needed to keep my head and treat this as seriously as it deserved to be treated.

Though Nick had told me to come over straight from work, which would be quickest considering the short distance between their apartment and the coffee shop, by the time my shift ended, I decided to run home first. I had saved a little money on groceries the last couple of days since Henry and Nick had been feeding me, so I splurged on a taxi, asking the driver to wait while I ran in, dropped off the flowers and chocolates from Henry, and quickly changed my clothes.

'Just because I'm changing doesn't mean I expect anything to happen tonight', I told the girl in the mirror as I touched up my makeup.

'You are such a liar', she smirked back at me.

The taxi dropped me off in front of Nick and Henry's gleaming building, and I marched up to the security desk as confidently as I could. "Hi, how are you? Nick said he'd leave a key here for me?"

The woman in her 40s looked up at me with a complete poker face. "Nick?"

Oh, shit. I hadn't realized until now that I had no clue about his last name. I slept with the man last night and I didn't know his last name, nor had I told him mine. What happened to my life?

"He's in apartment 2202," I explained, thankful that at least I remembered the apartment number.

"And your name?"

"Kimber Page."

Finally, the woman cracked a bit of a smile as she reached down and picked up an envelope from next to her computer. "That's a great name. Are you a relative of Nick's?"

Of course she wouldn't assume I had any romantic reason for being here, since she must know about Henry. "Just a friend of both Henry and Nick."

"They are the nicest men," she told me, leaning forward conspiratorially even though we were the only ones around. "Most of the people who can afford to live here are snobs but they're not like that."

She could say that again. I'd never met two less pretentious men, no matter the size of their bank account or how gorgeous they were. "I completely agree," I assured her. "What's your name?"

"Kelly. It's not as pretty as Kimber."

"It's nice to meet you, Kelly." I gave her a warm smile and we chatted for a few more minutes about her job and about ridiculous housing prices in Vancouver before I excused myself to go upstairs. It pleased me to know that my initial impression of both Nick and Henry seemed to be right: they were genuinely nice guys, and I couldn't help wondering what Kelly would think if she knew exactly what had gone on between us.

"Hello?" I called out when I entered the apartment, not too loud in case I'd arrived before the end of his nap, but loud enough that he could hear me from the kitchen or the living room. Silence greeted me in reply so I quietly slipped off my shoes and headed into the kitchen with the cake I had brought from work.

A moment later, a door closed somewhere deeper in the apartment, so I stuck my head back out into the hallway.

"Nick?"

Still nothing, so I took a few more steps towards the bedroom, not wanting to startle him if he hadn't heard me come in.

"Nick? Are you up?"

The bedroom door stood open, and a moment later, I heard the shower being switched on in the bathroom attached to their bedroom. That must be why he didn't hear me, I realized, and he'd be busy for a while now. I would wait for him in the kitchen.

As I turned to head back, the front door opened and Henry walked in, immediately catching sight of me in the middle of the hallway. "Kimber! Hi. I'm glad you could make it. Is Nick up?"

He gave me a smile but also a slightly curious look, probably wondering what I'd been doing, and my cheeks heated up as I realized what it looked like.

I stuttered out a flustered reply. "He, uh... he just got in the shower, I think. I thought I would... I mean, I thought I heard... I didn't know where he was, but as soon as I realized, I left." I couldn't possibly sound any more guilty, I thought as I winced.

Thankfully, my embarrassment only made Henry laugh. "Usually I'm the tongue-tied one," he teased me. "It's okay, Kimber. I don't think you were spying on Nick in the shower, though if you were, I couldn't blame you. I've done it a few times myself."

"That's different. You're his boyfriend, and I'm just some random girl off the street."

He shook his head, his brow creasing a little. "That's definitely not how we think of you. Here, come on."

He came up to me, holding out his hand, and I looked at it in confusion. "Come on what?"

"Come with me," he clarified, extending his hand once more, and this time I tentatively placed my hand in it.

"Go with you where?"

He gave me a wink. "To enjoy the view."

~Nick~

I usually had no problem having a quick nap after work to refresh myself. My work day started at six o'clock in the morning, meaning I usually got up at four to fit in a workout before I headed into the office. Unless I had a nap when I got home, I'd be dropping off by nine o'clock at night, which wouldn't leave much time to spend with Henry, so the one or two-hour sleep before he got home worked out best for us both and I'd trained my body to expect it.

But today, my mind refused to switch off. I had a lot to think about.

Work topped that list, of course. As I told Henry over lunch, gossip swept through the office after management made the announcement about the positions becoming available. Now that my mood had balanced out since Mr Montgomery told me about it yesterday, the whole thing pissed me off more than ever. I deserved that promotion, yet if I got it simply for being gay, it would feel like I hadn't earned it, even though I had. Like Henry said, the whole thing would be tainted; he'd found the perfect word for it.

The situation with Henry's parents came second on my list of concerns. I hadn't made a big deal about it because I could see that he did genuinely feel bad, but his reluctance to acknowledge our relationship still hurt anyway. My parents knew all about Henry, not that they cared. Though I'd told them his name many times, I bet they'd fail the question if they were given a pop quiz. Henry, on the other hand, had dinner with his parents every week. How could he have never mentioned anything about what we were to each other? I knew he loved me, but that only made it more confusing. Why did he feel he had to hide it?

And finally, uncertainty still lingered around the situation with Kimber. She had agreed to come over to see us today, but why? She said she wanted to talk to us, but could it be more than that?

Everything felt unsettled and, after staring at the ceiling for an hour, I finally gave up and went to have a shower instead, figuring I could try to revitalize myself that way instead before the other two got here.

Like everything else in the apartment, I'd spared no expense on the shower. Large and top-of-the-line, it could have fit four of me easily as I stood in the centre of it, my eyes closed and my head back, letting the warm water fall onto my face as I tried to clear my mind. Kimber should be here soon, I thought, and my body immediately reacted to the idea, my cock beginning to twitch as the blood flow to it increased.

I couldn't pretend not to be hoping for more to happen between the three of us tonight. Henry had got to have sex with her but I hadn't yet. I wanted to feel her coming on my cock, watching her face as she did. Unless I had Henry's cock in my mouth at the same time, in which case it would block my view. So many possibilities existed, and my own cock grew even harder at the thought of them. Reaching down, I gave it a firm stroke, groaning as I did.

A giggle made my eyes shoot open, and only then did I notice the two figures standing outside the shower, by the bathroom door. My heart raced faster, in surprise but even more in anticipation. Were my daydreams about to come true?

"You two enjoying yourselves?" I asked as I switched the water off. Henry still wore his coat, so he'd obviously just got home, but Kimber had her shoes and coat off. How long had she been here?

How long had they both been standing there?

"Not as much as you're enjoying yourself, apparently," Henry teased me, and I followed his gaze down to my rigid cock which proved his point. "We were just hoping to sneak a peek at your ass, but this is so much better."

I stepped out of the shower, not bothering to dry off or to cover myself. It hardly seemed necessary. They'd both seen me this way before, and they were the ones who came to see me anyway.

Though Kimber's cheeks were flushed, she held my gaze as she offered me a simple greeting. "Hi, Nick."

"Hi. I didn't hear you come in but I'm happy you're here."

"Obviously," Henry replied, his eyes dropping to my cock again before looking back up at me, a smile on his face. "You need some help with that?"

My eyebrows raised as I looked between him and Kimber. I certainly wouldn't object, but I didn't want to put any pressure on if she hadn't come here with that in mind.

Since no objections came from her, I answered honestly: "From you? Always."

Henry gave Kimber a wink as he shrugged his coat off and handed it to her. Walking straight over to me, he gave me a kiss before dropping to his knees in front of me, at an angle where we could both still see Kimber.

"Fuck, yes."

The words rumbled out of me as Henry's warm mouth wrapped around my head, licking every drop of water off me, and I gripped the back of his head tightly as I looked back over to Kimber. She held Henry's coat tight against her, her knuckles white as she clenched her fists. Between that and the look in her eyes, I could tell this turned her on too. Not quite as much as it did for me, obviously, but it had potential.

After all, she could take part too, if she wanted to, so I offered her a subtle invitation to join us now. "Henry is so good at this, you'd never know he hadn't done it before me."

The man in question looked up at me, his mouth still full and his eyes shining in appreciation at the compliment. His tongue stroked me firmly and I stifled another groan.

As I hoped, Kimber got my drift immediately, and she put Henry's coat down on the vanity before taking a step towards us. "Maybe you can give me some tips, Henry?"

He pulled back just enough to smile at her. "I'd be happy to. Come here."

He held out his hand to her and she took it, lowering herself down until she knelt next to him, both of them eye level with my cock which ached in anticipation thanks to all the attention being shown to it.

"Now, I can't speak for all men," Henry told Kimber, stepping into the teaching role naturally, "but Nick loves having his balls licked, and he's especially sensitive right here."

His tongue reached out and flicked across the vein on the bottom side of my shaft, right at the ridge of my head, and my cock jumped happily, making them both giggle, sharing a conspiratorial grin.

"That looks like fun," Kimber said, smiling at Henry before looking up at me, her blue eyes heated and hopeful. "Can I give it a try?"

The sight of the two of them down there together, sharing this experience, nearly killed me with pleasure. "Be my guest," I managed to say, my voice tight as I tried to hold back my arousal. I didn't want this to be over *too* quickly.

Kimber licked her lips first before leaning closer to me, and as her tongue connected with my skin, my eyes closed of their own accord. The feel of her differed significantly to Henry, the action of her tongue softer and gentler. I couldn't say which I preferred; they were different but both amazing.

"Like this?" she asked, and I opened my eyes again to see her tongue moving across my cock, looking to Henry for approval.

"That's really good," he assured her, and I could hear the tightness in his own voice. His own desire had obviously taken hold. "And of course, a bit of variety is always good. You can't go wrong with some basic up and down."

Moving along one side of my shaft, he licked all the way down to my base and back up again, meeting Kimber back at the tip. This time when he moved back towards me, she did too, on the other side, both of their tongues caressing me at once, sending a surge of desire through me. Fuck, I felt like the luckiest man in the world right now. All my other worries were forgotten, nothing in my head but the amazing feel and sight of the two of them sharing my cock between them.

When they reached the tip again, Henry reached over and gently took hold of Kimber's face, pulling her into a kiss around the head of my cock. Their tongues moved against me and against each other as I inhaled sharply. So much for holding back. I'd rarely been so desperate for release.

As they broke their kiss, Henry whispered something to her, something I couldn't hear, but it became clear soon enough as they both licked down my shaft again, down to my balls. As they both began to suck on them at the same time, I nearly lost it right then and there.

"Holy shit," I groaned, holding onto them both to keep my balance. My cock throbbed, my whole body pulsing with need, and Henry obviously knew it.

"You can go and finish him off," he told Kimber. "I'll stay here."

She quickly complied, returning to my cock while Henry continued to work his magic on my balls, and when Kimber took me fully into her mouth, eruption was imminent.

"It's not going to take much," I warned her, but that didn't put her off at all. Her eyes fixed on me, she began to pump me with her hand, her mouth following immediately next to it, and my orgasm built strong and fast. My balls were still in Henry's mouth as they tightened, and my head fell back as lights danced in front of me, my body surrendering to the pleasure they were both giving me as I came hard into the warmth and wetness of Kimber's mouth.

She continued to suck me gently as my pulsing stopped, and when her mouth finally left me, Henry kissed her, sharing the taste of me with her, just as he and I had done with her sweetness last night. Though I'd literally *just* come, the sight of their tongues tangling had desire running through me again. There was still so much more I wanted to do with them, so many things we could try.

I took a step back, finally grabbing a towel to dry myself off. "So, Kimber, you wanted to talk to us about something?"

They both smiled as they pulled their lips apart, and Henry got to his feet, helping Kimber up afterwards. She looked between us with an expression almost entirely composed of lust, making it perfectly clear how much she'd enjoyed that. "I did, but maybe it can wait for just a little while longer?"

That worked for me. With no further words, I dropped the towel again, walking over to the two of them and kissing them both at the same time.

~Kimber~

Though I honestly hadn't come over here with this in mind, at least not right off the bat, as Nick took my hand and led me back into their bedroom, I couldn't bring myself to complain about it. All reason and self-control seemed to fly out the door as soon as he stepped out of the shower, every inch of him hard and firm and glistening wet.

It would have taken a saint or a nun to resist that, and I belonged to neither of those job descriptions.

When Henry went down on Nick, getting down on his knees in front of his naked boyfriend, still dressed in his suit from work, I thought that might have been the sexiest thing I had ever seen. But when they invited me to join in and I looked into Henry's eyes as we both worked together to bring Nick to his climax, I knew I'd been wrong: *that* was the sexiest thing I had ever seen.

At least for now. I had a feeling I might change my mind again before the night came to an end.

When we reached the bed, Nick kissed me, hard but not too hard, while Henry got undressed behind me, the rustle of his clothes as they came off almost as much of an aphrodisiac as Nick's kiss.

"I'd really like to have sex with you tonight," Nick told me in that blunt, to-the-point way of his that flooded my whole body with warmth. "But it's going to take me a little while to be ready for that after what you guys just did to me. That felt incredible."

I gave him a smile filled with pride. I'd never made a guy come so fast with a blow job before, though of course I knew I had to share the credit. Me and Henry together made it good for him, just like they had both made me come in record time last night.

"So, before we get to that," Nick continued, "Henry's going to go down on you again while I suck him off. Is that okay?"

I couldn't think of anything he might suggest that wouldn't be okay, but I glanced over at Henry anyway to make sure he felt the same. His naked body looked just as enticing as Nick's and his dark eyes were bright with anticipation. Mine must look just the same. We all wanted this just as much as each other, which made it even better.

"It sounds amazing," I answered truthfully, turning back to Nick, and the words were no sooner out of my mouth than his lips were on mine again, firm and assertive.

Two sets of hands began to remove my clothes, one pair undoing my pants while the other pulled my shirt up and over my head. Nick broke the kiss long enough to get my shirt off but his lips came right back, kissing me hard while undoing my bra as Henry gently pulled my panties down. Their touch felt insistent and needy, and yet, I knew if I asked them to stop, they would without question. Though they had me at their mercy, it was only because I'd agreed to it, because I wanted it.

And God, I wanted it.

When my clothes had all disappeared, leaving me just as naked as they were, Nick laid me down on the bed in the proper direction this time rather than across it as I had been last night. My feet were flat on the bed, my knees pressed together as Henry crawled up onto the bed after me on his hands and knees. Though Henry's heated smile drew my attention, I could also see Nick position himself at the bottom of the bed, also on his back, between Henry's legs, his hands around Henry's hips. Although I couldn't see exactly what happened, from Henry's reaction I could guess the exact moment when Nick's mouth made contact with his cock and, with a smile half sweet and half sinful, Henry gently prised my legs apart and dove in.

~Henry~

I honestly hadn't expected the three of us to be fully naked less than half an hour after I got home, but I couldn't be happier with the way things were turning out. Nick's good mood cheered me, for a start. All afternoon, I'd been worried that his hurt over what I told him at lunch might grow stronger the more he thought about it, but at the moment, there were no signs of him holding a grudge. Perhaps the blow job helped to distract him.

Kimber clearly had no complaints either. I hadn't meant to distract her from whatever she wanted to talk to us about, but when she told me she heard Nick go into the shower, I just couldn't help myself. We were only going to go take a peek, but then Nick caught us, one thing led to another, and now here we were, naked and arranged on the bed in a way to give all of us a maximum of pleasure, given that Nick's cock was temporarily out of operation.

On my hands and knees on the bed, Kimber in front of me and Nick beneath me, once again I occupied the middle of our ménage and I loved it. No one had ever accused me of being particularly adventurous in the bedroom before, but safe and secure between two people I liked and trusted, I felt a lot more bold than I ever had before.

As Nick's tongue connected with my already stiff shaft, I parted Kimber's legs, exposing her to me, and took a deep breath, inhaling her sweet scent before my own tongue followed, licking a wide stripe along her pretty pink lips.

A stuttering laugh came from above me and I raised my head to look at her, slightly confused. "What's so funny?"

Kimber smiled down at me, her eyes full of both affection and need. "Whenever you'd sniff my baking at the coffee shop, I would daydream about you smelling me like that. I can't believe it's really happening."

Nick chuckled from below me. "He's definitely a sniffer. He has to smell everything before he puts it in his mouth."

They were both teasing me now and my cheeks flushed with embarrassment, desire, and pleasure, all mingled together. "I like to engage all my senses. Is that a problem?"

"No," they both agreed in unison, and Kimber bit her lip as my head dropped again, burying my face between her legs.

She *did* smell wonderful, and she tasted even better. My tongue swirled around her sensitive skin, flicking lightly over her clit as she sighed above me.

Then Nick sucked me in hard, his mouth as strong as always, and I nearly lost my balance, my mouth pressing more firmly against Kimber's wet, warm centre, and I took advantage of the situation to kiss her deeper, sticking my tongue deep inside her. Damn, this felt amazing. I loved the way Kimber squirmed as my fingers pressed into her, thrusting into her in time with the movement of Nick's mouth on me, and when I sucked down on her clit, her back arched off the bed and she called out my name.

"Oh, God, Henry!"

I could feel Nick's chuckle as much as hear it, his throat vibrating around my cock. "Mm hmm," came his hummed response, his mouth too full to say anything else.

I had just said I liked to have all my senses engaged and that explained exactly my current situation precisely: the feel of Nick's mouth on me, the sounds both he and Kimber were making, and most of all, the taste and smell and sight of Kimber's pussy, it all combined to make a buildup of pleasure more intense than anything I could remember.

Kimber's legs began to tremble and I pushed in harder, finding her g-spot as I clamped down on her clit once more, and she contracted around my fingers just in time as my own peak hit, my body contracting and releasing as my vision went black, and I whispered both their names against Kimber's skin. I owed that orgasm to both of them, to the combination of them that turned me on so much.

Still panting, I gasped in surprise as Nick flipped me over, my back hitting the bed as he kissed me hard. My taste lingered still on his lips, as Kimber's did on mine, and they mixed and mingled between us as his mouth moved against mine.

When he finally pulled back, I opened my eyes to find him grinning over at Kimber, who watched us with that sweet, satisfied smile on her face, looking as though she felt just as good as I did.

Overall, that seemed to have been another massive success all around, I would say.

Nick seemed to agree, a smile on his face as he sat down on the bed between us, the three of us taking up nearly the entire space now.

"So," he said to Kimber conversationally, like she had just arrived and ignoring the fact that we were all naked after being incredibly intimate with each other. "You wanted to talk to us about something?"

Chapter Eight

~Kimber~

The tail end of another amazing orgasm still reverberated through my body when Nick asked what I had come here to talk about, and I had to laugh. I had certainly let myself get distracted from my original purpose, but I doubted many women in the world would blame me.

I had never felt as comfortable being naked as I did around Nick and Henry. They didn't show any negativity about my body, never shying away from any of the lumpier parts of me. In the past, men I'd slept with would avoid my stomach or anywhere my skin folded, but not these two. With every touch and every action, they made me feel sexy and desirable, and I wanted to hold onto that feeling just a little bit longer.

Maybe that explained why I let myself get distracted, or maybe it was simply that they turned me on so much I forgot how to think; both sounded plausible.

In any case, I really *should* talk to them, and it would be a whole lot easier to concentrate if we weren't still naked, which I mentioned to them now. "Do you mind if we get dressed again first?"

Henry immediately nodded at me while Nick smirked. "That's fine, but don't forget what I said earlier."

How could I? He told me he wanted to have sex with me; a woman doesn't forget something like that, especially from a man like him.

We all put some clothes back on, though Nick only put pants on, making it more than clear that he fully anticipated removing his clothing again later, and we went into the kitchen where Henry pulled out some food to start making supper while Nick and I took a seat on the stools at their kitchen island. The sleek marble countertop felt cool beneath my arms, my body still overheated from our activities in the bedroom.

I had their full attention as I began to explain the reason for my visit. "I got a call from my agent today, and I'm up for a pretty big role on a major TV show."

Henry's eyes lit up with pride and happiness as he congratulated me, while Nick smiled over at me in approval. "After that scene you did for us yesterday, I'm not surprised. You deserve it."

Their unbridled support nearly brought tears to my eyes. Besides Rocco, not many people really believed I could make it as an actress. My parents thought my dreams were unrealistic and the few other friends I had here were mostly actors too, meaning that although they pretended to be happy for me when things went my way, jealousy always lurked behind it.

The genuine delight that Nick and Henry showed made a nice change.

Still, they were getting ahead of themselves. "I don't have the role yet," I cautioned. "They're just interested in meeting with me, but my agent said something else that got me thinking, and that in particular is what I wanted to talk to you about."

"What is it?" I had Henry's full attention even as he moved around the kitchen preparing our meal.

"Someone else had previously been offered the role, but her contract has been terminated because they found out she starred in an... adult film."

Nick's eyebrows raised curiously. "Do you know the name of it?"

"I haven't... I don't... what?" The question caught me completely off guard and both men laughed at my stuttered response while I shot Nick a dirty look. "That's not the point."

"So what's the point then?" Nick asked, leaning forward as Henry offered him a sugar snap pea, opening his mouth so his boyfriend could pop it in. The two of them were like a perfectly choreographed dance, completely in sync, communicating without words. It left me a little bit in awe of them, and I felt a pang of envy too. They had just what I always wanted and it had never felt so tantalizingly close as it did right now.

Taking a deep breath, I tried to focus back on my own conversation. "The point is that they specifically told my agent they wanted someone 'wholesome' for the role, someone with no dark secrets that might come out and ruin the show's reputation."

Henry put the pieces together first. "And you don't think what we've been doing is particularly wholesome."

He'd hit the nail on the head, and I nodded sheepishly while Nick's lips tightened.

"What you do in private is none of their business. It's no one's business."

"I agree that's how it should be, but when someone's in the public eye, it doesn't work that way. There is no such thing as a truly private life."

"So, you're saying you don't want to do this again?" Disappointment coloured Henry's voice so strongly that I wanted to get up and give him a hug right there and then. He always brought out my protective side.

"It's not that I don't want to," I assured him. "After what just happened, I think it's pretty clear that I do."

They both had to concede that point, exchanging a small smile with each other.

"I'm just trying to be realistic. These kinds of roles hardly ever come around for someone like me, and I don't want to mess it up over something which, while amazing, is only temporary."

That sounded a little harsher than I meant it to as the words came out of my mouth. They had been completely upfront with me from the start about the nature of this arrangement so I couldn't be upset about it. I simply wanted to be practical.

Again, Henry and Nick looked at each other, communicating without speaking, and Henry relayed the agreed-upon message to me. "Of course it's your decision, Kimber, and we'll respect it no matter what you want to do, but please don't think this doesn't mean anything to us. We've never done anything like this before with any other woman, and it's so much better than we expected. Not just the sex, although that is *great*, but just spending time with you too. It feels natural. Our relationship felt complete before, but with you here, it's better somehow."

Nick nodded in firm agreement. "I don't tend to connect with people on a deeper level, Henry being an obvious exception, but you and I have just clicked. I know Henry feels the same, and the fact that we all like and lust after each other is a lot more rare than you might think. I don't want this to be just a passing fling."

I appreciated their words more than I could say, especially since I felt just the same about the two of them, but I didn't understand what else it could be. "So what *do* you want?"

Nick held my gaze as confidently as ever. "I think it's a little too early to put any kind of label on it, but I'd like to find out what it could be. I'm not worried about what anyone else thinks, Kimber. You're never going to please everyone, so you might as well please yourself."

That kind of attitude inspired and invigorated me, and clearly Henry thought so too as he smiled over at me. "I agree with Nick, even though I don't always do it myself."

They exchanged another glance there, full of meaning, and I had to ask: "That sounds like you're talking about something in particular."

With a grimace, Henry explained to me the situation with his parents and this party he had invited me to next week. "I've been afraid of what they'll think for a long time," he admitted. "But Nick's right: I can't live my life for them. I'm happy being with him, so they can accept it or not but it's not going to change a thing about the way I feel."

Nick gave him an approving nod. "It's always the same bullshit," he told me. "Even at my work, everyone's focused on who I'm sleeping with."

His turn came to fill me in on his dilemma at work, and I had to point out the irony. "So Henry's worried about being punished for being gay, and you're worried about being rewarded for it."

They both smiled ruefully, exchanging amused yet pained looks with each other. "Pretty much," Nick agreed. "I wonder what they'd do if I..."

He trailed off as something occurred to him, made clear from the way his eyes widened as he looked away, thinking things over. When he turned back to me, a new mischievousness twinkled in his gaze.

"How would you like a new acting role, Kimber?"

He had lost me on his 180-degree subject change. "Besides the one I'm already up for?"

He nodded eagerly. "This one would be very short-lived. There's a drinks reception next week for the top performers at my company, and the rumour is that the board members will be there to scope out their picks for the vacant positions."

I still didn't understand. "Okay?"

"What if I took you to the party and introduced you as my girlfriend?"

This time, Henry and I exchanged glances. He looked just as confused as me, but more intrigued than upset.

"Why would you do that?" I asked.

"The rumour is that they want me because I'm gay, right?" Henry and I both nodded. "So what if they think I'm seeing a woman instead? It would put them on the spot, and if they changed their mind because of it, everyone would know how biased they were."

"Nick," Henry admonished him gently. "You want this promotion. Wouldn't it be better not to rock the boat?"

Nick shook his head just as firmly as he'd nodded a moment earlier. "If I get it, I want it to be for the right reasons. I'd rather expose them than get the job just to be their token homosexual on the management team."

His conviction was addictive and I heard myself agreeing, swept up in the moment. "If that's really what you want, then of course. I'd be honoured to go with you."

"Kimber!" Henry looked over at me in surprise. "What about your own image? Nick isn't exactly low-profile. There could be talk."

There could be, but so what? They couldn't prove anything other than that I went on a date with a handsome, rich, successful man. What harm could it do? And the role wasn't even guaranteed anyway. What if I turned the two amazing men in front of me down now and didn't even get the job? I would feel like a complete idiot then.

"One date won't hurt," I assured him. "Especially not when I have bigger things to worry about."

Concern flashed across both their faces. "Like what?" Henry asked.

"Like how I really like you both too. I'm not ready to give you up just yet."

My eyes dropped to the floor as the words came out of my mouth, scarcely able to believe I just admitted that to them. For them to each say they liked me was one thing, but for me to confess that I liked them both seemed different. Maybe because they were already together, because they came as a package. It felt greedy and a little wrong, but completely right too.

A gentle finger reached under my chin, lifting it back up, and when I raised my eyes, both of them were right there, Nick's hand the one touching me. And before I could say or do anything else, Henry bent down and kissed me.

His soft and sweet kiss soothed any uncertainty I felt, and as soon as his lips left mine, they were replaced with another pair, harder and firmer.

When Nick pulled back, he gave me a wink. "I'm really glad to hear you say that," he said, his voice deep and husky as he leaned closer to me. "Because there are still an awful lot of things we haven't done yet."

~Nick~

Somehow, despite our mutual titillation, the three of us managed to finish cooking and eat supper, which would come in handy since we were all going to need some energy for the evening. The atmosphere around the dining table felt electric, the conversation filled with innuendo, each one of us brimming with anticipation for what awaited us back in the bedroom.

I was grateful Kimber had opened up to us about the things bothering her, and of course it pleased me enormously to hear that she felt something for us too. From the way he had spoken about her in the past, I knew Henry had at least some feelings for her even before all of this began, though I also knew without a doubt that he never would have acted on them if I hadn't suggested the whole thing. And even though I'd only really known Kimber for a few days now, that time cemented my certainty that I wanted to know her better. I meant what I said when I told her I didn't want this to be just about sex. What it might be, I couldn't say for sure yet, but I wanted to figure it out together, as a set of three.

Finally, supper finished and we all got up at the same time, carrying our dishes over to the sink.

Henry gave Kimber and I an inquiring look. "Should we do dishes now or later?"

When Kimber glanced over at me, the amusement and anticipation in her eyes mirrored my own. "Later," we both declared in unison and, laughing between us, we all made our way back to the bedroom.

For a long time after I moved in, this room had seemed impersonal and cold, but ever since Henry joined me, the ambiance had completely changed. I'd never lived with a lover before Henry. I'd dated before him - a lot, some might say - both men and women, but there had never been anyone I felt comfortable enough with to want to share my whole life with them. I liked parts of them and they liked parts of me, but never the whole package. They were, without exception, all upper-middle-class like me, with similar upbringings and similar social lives. Maybe we were just too similar.

Henry didn't fit that mold. His background had nothing in common with mine, nor did his work. Sexy, yet also sweet, confident but insecure, honest but discreet, he was a walking contradiction, a puzzle for me to solve, and the more I got to know him, the more I liked him. His trust took some time to earn, but once I did, it never wavered. He always had my back, always supported me, letting me rant and rave about anything I wanted to and then quietly offering his suggestions, which were usually just what I needed to hear.

We complemented each other in a way that simply worked, and I had every intention of marrying him someday even if I hadn't told him that yet.

So finding out today that he hadn't told his parents about me because he thought we might not last really stung, but I did my best to see it through his eyes too. As a peacemaker and a natural caregiver, he hadn't wanted to upset his parents, and I understood that, but they shouldn't be upset about their son being in love. I would gladly take on anyone who thought otherwise.

So overall, our relationship completely satisfied me. I hadn't thought we lacked anything, but adding Kimber to the mix truly surprised me. She fit in so naturally with us, amazingly well, in every way. When I had suggested involving a woman, I had only been thinking of the sexual angle, but now, new possibilities were presenting themselves. Her calming presence, her humour and kindness and honesty, provided a middle ground between my bluntness and Henry's reticence.

And the fantastic sex only made it better. Those were the thoughts that filled my mind right now as Henry and I got to work undressing Kimber again.

She giggled as I kissed her neck from behind her while undoing her bra. "You know, I can undress myself. I've been doing it for more than twenty years."

"It's so much more fun this way though," Henry said before kissing her gently too. "And I love that you trust us to let us do it."

That was what it came down to: trust and vulnerability. Putting yourself in someone else's hands and having faith that they wouldn't hurt you could be one of the hardest things in life, but with Henry and Kimber, everything felt safe and secure, and it made me so happy that she felt it too.

Once her clothes were gone, Henry and I quickly removed ours. My cock stood hard already again, thanks to the anticipation that had been building ever since Kimber said she wanted to do more with us.

I only had my pants to remove which meant I finished undressing faster than Henry, and I took advantage of it by taking Kimber's hand and leading her over to the bed. "You remember what I told you before?"

The heat in her eyes told me she did even before she nodded. "You want to have sex with me. I want that too, Nick. I can't wait to know how you feel inside me."

A groan rumbled in my throat as my cock jumped. That directness really turned me on.

I would be just as direct with her in return as I got onto the bed first, lying on my back with my head on the pillow. "Get on top of me."

In contrast to the boldness of what she'd just said, uncertainty flashed across Kimber's face. "Are you sure? I don't want to hurt you."

Hurt me? It took me a second to realize what she meant, but when her hand moved to her stomach self-consciously, I figured it out. Her weight hadn't come up at all in any of our adventures in the bedroom so far, and honestly, I had completely forgotten about her size as a negative thing. When I looked at her, I saw so much more than that.

She wouldn't want me to say anything sappy like that though, so with a smirk, I flexed my biceps for her. "Look at me, Kimber. Do you really think you're going to break me? Now get over here and get on my cock before you really hurt me by making me wait any longer."

She rolled her eyes at my shamelessness, but it seemed to work since she did as I said, getting onto the bed and stradling me. Her wetness could already be felt as her pussy pressed against my hard shaft which lay against my body.

"Kiss me," I instructed next, and she readily obeyed, leaning down over me, her long dark hair forming a curtain around us as her soft lips pressed against mine. Her breasts pressed against me too, her whole body soft and supple against my firm frame, a perfect match.

The bed dipped next to me, letting me know that Henry had joined us. I had plans for him too, but first, I needed to get Kimber in position.

"Henry," I murmured to him, my mouth still against Kimber's. "Why don't you check and see if she's ready?"

Kimber whimpered in anticipation as Henry moved down the bed, gently raising her hips and, I assumed from her reaction, pushing a finger or two inside her.

He chuckled softly as he returned to the head of the bed. "Definitely ready," he confirmed, holding out his index finger when I turned to look at him. "See for yourself."

Though I could see the dampness, just to be sure, I reached out and pulled it closer to me, taking it into my mouth and tasting her sweet essence, my eyes on Kimber the whole time. Her lips were parted and her eyelids heavy, her own desire growing stronger each second just like mine.

"What are we waiting for, then?" I asked her, my eyebrows raised. "Climb on me."

"I got it," Henry offered, moving back to take hold of my cock and guide it into place, letting Kimber keep her eyes on me.

As she sank down onto me, warm and wet and tight, we both moaned in pleasure. I'd never gone quite so long without being inside a woman before, and fuck, it felt good.

"You okay?" I asked her, knowing my cock was thicker than most; Henry had told me so multiple times and I'd been with enough other men to be able to compare.

She nodded, closing her eyes for a moment and taking a deep breath. "I'm so much better than okay."

I grinned up at her as she began to move, still leaning down over me, raising her hips as she slid almost all the way off me, and then dropping back again, letting me feel each inch of her as she savoured every inch of me.

The angle was wonderful, but it wouldn't work for what I had in mind. "Sit up," I instructed her instead. "All the way up."

Obediently, she raised herself until she sat astride me, my cock still buried in her completely.

"Henry, on your feet."

He gave me a curious look, examining our position, until he figured out what I intended. Eagerly, he got up, his own cock hard already as he stood on the bed, his feet on either side of my chest, his cock at Kimber's eye level.

They both knew what came next, but I spelled it out anyway. "Kimber, you focus on Henry, suck him until he comes. I'll take care of the two of us."

From my vantage point, I could see Henry's ass cheeks tighten as Kimber's mouth connected with his cock. I couldn't see exactly what they were doing from this angle, but I had other things to worry about anyway. My hands went to Kimber's hips, raising her just enough that I had room to move, and then I thrust up into her, hard.

Kimber's moans were muffled by Henry's cock as I got into a rhythm, finding the angle that worked best for us both. I had missed fucking a pussy, I had to admit. It felt incredible to have her wrapped around me, and my view didn't hurt either, with Henry's ass just above me. After a couple of minutes, I couldn't resist the temptation, and I pulled one of my hands back, coated my finger with my saliva, and reached up to press it into Henry's hole.

"Shit, yes," he groaned as I worked it in and out, his cock still in Kimber's mouth, my cock still inside her, the three of us connected in the most intimate way imaginable as we all propelled each other towards a mutual ecstasy.

Kimber broke first, her body clenching my cock hard as she came, and I exhaled hard. Feeling a woman orgasming around me definitely topped the list of the best part of having sex with a woman.

"Fuck, Kimber." With both Henry and Kimber moaning above me, I finished in record time.

Through my taste of heaven, I was vaguely aware of Henry finishing himself off, draping his cum across Kimber's breasts, though I couldn't see it for myself until he stepped aside. Her eyes were hazed, her cheeks red as she looked down on me, and with one arm around her waist, I raised myself up and swept my tongue across her chest to lap up the evidence of his fulfilment. They both groaned once more as I licked her completely clean, and when I had the last drop in my mouth, I kissed her to share the spoils of our pleasure with her.

Gently, Henry and I both helped Kimber down, settling her onto the bed next to me while Henry lay on her other side, all of us staring up at the ceiling as we caught our breath.

"So, uh... is that what you guys do every night?" Kimber asked with a short laugh. "Maybe that's why you're in such good shape."

"It doesn't hurt," I agreed. "You think you can keep up with us?"

She smiled over at me, turning her head to face me. "I don't know, but if anything is going to kill me, I can think of worse ways to go."

Laughing, Henry rolled onto his side, pressed up against Kimber, and stretched his arm out to me, so I quickly did the same, embracing them both at the same time as we lay together in comfortable silence.

I honestly couldn't remember ever feeling more satisfied than I did right now.

Chapter Nine

~Henry~

Although the sun hadn't begun to set yet, as the three of us lay together, naked and wrapped up in each other, I noticed Nick's eyes closing for longer and longer periods each time he blinked.

"Did you rest this afternoon?" I asked curiously. His nap usually gave him a lot more energy than this.

"No," he admitted, giving me a rueful smile from Kimber's other side. "I tried, but I had a few things on my mind."

I could guess what some of those things might be, and guilt ran through me for adding to his worries. "Do you want to talk or sleep?"

Kimber laughed between us. "That's a great question. Do I get that option too?"

"Whenever you need it," I assured her. "But you're not the one who looks like she's about to fall asleep."

Nick groaned as he rolled over onto his back, covering his eyes with his hand. "Yeah, it just kind of hit me. If you two don't mind, I might bow out now."

Of course I didn't mind, and neither did Kimber. I gave Nick a kiss and wished him goodnight, and Kimber did the same before she and I got up and got dressed again for the second time tonight, turning off the light as we left the bedroom so that Nick could sleep.

"What do you do when Nick goes to bed early?" Kimber asked as we got back to the living room, her eyes darting to the window and the magnificent view once again. "What does a Friday night look like for Henry Zhang?"

She always had a way of phrasing things that made me smile. "They're usually pretty tame. My life before I met Nick had a lot more quiet nights, a lot less glamorous than all this might seem. I used to live over in Kitsilano and go out to the beach sometimes to watch the sun go down." I winced as I heard the words come out of my mouth. "That sounds really cheesy, doesn't it?"

Her blue eyes were warm as she smiled over at me. "I think it sounds amazing and I haven't ever really done that before. Kits Beach is a bit out of the way but English Bay is pretty close to my apartment. We could go there if you want?"

"You mean now?" I hadn't realized we were talking about actually going out.

Her smile faded at my surprise. "I mean, we don't have to. I can just go home if you've got other things you want to be doing."

Shit, I hadn't meant it like that. "No, Kimber, I'd love to go, the invitation just took me by surprise. Let me leave a note for Nick so he doesn't worry if he gets up and finds us gone."

Nick and I had a whiteboard in the kitchen where we left reminders and notes for each other since our working hours were so different, and I left him a quick message there now. I read it back a couple of times before adding one more line. *Took the car.*

After grabbing the keys, Kimber and I took the elevator down to the parking garage. Nick had a premium parking space to go along with his top floor apartment, and both excitement and nerves ran through me as I took a seat behind the wheel of his car. I'd never driven it without him before, though he had always told me I could use it anytime I wanted. I had sold my own car when I moved in with him, partly because he only had one parking spot, and partly because it would have looked wildly out of place among all the luxury cars in his building anyway.

Cautiously, I navigated us out of the garage and onto the downtown streets and Kimber gave me a knowing smile as we pulled up to a red light. "You don't usually drive a stick shift, do you?"

"Is it that obvious?" I thought I'd been doing pretty well, actually.

"It could be just a *tiny* bit smoother," she teased me. "Do you want some pointers?"

"How do you know how to drive a stick?" I assumed she didn't have a car of her own, since she'd been walking home in the rain the other day and had taken a taxi to see us today.

"I grew up on a farm," she reminded me. "The first vehicle I learned to drive was a tractor."

I couldn't imagine such a thing so I had to bow to her superior knowledge. "So what am I doing wrong?"

"Well, for a start, you're in first gear right now," she pointed out. "Put it in neutral when you stop and use the brake rather than the clutch."

It took a few seconds for me to figure out what she meant, but the next time we stopped, I tried it her way and had to admit it worked better. She gave me a few more tips as we made our way towards the park, laughing and joking with each other.

The sun hung low in the sky by the time we parked and made our way to English Bay. For a Friday, the beach had plenty of space, and we found a spot on one of the large logs laid out in the sand.

"So, you're going to come out to your parents at your mom's party, eh?" Kimber asked as we both looked out over the water. The setting sun painted a wide golden stripe across the gentle wave, and the call of the seabirds and the salty tang of the air made the bustle of downtown feel far away, though we could be back there in a matter of minutes. "You never struck me as the dramatic type before."

Her teasing tone made everything feel lighter. "Actually, I'm hoping by doing it this way, I'll avoid some drama. If there are a lot of other people around, they can't make a scene."

"They must not be like my mom, then. She could make a scene no matter where she is or who she's with. But why haven't you told them before? You and Nick are pretty serious, aren't you?"

"We are." I really didn't have a good explanation for why I had kept silent so long, but I tried to explain myself anyway. "They just have a lot of traditional ideas and I really don't know how they'll react to this. We don't talk about this kind of stuff. Nick is the best thing in my life, and it feels like if I put it out there and they don't approve, it will be... stained, somehow. Right now it's perfect and I don't want anyone to think otherwise. I don't know if that makes any sense."

"It makes complete sense," she assured me, linking her arm through mine supportively. "It's not exactly the same thing, but I kind of feel the same about this whole thing with you and Nick. It's amazing and I'm so happy to have met you both, but if other people found out and started judging it, it would take away some of the joy of it, even though it really shouldn't matter what anyone else thinks."

"That's exactly it." It relieved me so much that she understood. Nick lived by his own rules and had for so long that even when he tried to see my point of view, he couldn't entirely relate. "But it's time I stopped hiding. I'm going to tell them, no matter what, so if you want to back out of the party now, I would understand."

She smiled up at me with those bright blue eyes. "And miss the drama? Not a chance."

The sky began to turn pink as the sun dipped lower and we talked more about our childhoods and the expectations of our parents. Kimber told me no one in her family believed she could make it as an actress.

"They basically think my whole career is a waste of time, and sooner or later I'll slink home with my tail between my legs and admit that they were all right."

"What made you want to be an actress in the first place?" It seemed like an unlikely ambition for a small-town girl from the middle of nowhere.

"I got teased a lot as a kid," she said matter-of-factly. "So I made up this whole persona for myself so that it wouldn't bother me. I pretended to be a secretly beautiful girl who had to wear a mask so that no one knew it. When the other kids made fun of me, it wouldn't bother me because I knew the truth and they didn't. It sounds really stupid now but it worked for me at the time, and I found I really liked pretending to be someone else. And when I started doing school plays in high school, that clinched it. I knew right away I wanted to do that forever. I never got cast as the lead, of course, since they always chose the thin, pretty girl who couldn't even remember her lines, but the time I spent in character, I could forget everything else and just live someone else's life for a bit. It's an amazing feeling."

I had never thought about it like that before, but I could see her point. It bore some similarities to how Nick made me feel like a different man when we were together.

"Looks like those other kids missed out in the end," I told her. "You're going to have an amazing career, and you're beautiful too. They just couldn't see it."

Her gaze dropped down to the sand at our feet. "Not everyone would agree with the second part of that, but you certainly make me feel that way, Henry. Both you and Nick, the way you look at me... no one's ever really looked at me like that, even in private."

If that was true, then the men she'd met before must be blind. "Well, maybe we're in on the secret too. Maybe we can see that woman inside. I'd be proud to tell anyone that she's with me."

When she raised her eyes to me again, the look of vulnerability in them almost took my breath away, and I couldn't help myself. As the sun disappeared over the water, I kissed her, soft and slow.

I could really fall for this woman. I had already started to.

What would my boyfriend think about that?

~Kimber~

Sitting on the beach and watching the setting sun with one of the most handsome men I'd ever seen felt like a dream. If those small-town kids who had always judged me based on my appearance could see me now, they wouldn't believe their eyes. Or their ears, once he started saying the sweetest things I could imagine, his dark eyes shining with sincerity. Lost in those eyes, I told him things I'd never told anyone before, and when he kissed me, I'd never had anything so close to a true fairytale moment.

Except this wasn't my fairytale. This happy ending didn't belong to me, not when the man in front of me already loved someone else. So when those butterflies built up in my stomach and my heart began to melt, I forced myself to pull back, not because I wanted to, but because I had to try to protect myself.

It felt like we were right on the edge of something profound, something perfect and dangerous at the same time.

What would happen if we fell?

"Are we supposed to be doing this?" I asked him, our faces still only inches apart.

Henry's fingers stroked my cheek softly. "I don't know," he admitted. "I just needed to. I hope it didn't make you uncomfortable."

Not unless perfection counted as uncomfortable. "I loved it, Henry, I just don't know what it means. I don't want to mess things up."

He knew exactly what I meant without me having to explain, and he turned away, looking out over the water, the emotions playing across his face a mirror image of the ones inside me: happiness, desire and confusion. "I don't want that either, but I also feel like it might be okay? I really don't know. I've never done anything like this before, Kimber, but it feels right. I need to talk to Nick."

That sounded like a good plan to me. My feelings were secondary to the relationship they already had between them, I'd known that from the start. "I'm working tomorrow and Sunday, and I'm going out with some friends tomorrow night. One of them just landed a new role and we're celebrating. So maybe it's best if we take the weekend off from... whatever this is... and you guys can see how you feel afterwards?"

The idea that they might change their mind with a bit of distance caused my chest to tighten painfully, but I also needed to know. Were we all just getting swept away in this without really putting it in perspective? Besides work, I'd barely had a moment over the last few days that hadn't been spent with one or both of them. Maybe we all needed a break and a bit of time to reflect.

If they decided to end things, it would hurt, but it would be better in the long run that I hadn't gotten in any deeper. And if they decided they wanted to keep going, then I would know they really meant it.

That seemed like a chance worth taking.

I wanted to make one more thing clear. "But no matter what you decide, I still want to go to your parents' party, and to Nick's work drinks too, if he still wants me to. That won't change."

He flashed me a grateful smile. "You're amazing, Kimber. Thank you."

No man had ever called me amazing before, unless they meant it sarcastically, but from Henry, it couldn't have sounded more genuine.

With him and Nick, I felt amazing. The things we had done in their room were so much better than anything I could have imagined. With Nick inside me and Henry in my mouth, gazing down at me in admiration, I felt just like that secretly beautiful woman I had always pretended to be.

I wanted more of that feeling, but not at the cost of hurting either of them. I had to put the decision in their hands and take a step back.

Henry walked me the few blocks to my apartment like the gentleman he was, kissing my cheek at the door, before he left to go back to his car and back to his life in the flashy apartment with the gorgeous man already waiting in his bed. Meanwhile, I walked up to my tiny studio which seemed quieter and lonelier than ever, hoping with all my might that the outcome of Henry and Nick's conversation would be in my favour.

Now that I had got a taste of how good life could be, could I ever go back to how it had been before?

~Nick~

The morning sun streamed through the large windows of my bedroom when I opened my eyes again, bathing the whole room in golden light. I couldn't remember the last time I'd slept so long, or so well. Although I still had things to worry about, everything seemed a little bit lighter since Kimber had come into our lives. Having her around smoothed out the rough edges in a way I hadn't known was possible.

Henry sat next to me, already awake, his chest bare with his laptop balanced on his knees, his brow furrowed in concentration as he read over something which must be for work.

He hadn't noticed that I'd woken up yet so I took this rare opportunity to watch him without him being aware of it. His black hair stuck up in a few places, adorably mussed from his sleep, a hint of stubble lined his chin, and he wore his reading glasses which he hardly ever used outside of work. The sunshine highlighted his muscular arms and chest, and he couldn't have looked any sexier if he tried.

The fact that he never really tried made the whole thing even sexier.

"How's the environment doing today?" I asked, and his eyes widened in surprise as he looked down at me.

"Good morning." The look of surprise melted into one of affection as he quickly pulled off his glasses and closed his laptop, placing them both on his bedside table. "It's not great, but I'm also not going to get it fixed before breakfast. How did you sleep?"

He leaned down to kiss me, his breath already fresh, which told me he must have been up for a while already.

"I slept great. What time is it?"

"Nearly nine."

Nine? I must have been out for almost twelve hours which couldn't be more unusual for me. "What time did Kimber leave?"

He gave me a sheepish smile. "So you never saw my note? She and I went out for a little while just after you went to bed. I took the car."

The surprises kept on coming. He'd never been confident enough to take my car before. "Where did you go?"

"Just down to the beach to watch the sunset." My eyebrows raised and he laughed. "I know, it's cheesy, but we enjoyed it."

He had never told me he wanted to do things like that, but then, it had never crossed my mind to ask either. "And she went home from there?"

Henry nodded in confirmation even as his expression grew more uncertain. "Yes, but there's something I want to talk to you about. While we were on the beach, something happened."

"Something?" I needed a little more detail than that.

"A kiss. I kissed her." Guilt flashed across his face as he confessed it. "It just felt right in the moment, but then I didn't know if I should be doing that? Do we only kiss her when we're together? I'm a bit confused, Nick, and I don't want to complicate things or screw up."

He'd obviously been worrying about this, so I pulled him down to kiss him myself right now. "The fact that you're telling me just goes to show that I've got nothing to worry about. I know you love me, Henry, but I know you like her too."

"So what do we do?" he asked, shuffling down so that his eyes were level with mine, his head next to me on the pillow. "Kimber suggested that we take the weekend to talk things out between us and spend a bit of time together on our own, to make sure we were on the same page. We won't see her again until next week."

A pang of disappointment ran through me with that news, stronger than I would have expected, but I could appreciate the sentiment behind it too. She had said she didn't want to impact our relationship, and that selflessness explained exactly why she wouldn't.

"Well, I don't want to put words in your mouth, but I think she brings something different to the table. She's not like me and she's not like you, but she fits in with us anyway. I like the way I feel when she's around, and I like the way she makes you smile."

The look of complete understanding in his eyes told me he felt just the same. "And how do you feel about me kissing her?" he asked tentatively.

A serious question like that deserved a serious response, so I took the time to come up with one. "I guess it makes me... happy? I mean, I want you both to be happy, so if kissing each other does that, then I don't have a problem with it. I like kissing her too, but it doesn't make me want to kiss you any less."

My slightly convoluted reasoning made him smile. "That's what I thought too. I tried to imagine how I would feel if you told me you'd kissed her, and I didn't feel jealous at all. Isn't that weird though? Shouldn't I?"

"Who gives a fuck about 'should' and 'shouldn't'?" I asked, completely seriously. "As long as we all understand things the same way, there isn't a thing wrong with it."

"But where's the line?" he prompted. "Is there one?"

I turned the question back on him. "Where do you think it is? If I had sex with her, without you there, would it bother you?"

Just as I had done, Henry took the time to really think it over, and when he answered, his answer both surprised and pleased me. "I don't think so. Anyone else in the world, yes, but Kimber? It wouldn't bother me because I trust her and I know she respects us both."

Therein lay the crux of the matter, trust and respect, and I completely agreed. "So it sounds to me like we're talking about getting into some kind of real relationship with her, one that has both a threesome component, but also three separate couples."

He took a moment to sort that out in his head, counting on his fingers to determine who the three couples were. I could practically see the wheels turning. When he had it figured out, he gave me another tentative smile. "That sounds amazing, but does that really work? Do people really do that?"

"They do," I assured him. "And even if no one else does, who cares? We can do what we want. These are our lives, Henry, and if we're not hurting anyone else, it's no one's fucking business."

"You're incredible," he whispered to me, his eyes full of appreciation. "I'm so glad I found you."

With those words, I couldn't stop myself from kissing him again, much harder this time.

My cock immediately began to harden as Henry returned my kiss, just as willingly and eagerly, and when my hips pressed against him, I could feel him getting stiffer through the thin fabric of his pajama pants. I hadn't bothered to get dressed again last night before going to sleep so I had nothing holding me back. My hands went to his hips, pulling him even tighter against me as our shafts rubbed against each other, his arousal feeding mine.

I was so glad I had found him too.

With a growl of anticipation, I threw the covers off entirely and pulled Henry's pants off, exposing his long, perfect cock to me, my mouth watering in anticipation as I lay down beside him, top to tail, his cock at my eye level and mine at his.

Groaning in satisfaction, I took him in at the same time he wrapped his lips around me. We knew each other well enough at this point to know exactly how to turn each other on, where our pleasure points were. When he gave Kimber instructions on how to blow me, it had been incredibly sexy, but I knew him just as well as he knew me. I could teach a course on how to make him gasp and I did it now, flicking my tongue roughly across the underside of his shaft while I took him in deeper. His muffled moan, muffled by my cock in his mouth, only turned me on more.

As my mouth moved, I pulled lightly on his balls and then pressed my fingers hard just beneath them, inching close to his ass, and when I ran my finger around his rim right as his cock hit the back of my throat, he shuddered against me.

Not that any of this was one-sided. I had no immunity to his actions either. His hand took over the work of pumping my shaft as he sucked my balls, and my groan made my whole mouth vibrate around him. We could go on like this forever or we could make it quick, and today, I wanted it fast and dirty.

As my orgasm approached, I pulled out my secret weapon, taking his whole length down my throat, and his balls immediately tightened as his mouth took me in once more.

A moment later, he came, with me right behind him, the taste of his cum in my mouth putting me over the edge, both of us swallowing and moaning together.

Fuck, that felt incredible. It had been a while since we were quite that in tune with each other, and I had to assume it had everything to do with how together we were on everything else in our lives.

Though it had only been a few days, Kimber had definitely already changed things for the better.

~Kimber~

Saturdays were always busy at Rocco's coffee shop, so my first chance to check my phone came on my lunch break, and when I pulled it out, I found it full of messages.

The one from my agent, I opened first. It confirmed the date and time for my audition for the new role she'd told me about, for Wednesday afternoon this week. I called out to Rocco behind the counter to see if I could have the day off, not expecting it to be an issue since he never refused me for an audition, and he quickly gave his approval. I sent a short text back to confirm I had the information and would be ready for it.

Beneath my agent's message was a flurry of texts from my family, celebrating the fact that my younger sister had just got a promotion at work. Already engaged and living in her own house, just a 10-minute drive away from my parents, they couldn't be prouder of her.

As the undisputed black sheep of the family, my accomplishments paled in comparison, but I sent my sincere congratulations anyway. Working at the coffee shop might not pay as well as her new position, but I would much rather be chasing my dreams than settling for the kind of life my parents thought suitable for someone like me. As Nick said: who cared what anyone else thought? Taking a chance on what made me happy was worth it.

Next up, I skimmed through a bunch of back and forth chatter about the get-together I had to attend tonight, but the texts beneath it were the ones I really wanted to read: the ones from Nick and Henry, both sent on the group chat between the three of us.

Henry: *Hey Kimber, just wanted to let you know that Nick and I have talked and everything's good. We'd like to talk to you too, whenever you're ready. Hope you're having a good day.*

Nick: *I'd say I hope you're feeling okay, but I don't. I hope you're sore and that every time you limp, you think of me.*

Henry: *Seriously? She's probably reading this at work.*

Nick: *Good. A little sexting always makes the day go faster.*

Henry: *Sorry, Kimber. I'd say he doesn't mean it, but we'd all know that's a lie.*

Nick: *Of course I mean it. That's why you love me. That, and my ass, of course.*

Henry: *...*

Henry: *So, yeah, Kimber. Whenever you'd like to talk, we'd love to see you.*

By the time I got to the end, my grin took up my whole face. I could hear both of their voices so clearly, their different personalities and the way they teased each other. They were each such amazing men in their own way, and even better together. And the fact that they were including me in their lives, that they were obviously thinking about me even when they were together, seemed far too good to be true, even if I had the proof right there in my hands.

Henry must have told Nick about the kiss last night and, based on his messages, Nick seemed totally fine with it. Although I would have loved to talk to them right away and find out what they wanted to speak to me about, I felt we should stick to the plan too. Taking the weekend apart still seemed like a prudent idea, no matter how much my body tingled at the idea of seeing them again.

With some reluctance, I therefore sent them a simple message back: *I'm doing great, thank you for checking in. I've got Tuesday and Wednesday off this week, so maybe we could talk Monday evening if that works for you guys.*

After hitting send, I couldn't resist adding one more quick note.

I'm walking just fine today, btw. Don't flatter yourself, Nick. ;)

Henry's typing bubbles immediately popped up, followed by a laughing emoji. *That's right, Kimber. Keep him humble. He needs it.*

You can deny it all you want, Nick's reply read. *I'll have you both begging for it soon enough.*

A shiver of anticipation raced through me as I grinned once more. Why his cockiness should be so appealing, I really couldn't explain, but I loved it.

The rest of the weekend went relatively quickly. Nothing surprised me about Saturday's get-together: other actors pretending to be happy for the good fortune of one of our colleagues while many of them made snide remarks behind her back. I used to dream about throwing an event like this when I got my big break, but now I thought I'd rather just celebrate with the people who truly supported me and would be genuinely happy for my success, people like Rocco, Henry and Nick.

I heard from them again on Sunday, just funny, casual texts, and again on Monday while we were all working. Henry came in for his usual coffee on Monday morning, giving me an almost shy smile as he came up to the counter.

"I hope this is okay. I stayed away this weekend since you said you wanted some space, but I really need my caffeine for the work day."

I certainly didn't want him to feel unwelcome. "I'm always glad to see you, Henry. I just wanted you and Nick to have time to yourselves."

"We did," he assured me. "And we enjoyed it, but we're both looking forward to seeing you later."

"I'm looking forward to that too."

He promised to come back and pick me up when I finished work for the day, and the smile stayed on my face for at least half an hour after he'd left.

"Are you going to tell me yet what's going on between you two?" Rocco's question managed to be both curious and unobtrusive as our morning rush died down. "I know that look he's giving you, Kimber. He cares for you, and you care for him too."

I glanced around to make sure we couldn't be overheard. The customers all seemed caught up in their own conversations, no one paying us any attention. "It's not quite that simple, Rocky. He's already in a relationship."

The older man's eyebrows shot up. "Does his girlfriend know about the flowers and the lovesick looks?"

I rolled my eyes at the exaggeration. Henry was hardly lovesick over me. "Actually, he doesn't have a girlfriend. He has a boyfriend, and yes, he knows about the gifts."

Rocco's eyes went even wider. "He's gay? I had no idea. I would have gone after him myself."

"Rocky!" A few of the customers at the tables looked up at my outburst, so I quickly lowered my voice, but I couldn't keep the surprise out of my reply. Rocco had never mentioned dating anyone, man or woman, so I'd had no idea about his orientation either. Apparently, my gaydar really needed some work. "You never said anything."

"Looks like we can both keep secrets." He gave me an appraising look. "Gay or not, that man has feelings for you though."

"I know." With one more surreptitious look around, I leaned even closer. There weren't many people on earth I could admit the truth to just yet, but I trusted Rocco, especially now that I knew just how private he could keep things. "I've actually kind of been seeing them both. Together."

I expected my friend and employer to look completely shocked or even horrified, but instead, his face lit up with delight. "Good for you! It's about time someone saw how wonderful you are. You deserve to have some fun, and that boy looks like fun."

My cheeks reddened at the reminder of exactly what kind of fun I'd been having. "You don't think it's weird?"

"Personally? I think it's wonderful when people make each other happy, no matter what that looks like. But if you're asking me if everyone will feel the same, I think you already know the answer to that, Kimber."

He had a point; I did. There were people who would not only find it weird, but wrong. People who would judge me for it, just like I'd always been judged for the way I looked or the career I'd chosen.

But maybe Nick also had a point. Maybe it really didn't matter what anyone else thought. They made me happy, both of them, and it seemed I did the same to them too. So, instead of scaring me off, Rocco's words only spurred me on more. If Henry and Nick were going to tell me tonight that they wanted to continue our relationship, then I would happily agree.

Hopefully, I had interpreted the invitation correctly. Hopefully, I wasn't getting my hopes up for nothing.

Hopefully, all three of us could be happy together.

Chapter Ten

Things had been so comfortable and settled with Nick for so long that I'd almost forgotten how nerve-wracking making that initial declaration of feelings could be. Even though Nick had been, as usual, completely up front with me about how he felt right from the start, admitting to him just how hard I'd fallen for him still took a lot of courage. I liked him so much that his rejection would have crushed me, and putting that much power in another person's hands frightened me.

So even though I knew Kimber felt something for me, and for Nick too, my stomach still felt tied in knots as I made my way back to the coffee shop to pick her up. Were her feelings strong enough to want to pursue more than just a physical relationship with us? I still had no idea how we would present it to the outside world, but with Nick's encouragement, I pushed past that part. People would think whatever they were going to think and nothing I could do would change that. All I could control was my own happiness, and right now, that included having Kimber in our lives.

She stood behind the counter when I walked in, chatting with Rocco and another of their co-workers who had come in to work the later shift. Kimber glanced towards the door when it opened, and when she saw me there, her eyes lit up in a way that made my heart leap. She looked just as hopeful as I felt.

Maybe we were all on the same page after all.

With a smile, she untied her apron and grabbed her jacket from the back room, saying goodbye to her co-workers and some of the customers too as we headed out together onto the sunny street.

"They all think we're dating now," she warned me. "First the flowers and now you're picking me up after work? They're all going to get the wrong idea."

I actually hoped they had exactly the right idea, but we still needed to talk about that.

She told me about her weekend as we walked the short distance to my apartment, and she surprised me by greeting Kelly at the reception desk of our building by name. The warm smile Kelly gave her in response was even more unexpected. How did Kimber win people over so quickly? It had taken me months to get on a first-name basis with Kelly, but Kimber just made people feel comfortable. She certainly did with me.

The silence that filled the air as we stepped into the apartment usually indicated I'd arrived before Nick got up. "Should we let him rest or go wake him up?" I asked her, and her eyes sparkled at the possibility of taking Nick by surprise.

"As much as I love the idea of catching him off guard, maybe we should let him sleep," she reluctantly decided. "I could help you cook supper instead?"

That sounded like almost as much fun, so we got ourselves set up in the kitchen, chatting about cooking and baking and the differences between them as we worked. Soon, Nick appeared in the doorway, though I couldn't guess whether our laughter woke him or the smell of the food cooking.

He wore only his pajama pants, his hair adorably messy, and the look on Kimber's face when she saw him made it abundantly clear just how attractive she found the whole picture.

I couldn't blame her. I'd never seen a sexier man either.

"I can't decide which I'm hungrier for," he said to us both as he walked over to us. "Whatever you're cooking, or the two of you."

Kimber rolled her eyes at me, making me laugh, but I noticed the way her cheeks flushed as Nick gave her a kiss on the cheek to say hello, the same way my own body heated at his words. We could pretend we didn't like his blunt expressions of interest, but it would be a lie. She liked it just as much as I did.

"What are you talking about?" he asked me as he gave me a kiss too, and I knew exactly what his question really meant. He wanted to know if I'd broached the subject we wanted to talk to Kimber about tonight, but I hadn't. I'd been waiting for him.

"Just food," I answered truthfully. "It'll be ready in just a few minutes. Why don't you guys grab something to drink and set us up out on the balcony?"

They quickly set to work, returning to the kitchen just in time for me to plate up the meal and we all carried our own plates back out to the balcony, with the mountains in the distance and the warm early-summer evening air dancing over our skin in a light breeze. Kimber sat between Nick and me, and as we ate and talked and laughed, sharing stories about our days or funny things that we'd seen, I couldn't remember ever feeling as at home as I did right now.

Normally on a Monday, I would be having dinner with my parents, but I had cancelled tonight since I would see them at the party this weekend. Our dinners were never like this, where I felt free to say anything that came into my head, knowing it would be received with warmth and interest. Kimber and Nick might tease me but affection always lay beneath. There was no judgement, no expectation, no censure.

Everything about this felt so right.

When the meal had ended and the three of us sat there with our wine, I looked over at Nick to see if he wanted to move the conversation onto more serious ground, and he gave me a nod, in complete sync with me.

"So, we did what you suggested this weekend," I told Kimber, clearing my throat as I put my wine glass down. My nerves made my hand tremble and I hoped she wouldn't notice. "Nick and I talked about this whole situation and our relationship and what we want to do going forward."

She nodded, licking her lips as she took a deep breath. "And what did you decide?"

I had my mouth open to reply, but Nick cut me off. "Wait. I'd like to hear how you're feeling first, Kimber. You've had the weekend to think things over too, about us, about your public profile as an actress, about everything. What have you decided?"

It didn't feel entirely fair to me to put her on the spot like that before we said how we felt, but I couldn't deny my curiosity about what her response would be, so I stayed silent, letting Nick take the lead.

Kimber looked between the two of us with a soft smile on her face. "Well, I wouldn't be here if I'd decided I never wanted to see you again, would I?"

That made me smile too, but Nick appeared unsatisfied. "See us how? As friends? As lovers? What do you want out of this, Kimber? Tell me what the absolute best-case scenario is for you. Pretend this is your fantasy and you can have whatever you want. What would it look like?"

That was another tough question. She glanced over at me, her expression open and vulnerable, like it had been on the beach on Friday night, and to her immense credit, she answered him truthfully. "Well, I guess for me the best-case would be moments like this, the three of us comfortable and enjoying each other's company, followed by nights like the ones we had last week. I've never been in a relationship that felt as natural as it feels to be here with the two of you. So without worrying about feeling greedy, or what anyone else thought, that's what I would want: just this."

"Greedy?" I repeated curiously. "Why would you be greedy?"

She gave a self-deprecating shrug. "Because I'm inserting myself into your relationship, trying to take something that doesn't belong to me. Because most women have trouble finding one good man, and I want to have two. Because I love being intimate with both of you. Take your pick."

"That's not being greedy, Kimber," Nick said, his voice low and firm. "You didn't insert yourself anywhere. We invited you in, and now that you're here, we want you to stay. We want this too, just like this. We want a real relationship with you, not just sex."

Her eyes widened in surprise, as though she really hadn't expected that response. "But... how would that work? I mean, for a few nights, I understand, but in the long term..."

"It'll work how we make it work," I said, borrowing Nick's language, and he gave me a nod of approval. "We all want this, so what's stopping us? We'd like you to be our girlfriend, Kimber. We'd like to be your partners, both of us. And if you'd like to..."

I trailed off, looking to Nick for confirmation before I went all in, and he nodded again, smiling in agreement.

"We'd like you to move in here with us. At least temporarily, to see how it goes."

Her eyes couldn't have got any wider as she looked between us again. "Are you serious?"

"Completely," Nick assured her. "Like Henry said, we all want this, so why waste time?"

"But... it hasn't even been a week since this started." Her eyes came to me, appealing to me to be the voice of reason, but Nick and I fully agreed on this.

"One of the best weeks of my life," I told her honestly. "I don't regret moving in with Nick for a second, and I don't think you will either. You don't need to decide right now, but at the very least, you can stay here tonight. Spend the whole night with us and see what it could be like. Please, Kimber. Give it a chance. Say yes."

~Kimber~

I never expected anything like this.

With the offer to come for dinner tonight, it felt like Nick and Henry were going to tell me that they wanted to continue with what we'd been doing, but I stopped my imagination from going any further. I enjoyed being a part of their lives and I wanted to keep doing it; I wouldn't allow myself to hope for anything more.

So, for them to say that they actually wanted a real relationship hit me completely out of the blue.

I didn't know anyone in a three-person relationship, not like the one they were proposing. If someone had suggested this kind of thing to me a week ago, I would have thought they were crazy. How could three people be together with no one feeling left out? How could everyone feel satisfied?

But having spent the time together with them that I had, it made a lot more sense to me now. I liked spending time with Henry on his own, and I liked spending time with Nick too. Not a drop of jealousy flowed in my blood at the idea of them spending time together without me; in fact, if anything, the thought made me happy since I knew how happy they made each other.

And most of all, I liked spending time with both of them together.

It felt like, at least within the walls of this apartment, what they were proposing could be completely possible. And sexually, I already knew there were ways to keep all three of us satisfied at the same time, and I imagined there were even more ways that I hadn't thought of yet.

So, although their suggestion truly surprised me, I could see it working, and the thought filled me with a joy I'd hardly ever known before. This was about more than sex and more than simply me being a woman. They could have approached any woman, but they asked me. They liked *me*. They wanted a relationship with *me*. They felt something for me, just as I did for them.

And just when I had started to recover from the shock of that, Henry asked me to move in, and I thought he must be joking. Nobody moved in with someone they'd just met, and certainly not with two men! What would people think?

I recognized that voice in my head, my mother's voice, my default reaction, and I tried to push it aside and think more like Nick. Who cared what people thought? The more important question would be: did this make me happy? Did I want to wake up to Henry and Nick in the morning and come home to them in the evening, in this incredible apartment?

Did I really have to think about that?

But as much as I wanted to agree, I tried to think of practicalities too as they both watched me, Nick's blue eyes and Henry's dark ones, both of them eagerly awaiting my response.

"I don't have any clothes," I pointed out. "I've got nothing to wear if I stay here tonight."

Nick's lips twitched as he tried not to laugh. "I don't see that as a problem. Henry?"

Henry threw him a scolding look before turning back to me. "You don't work tomorrow, right? You could take Nick's car in the morning and go back to your place to pack up whatever you need, at least to get you started."

"Or I could just have some clothes brought over tonight," Nick suggested, pulling out his phone. "What size are you?"

"Nick!" Henry groaned. "You can't just ask a woman that."

He shot me an apologetic smile, but I simply shrugged. They'd both seen me naked; I had nothing left to hide. Besides, Nick had me curious about his intentions. "Size 20," I told him. "22 if it's for lounging around."

Nick didn't bat an eye as he entered the numbers into his phone. After tapping on the screen a few more times, he put the phone down and looked up at me with that teasing smirk of his. "Done. Any other objections?"

None that I could think of at the moment. My mind had begun to short-circuit and all I could think about involved getting back into their bedroom, doing whatever wonderfully filthy thing they had in mind, since I knew Nick must have a plan, and then laying around in bed with them until we all fell asleep, happy and satisfied.

It sounded like heaven.

"I'll stay tonight," I agreed, my heart leaping at the way their eyes lit up at my reply. "And we'll go from there."

Nick gave Henry a wink. "I think that's almost exactly what you said too, and you're still here."

Henry smiled at us both. "Best decision of my life."

It felt like one of my best too.

My whole body buzzed in excitement, wound up tight in anticipation, but to my surprise, no one made an immediate beeline for the bedroom. Almost as if they wanted to prove to me that this had evolved beyond sex, we sat for a while longer on the balcony, enjoying the view and the conversation, and then we took the dishes back into the kitchen and cleaned up together, laughing as Nick kept finding excuses to rub himself up against us both.

"Is he always this dirty?" I asked Henry as Nick reached over my head to put something away in the cupboard, his hardening cock firmly pressed against my ass.

"This is nothing," Henry warned me. "Wait until he does this in public."

The idea of being out with Nick in public, people seeing me and him together, wondering how a woman like me got a man like him, made me even hotter.

A firm knock sounded at the apartment door, and Nick let out a sigh of relief. "Finally."

Without another word, he left to go answer it, and I looked over at Henry in confusion as we finished drying the last of the dishes. "What's that about?"

"I imagine those are your clothes," he explained.

"What? How? Where? Who?"

My stunned reaction made Henry laugh. "Nick's got a personal shopper who's always on call for him if he needs anything last minute. But what he picked out for you, I have no idea."

I had no idea either, but I wouldn't have to wait long to find out once Nick returned with several shopping bags in hand. "Here we go," he announced, handing them over to me. "Something for you to wear tomorrow and a few extras. Maybe you'll find something you'd like to try on tonight."

The heated look in his eye gave me a very good clue about what kind of clothing he meant and, at his prompting, I took the bags into the huge bathroom attached to their bedroom while the two of them sat down on the bed to wait for me.

Sure enough, within the collection of bags, I found one from La Vie en Rose, a lingerie store just down the street.

A small collection of underwear filled the bag: two bras and some panties. To my surprise, he'd got me exactly the right bra size, though he hadn't asked me for that measurement. There were also some very comfortable looking pajamas, and the item that Nick must have had in mind for tonight: a black lace babydoll nightie.

I'd never worn this kind of thing in front of a man before. No one had ever made me feel sexy enough to want to, but Nick obviously wanted it, and I had no doubt Henry would enjoy it too. Without hesitation, I quickly shed my other clothes and put on the black panties and babydoll top. A bit of solid black material stretched across my breasts, the rest of it made entirely of lace.

Looking at the woman in the mirror, I could hardly believe how happy and confident she looked, and I gave her a quick wink before I opened the door to return to my waiting audience.

~Nick~

As Kimber took the bags into the bathroom, Henry and I grinned at each other in anticipation. This couldn't be going any better. Okay, she hadn't out-and-out agreed to move in with us right away, but only because society's expectations were overriding her true desires. Somewhere in the back of her head, a voice nagged her, saying we were moving too fast or that people would talk, but that didn't matter a bit to me and hopefully, once she felt more secure in the sincerity of our offer, it wouldn't matter to her either.

I kissed Henry while we waited, my hand straying to his pants where his cock had already started to harden in anticipation, matching my own.

"What did you buy for her?" Henry asked curiously, glancing towards the still-closed bathroom door.

I shrugged. "I have no idea. Sarah picked it out."

The text I'd sent my personal shopper earlier only told her I had a female friend staying with me for a few days so I wanted whatever she'd need for that time. I sent her clothes sizes, including her bra size that I remembered from when Henry did Kimber's laundry last week, and Sarah took care of the rest.

I paid her well for these kinds of rush requests, but when Kimber opened the door and stepped out in her black lace nightie, her cheeks adorably flushed, I knew Sarah had earned herself a tip too. Kimber looked fantastic, and more than that, she felt it too. The blush told me that she knew exactly how quickly that outfit would work on us.

"You look amazing," Henry said, getting to his feet awkwardly thanks to his growing erection.

I followed right behind him as we both came to stand on either side of her. "Neither of us could pull off black lace," I agreed, running my hands down the material. "But it suits you."

As my fingers trailed closer to the black panties underneath, her eyes raised to mine, giving me all the invitation I needed. My mouth found hers as I pushed the fabric aside, finding her already wet and waiting, and she whimpered into our kiss.

"Henry," I murmured, my lips still against Kimber's. "Take over here. I need to get this underwear off before it's completely soaked."

I got a flash of Kimber's smile before Henry took my place, kissing her tenderly while I bent down to pull off the black panties, leaving the lacy babydoll in place.

My own clothes hit the floor next, and a simple touch on Henry's shoulder let him know when I was ready. He stepped aside to undress himself while I picked up where he left off, kissing Kimber and edging her backwards towards the bed, my hard cock pressed against her stomach. When she reached down and wrapped her hand around it, I groaned in pleasure.

"I love the feel of your hand on me," I told her. "I love the feel of all of you."

My hands cupped her breasts as I said it, my thumbs running against her hard nipples beneath the fabric, and suddenly I knew exactly what I wanted to do tonight: something that I definitely could not do with Henry.

"On your back," I instructed, pushing Kimber gently down onto the bed as Henry came up behind us, eager to join in the fun. "Henry, you're going to fuck her, once she's good and ready."

"You don't think I'm ready now?" Kimber asked, her eyebrows raised at me in challenge as she laid down in the middle of the bed, her head on the pillows. "And why are you always the one in charge? What if we want to tell you what to do?"

Henry nodded enthusiastically. "I think that's a great idea."

"For another night," I told them firmly. "Tonight, I already have plans."

Faced with my intransigence, neither of them put up any further argument, and Henry and I both climbed onto the bed, me between Kimber's legs and Henry beside her chest. Gently, he pulled the straps of her lingerie down, just enough to bare her breasts, and as he lowered his mouth to her puckered nipple, my fingers ran across her clit.

"Oh, God!" Kimber cried out in pure pleasure, and I soaked it in, watching her body writhe as my fingers slid across her wet, sensitive skin and Henry sucked and nibbled at her.

Intentionally or not, he'd positioned his body perfectly for me to reach out and stroke his cock with my other hand, and he moaned against Kimber's breast as I did it.

We played and teased each other a little longer until Kimber practically begged for some relief. "I thought someone was supposed to be fucking me? What's the plan, Nick?"

Her impatience made me smile. "Alright, I think you're ready now. Henry, you're up."

Releasing her nipple from his mouth with a pop, he got to his knees and shuffled over to take my place as I gave his cock one last squeeze.

"You'll have to stay on your knees since I'm going to be right in front of you," I explained. "Maybe we can use a pillow under her hips, or else you could..."

Kimber tossed a pillow at us, hitting me in the side of the head while Henry laughed. "Hurry up," she ordered.

We got the pillow under her, tilting her hips to give Henry better access. He hooked her knees over his arms as he got on his knees, and I watched as he slid into her, his cock disappearing deep inside her as they both exhaled in joint satisfaction.

With that taken care of, I moved back up to Kimber's face, kissing her as she sighed and moaned with each movement Henry made.

"Am I sucking you?" she asked, her blue eyes brightening at the thought. "Or is Henry?"

Both sounded pretty damn good, but weren't what I had in mind. "Neither."

Curiosity played across her face as she watched me reach over to the bedside table and grab the lube, coating myself in a thin layer before I straddled her stomach, on my hands and knees above her with my back to Henry as he thrust into her, slow and deep.

"Have you got enough room back there?" I asked him, turning my head to make sure he felt comfortable.

"Don't worry about me," he panted. "I'm doing just fine."

Kimber and I shared a smile over that as I lowered myself onto her and placed my cock directly between her soft, large breasts.

Finally, she clued into what I meant to do, and before I even had to ask her to, she used her hands to squeeze her breasts together, completely enveloping my stiff shaft.

With my own hands on either side of her head to steady myself, I began to slide in and out of the warm, snug cocoon she'd made for me with her beautiful tits, and it felt just as good as I'd imagined - different from a hand, or a mouth, or a pussy or an asshole, its own unique feeling, and when Henry picked up his pace, beginning to push into her faster, I did the same, keeping our rhythm the same, and soon all three of us were in complete harmony, our moans and sighs and groans making a musical language all their own.

"Oh God, I'm close," Kimber moaned from under us.

"Good girl." The words slipped out before I even realized I meant to say them, but from the way Kimber's lips parted, I could tell she didn't mind. "Come for both of us. Come with us."

Henry moved even faster, and a moment later, Kimber did just as I suggested, her body shuddering beneath us in fulfilment as we both continued to thrust, using her body in completely different ways but for the same end.

"Fuck, yes," Henry moaned from behind me, and I knew he'd found his release too, so I moved even faster, my own pleasure building with each thrust, and just as I spotted the finish line, Henry's finger pushed into my ass, sending a jolt of added excitement through me, and I lost all control.

I came hard, all over Kimber's chest and neck as she panted beneath me.

"Shit, that was good." With a groan, I rolled off of her, and Henry immediately leaned forward to take my place, still inside Kimber as he bent down to kiss her, and then, he bent lower and licked up my cum, his eyes watching me as he did it.

Fuck, he turned me on, and Kimber did too.

If night one of our relationship felt this good, I couldn't wait to see what tomorrow would bring.

~Kimber~

Once again, Nick managed to surprise me. When men said they liked big breasts, they usually meant big but also still somehow pert and gravity-defying, like the kind that pin-up models have. They didn't mean big and floppy, the kind that could slap me across the face if I tried to run without a bra on.

But both Nick and Henry had gravitated towards my chest every time I'd been naked, seeming to truly enjoy the sight and feel of my breasts, and when Nick fucked them just now, he left no doubt that he found it sexy. The warm cum along my neck backed him up. I certainly found it sexy too, seeing him so turned on and feeling his hard cock rubbing against my skin, pulsing with need.

Having Henry inside me at the same time definitely helped add to the overall experience, and all in all, I could chalk that up as another orgasm I'd never forget.

And as Henry pulled out to lay down beside me, him on one side of me and Nick on the other, all of us completely satisfied, I knew that any surprises in the bedroom with these two were going to be good surprises. Though my body had been perfectly sated, I couldn't wait to see what else they might have in store for me.

Henry seemed to be on the same page as he cuddled in close to me, nudging me gently onto my side so he could spoon me as I faced Nick, who lay on his back beside me. "Kimber, you sounded like you had something in particular you wanted to try before Nick took over again. What is it?"

Curiosity sparked in Nick's eyes. "Is that true? I want to know too."

Despite what we had just done and the fact that we were all still completely naked, I still felt a little awkward saying the words out loud. I'd never admitted to anyone that I wanted to try something like this, but they were both so honest and open with me, I wanted to pay them the same courtesy.

"Well, I've never given a ton of thought to threesomes before, but whenever I imagined two men and one woman, I pictured one thing in particular and we haven't done it yet."

As I would have expected, Nick caught my drift immediately without me needing to spell it out. "You mean double penetration?"

Forcing myself to maintain eye contact with him, I nodded. "I've never done it, I just thought it was kind of the standard thing."

His lips twisted into that sexy smirk of his. "I don't know if anything about what we're doing is standard, but that's certainly something we can try. Have you done anal before?"

Henry's hand moved down to caress my ass as Nick asked the question.

"I have once," I told him truthfully. "I didn't really enjoy it, but I feel like with you guys, it would be better."

His expression softened as if I'd paid him a compliment, though I only spoke the truth.

"Why didn't you enjoy it?" Henry asked from behind me, his chin resting on my shoulder so he could also see Nick.

"Well, the guy just kind of shoved it in without a lot of foreplay," I told them, wincing a little at the memory. "It hurt."

Nick's lips tightened as he glanced at Henry before looking back at me. "It sounds like you're being pretty generous in saying you 'didn't enjoy it', then. There should be some real prep that goes into it. It might feel uncomfortable at first, but it shouldn't hurt."

"Well, the guy in question cared a lot more about his own pleasure than mine."

"You don't have to worry about that here," Henry assured me, and I knew from everything we'd already done that I could trust him. "Nick is the best at foreplay. My first time had me so nervous, but he made it a really good experience. If you let him help, it will be good for you too."

I could feel Henry's smile against my cheek as Nick smiled back at him, clearly pleased with Henry's assessment.

"I actually thought maybe I could start with you," I told Henry. "Since you're not quite so... thick."

That made them both chuckle. "We'll figure it out together," Nick promised me. "And if you really don't like it, there are other ways to do double penetration too."

I frowned in confusion. "You mean one of you in my mouth? We've already done that."

Nick grinned. "No, that's not what I had in mind." His innuendo still went over my head, but Nick only laughed. "Never mind. In any case, there's no rush. We'll get there, and everywhere else we want to be. We've got time."

We did, especially if I really moved in here as they asked me to. It felt wonderful to know I could stay here tonight, that this wonderful feeling of belonging didn't have to end.

Right on cue, as if he'd heard my thoughts, Nick sat up. "I'm going to get ready for bed. Some of us work in the morning."

He gave me a wink as he got out of bed and headed into the bathroom. Henry moved away from me too, but only so I could lay on my back again and he could see my face, and concern clouded his eyes as he looked down at me. "You would tell us if we ever hurt you, right?"

The sincerity and thoughtfulness of the question melted my heart. "Of course I would. I was young and inexperienced with that other guy, and I let him do what he wanted in the hopes he'd decide he wanted to stick around. I know better now, and I know you and Nick respect me a lot more than that anyway. It's completely different."

That seemed to reassure him, and he leaned down to kiss me, his lips soft against mine and his scent flooding my senses as I inhaled. When he pulled away, he rested his head on his hand as he continued to look down at me. "You know, we haven't had a chance to talk about exactly what the three of us being in a relationship looks like, but Nick and I did discuss it a bit over the weekend."

"I'm all ears." I smiled up at him even as my heart beat a little faster. I had no idea how this would work and I definitely wanted to know what they were thinking.

"Well, obviously, whenever we can, we'll be together like this, the three of us." He gestured to the bed and to the bathroom to include Nick in the equation. "But when we can't, we could still spend time together with whoever's available. So when you're working on the weekends, for example, Nick and I might go out and do something together. Or, like we did on Friday while Nick slept, when he's unavailable, you and I could do something."

That made sense to me, and actually, in some ways it made an improvement on a regular two-person relationship. Now we had a greater chance of having someone always around if we needed them.

"Is that okay with you?" Henry asked, watching my reaction closely. "It wouldn't bother you if Nick and I do things without you?"

The question struck me as so ridiculous, I had to laugh. "Of course it wouldn't bother me. I know you two are together and I love how happy you make each other. You had this relationship first, so the bigger question is whether it bothers you and Nick to share each other with me."

Henry quickly shook his head. "I don't want you to think that, Kimber. It doesn't matter who met who first. Now that we're in this, everyone is equally important and equally a part of it. So not only would it not bother me for you and Nick to spend time together, I want you to. I'd like you to get to know each other better without me there. And I'd like for us to get to know each other better too."

So not only were we all dating as a group, we were dating each other separately too? "And you really think this is going to work? Out in public, I mean?"

A sheepish smile crossed his face. "Well, I'm not really one to talk about not caring what people think, but I'm working on it. And I don't want to have to hide anymore, not from my parents and not from everyone. I love Nick, and I care for you too. That's not a bad thing. In fact, it's a pretty great thing, and if people can't see it, it's their loss. The people that really matter shouldn't care."

Immediately I thought of Rocco's reaction, and how he said I should do what made me happy. That was one side of the coin, but on the other, I tried to imagine my family's reaction if I introduced them to these two men who were both dating not only me but each other too. It would be the talk of our small town for months.

And then I had to consider my work, and in particular the role that I would be trying out for this week. What would the people who wanted a 'wholesome' actress for the part think if they knew about my situation?

"We don't need to rush anything," Henry promised me. "But if you don't have other plans, I'd love it if you came and joined me for lunch tomorrow. Nick is always busy during the week. We could just grab something quick and go sit by the water or something?"

That sounded wonderful, and relatively innocent, so I quickly agreed. When Nick came out of the bathroom, I took my turn next, putting on the comfortable pajamas that had been bought for me. A toothbrush and hairbrush had also been included in the bags, along with some basic makeup and other toiletries. His personal shopper definitely knew her job.

When I had finished getting ready, I returned to the bedroom where Nick and Henry were speaking to each other quietly in bed, though they both smiled over at me as the door opened. Henry went into the bathroom after me, giving me a kiss on the way by, and Nick spread a welcoming arm over the bed. "Where do you want to sleep, Kimber? I'm going to take one side since I need to get up first, so do you want the middle or the other side?"

The bed could certainly fit the three of us, we'd established that already, but actually climbing in and going to sleep between Nick and Henry marked the start of something new. It felt like the first step in being in a real relationship, something significant and special.

"I think I'll try in the middle tonight, but I might change my mind later."

Nick's grin told me he had no problem with that, and I crawled in next to him. Henry returned soon afterwards, climbing in on my other side, and we chatted about anything that crossed our minds until sleep couldn't be put off any longer.

As my eyes drifted closed, I couldn't help thinking that no dream I could possibly have tonight could be better than my reality right now.

Chapter Eleven

~**Henry**~

The first thing I saw when I woke up in the morning was Kimber's face, fast asleep beside me. Her thick eyelashes rested against her skin, her pink lips were parted slightly, and her dark hair lay spread out beneath her. She had taken her makeup off before getting into bed last night, but I hardly noticed.

She still looked beautiful.

I could still remember the first time I watched Nick sleeping, and how vulnerable and handsome he looked. Letting yourself be so unguarded with another person constituted a real act of trust, and the fact that Kimber had agreed to stay with us last night both pleased me and made me proud. She felt safe with us, and I couldn't feel more safe with her.

Not wanting to wake her on her day off, I quietly got out of bed and got ready for work. Nick had left a long time ago, as usual. He never woke me either. On my way to the office, I made my usual stop at Rocco's coffee shop, though Kimber's absence made it less inviting. Previously, whenever I came in on one of her days off, I would always be curious about where she might be and what she did when she had time off, but today, I knew the answer. The mental image of her, warm and comfortable in my bed, made me smile.

The morning passed quickly, busy with meetings with a client for an upcoming arbitration hearing, and when I got back to my desk, I only had fifteen minutes before I'd agreed to meet Kimber outside. I checked my phone to see if she'd been in touch, to make sure nothing had changed, but I hadn't received anything from here. I did, however, have a message from Nick telling me he needed to work late today and couldn't say when he'd be home. It disappointed me, naturally, as I always hated to miss out on time with him, but at least now I had Kimber to spend that time with instead. Having her in our lives seemed like a better idea all the time.

When I came out the front door of my building, I saw her immediately, shining like a beacon in the small plaza in the pretty clothes Nick had bought from her. She held up a small bag in her hands as I approached. "I stopped in and picked up a couple of Rocco's sfogliatella for us. They're the best."

"You're the best," I countered, giving her a quick kiss.

Her eyes darted around nervously as I pulled back. "What if your co-workers see us?"

I had already thought about that. They all knew Nick and I were together, of course, but I meant it when I told Kimber that we were all equal in this relationship. I didn't want her to feel like she had to hide our relationship. I only felt pride about dating her, and I wanted her to know that.

"Then they see us," I told her, trying to sound as brave as Nick would be in my position, and I couldn't ask for a better reward than the smile that lit up her face.

Hand-in-hand, we walked over to Urban Fare to pick up some ready-to-eat poke bowls before heading on to Harbour Green Park in Coal Harbour. With the green grass, the shining sun, and the scent of salt water in the air, it made a perfect spot for a break, and we obviously weren't the only ones who thought so. We were surrounded by people: retirees, office workers like me, students, and parents with young kids, all looking like they'd rather be here than anywhere else.

"It must have been amazing to grow up here," Kimber said as we found an empty space on the grass, overlooking the water.

My experience had been quite different from the children we could see running around now. "Actually, as a kid, my world felt pretty limited. My parents hardly ever left Chinatown. We had a small apartment above my father's store and all my friends were local kids. I only went to North Vancouver for the first time when I turned sixteen and my parents started letting me go places on my own."

She took a bite of her salmon, listening to me thoughtfully. "They were overprotective?"

I wouldn't use that word. "I think they liked what they knew, that's where they were comfortable, and they thought I should be the same. And since I didn't want to cause them any trouble, I mostly did as they said."

Kimber smiled. "So you were a rule follower."

That was fair. "Yeah, I guess so. I pretty much always did what people expected of me, at least until I met Nick."

She smiled wider, the rays of the sun sparkling in her hair and in her eyes. "He's a bad influence, eh?"

I grinned back. "The worst. And the very best."

She asked about my work day and we talked about her audition tomorrow, and the time went so quickly that I could scarcely believe when my phone alarm went off, letting me know I needed to head back to the office. I had set it just in case we lost track of time, and it turned out to be a good idea.

"What's your plan this afternoon?" I asked Kimber as we walked back to my office.

"I still need to go to my apartment and pick up a few things so I'm going to do that now. Then I'll probably just rehearse a bit for tomorrow and try not to get too nervous about it."

I could hardly imagine. Getting up in front of an arbitration committee caused me enough stress at times, and at least they were just judging the strength of my arguments, not me personally. It awed me that she could put herself out there like that. "How would you like to go out for dinner tonight to take your mind off it?"

The smile on her face made it clear I had her interest. "All three of us?"

She hadn't heard from Nick? I thought he would have texted her too when he texted me. He must have been really busy if he hadn't. "No, Nick has to work late tonight. It would just be you and me."

Her eyebrows raised in surprise, but no hint of disappointment. She made me feel that spending time with me alone would be just as good. "That sounds like fun. Maybe we could go to Chinatown and you can show me all your old haunts."

Nick and I had never done that, only because I had always been afraid of running into my parents when they didn't know about Nick and Nick thought they did. My cowardice embarrassed me now, and I couldn't wait to make up for it this weekend. "Sure, sounds good. Why don't you come meet me back here at five o'clock and we can walk over?"

With that agreed, I kissed her goodbye and headed back inside. One of my colleagues stood waiting for the elevator, and she gave me a friendly smile as I walked up. "Hi, Henry. It's a nice day, isn't it?"

I couldn't have hid my happiness even if I wanted to. "It's perfect."

~Kimber~

After leaving Henry at his office, I made a slight amendment to my plans for the afternoon. If Nick had to work late, he might appreciate a little pick-me-up, so I stopped back in Rocco's shop and grabbed a couple more of his delicious homemade pastries before making my way over to Nick's office that Henry had pointed out to me earlier.

I intended to simply leave the treats at the reception desk for him, not wanting to disturb him if he had a lot of work to do, but as I explained the package to the receptionist, a very pretty and professional-looking blonde woman came up to the desk.

"This is for Nick?" she confirmed, gesturing to the parcel in my hand, and I nodded. "I'm his assistant, Erin. I can take it."

"Oh, it's really nice to meet you. I'm Kimber, Nick's..."

I trailed off, unsure how to introduce myself. Was I his girlfriend? He planned to bring me to meet his colleagues tomorrow and introduce me that way, but I didn't want to steal his thunder or cause any problems if he changed his mind.

"... friend," I finished finally.

If she noticed my hesitation, she gracefully ignored it. "Do you want to bring them in yourself? He's not with anyone at the moment and I have a feeling he'd like a distraction. It's one of those days."

One of which days? Although the words confused me, I accepted the invitation anyway, following her down the hall, past large offices with glass windows, feeling completely underdressed and out of place with all the important-looking people in their suits and ties.

"He's just in there," Erin told me, pointing to a closed door with a nameplate that read Nick Lewis. So *that* was his last name.

The solid door looked a little intimidating, but the thought of Nick's smile waiting on the other side made it seem a lot more welcoming. When I knocked, however, only silence answered me.

I glanced back at Erin but she had gone back to work, typing away on her keyboard and not paying any attention to me, or at least pretending not to, so I turned back and knocked again. "Nick?"

"What?"

The gruff voice that answered me bore little resemblance to the man I knew, but I took it as an invitation anyway and opened the door.

The darkness of the office took me by surprise when I walked in. The lights were off and the blinds half-drawn. Nick sat at his desk, his face illuminated by his computer screen as he glanced over at me, and his eyes widened in surprise as he saw me come in.

"Kimber?" He rubbed a hand down his face, as if he thought he might be seeing things. "What are you doing here?"

"Henry told me you had to work late," I explained, putting a smile on my face as I walked over to his desk. "I thought you might like a treat. Your assistant let me in, I'm sorry if I'm disturbing you."

"No, you're... it's just... I don't want..." He shook his head, as if the words refused to form, before he settled on a more simple sentence, though the words were still clipped. "Thank you."

"You're welcome." It seemed I had interrupted something and not wanting to make a nuisance of myself, I placed the package on his desk and stepped back. Just before I turned to go, though, something twigged in my memory. The way he looked now - the lines of worry across his face, the dullness in his eyes - matched almost exactly with the way he looked when I came across him in the bar last week. "Is everything okay?"

His jaw tightened as his eyes went back to his screen. "It's fine. I'm just busy. I'm usually busy. I don't have time for visitors during the day."

The rebuke and the cold tone of his voice made my stomach sink. Apparently, I had overstepped a boundary I hadn't known existed. "I'm sorry, Nick. I didn't realize it would be a problem. I won't bother you again."

Part of me hoped he would tell me I got it wrong, that he hadn't meant it like that, but he stayed silent as I turned and let myself out of his office. Erin looked up as I closed the door behind me, and I gave her a forced smile, thanking her for her help before I quickly returned the way I came.

~Henry~

"Which flavour is your favourite?"

Waiting in line at the bubble tea café, Kimber looked up at me with those sweet blue eyes of hers as she asked the question, and I couldn't help channelling a little of Nick's naughtiness. "Probably mango," I said out loud before leaning closer to her, whispering into her ear, "but it doesn't compare to the taste of you."

She rolled her eyes in exasperation, but as I hoped, her cheeks colored a little bit too. She liked me saying it, even if she didn't necessarily believe my words.

Even though they were definitely true.

This evening had been a lot of fun so far. After Kimber met me back at my office, we made the short walk over to Chinatown on the east side of Vancouver's downtown. I took her past my father's store, which had already closed for the day, and pointed out the apartment where I grew up. Now, my parents had a small house not far away and I hadn't lived with them since I went to university at UBC, but the place still had a lot of memories for me.

We wandered the streets as I told her stories from my childhood, and then we went to a small restaurant run by friends of my parents. Mrs Huang brought our meals out herself and we spoke in Mandarin for a short while as we exchanged the usual pleasantries, asking about each other's families, and she said how much she was looking forward to my mother's party this weekend. Switching to English, I introduced her to Kimber, not saying anything about the nature of our relationship. I needed to tell my parents about that myself. Kimber's usual warm vibe came through as strongly as ever and I could tell that Mrs Huang left with a favourable impression.

"It's kind of sexy hearing you speak another language," Kimber said when we were alone again, her eyes sparkling as she leaned closer to me across the table. "Maybe you could teach me."

"That's what Nick said too, but he only made it through three lessons before he gave up."

That made her smile, but I could see a bit of concern in her eyes too, and she quickly explained the reason for it. "I think I messed up with him today."

Hardly anything she could have said would have surprised me more. "What do you mean? What happened?"

With a grimace, she told me about how she went to see Nick in his office and the way he reacted. "If I'd known he didn't like to be disturbed at work, I wouldn't have gone. I guess I owe him an apology."

Her words completely floored me. He had never said anything like that to me in all the time we'd been together. "That's not like him. He loves it when I visit him at the office."

A look of embarrassment crossed Kimber's face. "So it's just me, then."

Shit, I didn't mean it like that. "No, not at all. He must have just been having a really tough day, but even so, it's not like him to take it out on someone else like that. I'm sorry, Kimber. I don't know why he acted that way, but if anyone is owed an apology, it's you. You were only being thoughtful."

She tried to shrug it off, but I could tell it still bothered her, just as it would have bothered me. We had quite a lot in common. "Does he have bad days like that a lot? His assistant said something about it being 'one of those days'."

My initial instinct was to assure her that they were rare, but when I stopped to really think it over, I had to concede there might be a bit of a pattern. "He's often not in a great mood when he has to work late, but it's unusual for him to be short-tempered like that. Usually when he's upset, he just withdraws and goes quiet."

"And does that happen a lot?"

Again, now that I thought about it, it might be more often than I had previously realized. "Maybe once a week or so?"

Kimber nodded thoughtfully. "And then the next day, he's back to normal?"

"Usually," I agreed. "Sometimes it can last a couple of days, but I think it has to do with work. He always works late on those days. I don't understand exactly what he does, so I don't know what upsets him."

I had tried asking him before, but he always told me not to worry and that he'd be back to himself soon. It always worked out that way, so I let it go. Talking about it with Kimber, though, made me feel like there might be more to it than I realized. She obviously thought so.

"I wonder if he's in a bad mood because he works late, or if he works late because he's in a bad mood?" she mused.

I honestly hadn't thought about it in those terms before. "I don't know, but if it's not work putting him in a bad mood, then what is it?"

"I think that's something only he can answer." She gave me a smile, letting me know she'd like to move on, and we did, talking easily for the rest of our meal.

After getting our bubble tea, we walked back to the apartment, enjoying the warm evening. We didn't get home until almost nine o'clock, and I thought Nick might be in bed already, but to my surprise, there was no sign of him.

"Is it typical for him to get home this late?" Kimber asked, sounding a bit worried.

"Not typical, but it does happen. I'll send him a quick text and make sure he's okay."

His reply took only seconds: *Almost there.*

When I shared it with Kimber, she chewed on her lip for a moment, thinking it over. "I might go downstairs and try to catch him, if you don't mind. I'd like to talk to him privately about what happened earlier."

Since they could sort it out without my help, I had no problem with that. I trusted them to work it out between them, so I sat down to find something that Kimber and I could watch on TV. Usually, I sat up by myself after Nick went to bed. Having someone else to hang out with really did make a nice change.

~Nick~

After shoving my phone back in my pocket, I stared down at the flowers in my other hand. I had always intended to pick them up today, to give them to Kimber as a good luck token for her audition tomorrow, but now they served another purpose too: they were part of the apology I needed to give her, even though I had no idea what to say.

As soon as my office door closed behind her, I knew I had messed up.

My bad days always felt worse when things were going well, and they couldn't have been going much better than they had been lately. Falling asleep with Kimber and Henry last night, I felt on top of the world, and it only made the low I woke up to this morning feel that much lower. I tried to shut it down like I always did: working out as hard as I could until the physical pain distracted from my thoughts, and keeping to myself in the office as much as possible.

Then Kimber showed up unexpectedly with her smile full of sunshine and a parcel of fresh baking, and I tried to hold it together, I really did. I could have said a lot worse. Sharper words were on the tip of my tongue, but I could tell from the way she retreated that I'd hurt her anyway.

In her eyes at that moment, in the surprise and the uncertainty, I recognized myself as a child. And when she walked away, I could see the walls I used to throw up whenever my mom's mood was unpredictable. Kimber or Henry shouldn't have to use their walls with me. I wanted to control it better than that.

I thought about sending her a text to apologize, but once I pulled my phone out, my fingers hovered over the keys indecisively. What if I just made it worse? My instincts often let me down on days like today. I relied on my gut day in and day out to guide me, both in business and in my personal relationships, but when I had days like this, I couldn't trust it, and it made me feel like a ship cut adrift with no way of navigating.

I put the phone away.

By the time the office had emptied out, when only me and the cleaning staff remained, I finally started to feel a little better. Supper time had come and gone, and I realized not only had I not texted Kimber to apologize, I never told her I wouldn't be home on time either. Henry would have filled her in eventually, but that didn't excuse the oversight. I owed her more consideration than that after I'd just promised to treat her as an equal in this relationship. Now, I owed her more of an apology than ever, and the flowers were just a part of that.

Still struggling to find the right words to go with them, I walked up to the front door of my building to find her sitting on the bench out front.

"Hey." She gave me a tentative smile as I approached, which made me wince. I knew that look too, the one that waited anxiously to find out if I would smile in return or bite her head off. She shouldn't have to wonder.

"Hey, yourself." When I smiled back, she immediately relaxed, and I held out the flowers in my hand. "These are for you. I'm sorry about earlier. My grumpy side got the better of me."

She looked genuinely touched as she took the flowers from me, but she made no move to stand up so I took a seat next to her instead.

"You and Henry are going to spoil me," she said, taking a deep sniff of the flowers. "I've only ever gotten flowers once before in my whole life, and you guys have done it twice in one week."

"Maybe it'll make up for lost time then." We smiled at each other again and I leaned in closer, feeling more relaxed now that I knew she would give me another chance. "I really am sorry, Kimber. You took me by surprise and my bad mood had nothing to do with you. I really appreciate that you came by to see me."

"Did you like the pastry?" she asked, and I winced again. I hadn't actually eaten them. Food tasted like ash on days like today, and combined with the guilt I felt, the thought of eating them made me sick. I'd thrown them away instead.

"I really appreciate the gesture." I hoped she wouldn't notice that I avoided the question. "Did you have a good day?"

"I did, but there's something I want to talk to you about, Nick. I'm not trying to pry or cause trouble, but I think it's important."

Pry? I hadn't expected that. "What is it?"

Kimber laid the flowers down in her lap, looking at them for a second before raising her eyes back to mine. "How often do these bad days of yours happen?"

Ah. She'd hit upon the one thing I didn't want to talk about, and I couldn't stop the defensive tone that crept into my voice. "Everyone has bad days."

"They do," she quickly agreed. "But some people have more than others, through no fault of their own. I saw you in the bar last week, remember? And now you had another one today, and Henry mentioned that it happens somewhat regularly."

I really didn't like the direction this seemed to be heading, or that she'd been talking to Henry behind my back. "I know you're trying to be helpful, but you don't know anything about it. I can handle a few bad days, Kimber. I have things under control."

"It shouldn't be something you have to control." Her gentle tone felt surprisingly firm. She obviously had no intention of backing down. "One of my cousins back home went through something like this. Most of the time, everyone loved to be around her, but then she'd have days that were really bad, days she couldn't deal with the world at all."

"Sounds rough." I refused to make the connection to myself, even though she obviously meant to.

And she did just that now. "That look she had on those days is the same way you looked today, Nick. Having control had nothing to do with it and neither did being strong. She finally went to a doctor and they diagnosed her. She got treatment, and now she's doing a lot better."

"I'm not sick." When anything made me as uncomfortable as this conversation did, I pushed back out of instinct. "You hardly know me,

Kimber, and I don't remember asking for your opinion. If I want it, I'll let you know."

I thought that would stop her. I'd said far less to her earlier and she had backed down then, but this time, she stood her ground.

"You asked me to move in," she reminded me, still speaking kindly but not yielding an inch. "You invited me into your life, and that means looking out for you. You might have hidden it well enough that the people close to you haven't noticed, but maybe a fresh perspective is what you need to help you see this isn't normal. You don't have to feel this way, and you don't have to deal with it alone."

Even if she had a point about me asking her into my life, I had no intention of backing down either. "So you think there's something wrong with me, but you want to stick around anyway? Which of us sounds crazy now?"

Her lips pursed, making her look almost as frustrated as I felt. "I never said you were crazy. And yes, of course I want to stay. I like you, Nick, a lot. I'm sorry that you're going through this, but it's nothing that you can't overcome if you take the step to get some help. I believe you're strong enough to do that, and Henry and I would be right there with you."

Henry. The idea of him thinking I needed help too nearly broke my heart, taking some of my anger away. In our relationship, I was the strong one, the one he could depend on. If I couldn't be that, I didn't know what I could give him. "Have you already talked to him about this?"

Kimber quickly shook her head. "No. I told him what happened earlier today, but nothing about the rest of it. He needs to hear that from you, Nick. He would want to help you if you let him."

An overwhelming mix of emotions - anger, frustration, guilt, sadness, and fear - all ran through me at once, leaving me feeling suddenly exhausted. "Look, I appreciate that you want to help, and I'm sorry again for being grumpy, but right now, I really just need to sleep. I'll feel better in the morning. I always do."

Disappointment clouded her eyes at that response, but she got to her feet, still holding onto the flowers, clutching them tightly as though they might disappear if she let go. "Let's go to bed then."

Chapter Twelve

~**Kimber**~

The next morning, I woke up to an empty bed again. Nick and Henry were both already gone for work but I had the day off, this time because of my audition later this afternoon.

Nerves and excitement fluttered around inside me as I took a long shower in Nick's incredible bathroom. The audition caused some of my anxiety, naturally, but part of it also stemmed from the way Nick and I had left things last night. I could understand his defiance, and he had a point: I had butted into a part of his life he clearly didn't want me to interfere in, but only because I genuinely cared about him. Hopefully, he would recognize my good intentions even if I'd overstepped with my actions. We still had some things to learn about the way each of us handled things.

When we got back up to the apartment last night, Nick gave Henry a kiss, asked about our evening, and then excused himself to go to bed. Henry and I stayed up for a while longer, watching TV cuddled up together on the couch just as I had always imagined during those months where I daydreamed about him after each coffee shop visit. He did ask if everything had been cleared up between me and Nick, and I simply said we had talked. I had said what I wanted to say to Nick, and it wasn't my place to tell Henry anything about it. If Nick wanted him to know, he would tell him himself.

Nothing sexual happened between any of us, but in a way, that relieved me. If we were really in this long-term, not every night would be an orgy, and the fact that I felt just as comfortable going to bed between them even without sex seemed like a good sign.

And though I still worried about how Nick felt after last night, there hadn't been any retraction of my invitation to join him at his work event tonight. In fact, when I went into the kitchen to get some breakfast, I found a note from Nick on the message board, wishing me luck today. Henry had scrawled his own good wishes beneath it too, and the thoughtfulness of the gesture filled me with warmth and helped to quiet some of the butterflies in my stomach. I snapped a quick picture of it with my phone as a memento and then sent them both a text to say thank you. I promised to let them know how everything went as soon as I finished.

The auditions were taking place at a studio in North Vancouver, and I went by public transit instead since I couldn't afford the luxury of a taxi. From the apartment, a short walk took me to Waterfront station where I got on the Sea Bus to Lonsdale Quay. When I had my first audition after moving to the city, getting around still flummoxed me at times, and when my agent told me I had to take the Sea Bus, I literally wrote down the letter 'C', thinking it stood for the name of the bus route. Only when I looked it up online later to check the route did I realize it actually referred to a boat. That memory still made me smile even though navigating the city had long since lost its novelty.

At Lonsdale Quay, I grabbed a quick lunch to make sure my stomach wouldn't growl at an inopportune time before taking a bus that took me close to the studio entrance. Putting on my best sunny smile, I walked up to the security booth and gave my name. The guard smiled back and wished me luck as he let me in, which I took as a good sign. People were on my side today and everything would go well.

No matter how many times I arrived at a studio, it thrilled me just the same, like walking into a completely different world. Each building contained soundstages and sets that had been created for the shows being made there, and each one represented a chance to experience a completely different life, to be someone other than myself.

Ironically for one of the biggest auditions of my life, right now, I wouldn't trade a single thing about my own life.

Since I had arrived a little early, the casting assistant offered me some coffee and I sat down in the waiting area, flipping through the scene I'd been sent to prepare, even though I already had it memorized front to back. Being well-prepared came naturally to me. There might be a million different reasons why I wouldn't get a role, but flubbing my lines would never be one of them.

"Kimber?" The assistant called my name and gave me a friendly smile. Another person rooting for me, I hoped. "They're ready for you now."

As confidently as I could, I followed her down the hall to the small, windowless room furnished only with a rectangular table with a phone and a few pieces of paper on it, behind which sat a group of three men. It was *always* men. I'd never figured out why more women didn't go into casting, but 95% of the time, I came up in front of a group of men.

Normally, a first-round audition would be a quick in and out – do the scene, maybe answer a question or two, and they'd be onto the next person. But in this case, since they had specifically asked to see me, it would be a little more involved. They'd asked me to prepare a scene of my own in addition to the one they'd provided, so as soon as I put my bag down and smoothed out my clothes, I strode over in front of the table and gave them a warm smile. They were all on my side too, whether they knew it yet or not. I just had to convince them of that.

"Good afternoon. I'm excited to be reading for you today for the role of Eliza."

None of them smiled back, but I held my own smile steady. I wouldn't let myself be intimidated today.

"Your first piece, then?" the oldest of the men said, and I immediately launched straight into it.

For today, I chose the same scene that I did for Henry and Nick last week when they asked to see me act. They both seemed to find it impressive, and I pictured them in front of me again as I performed it for the casting team now. I could almost feel them there with me, cheering me on.

All three men were completely poker-faced as I finished, but it felt like I had done a good job. Whether or not I got the role, I couldn't complain about how that went.

The man on the end pressed a button on the phone and a woman's voice immediately answered. In a clipped tone, he spoke only three words. "Bring Dale in."

I hardly had time to process that before the door opened again and a man walked in whom I had only seen on TV before: Dale Winters, one of the hottest actors in the city at the moment, and the star of the show. They must be seriously considering me if they brought the star in to read with me.

Playing it as cool as I could, I said hello and he smiled back at me in a genuinely friendly way before, with no further warning, he launched directly into the scene. "What do you think you're doing, coming over here when I specifically told you I didn't want to see you again?"

My surprise only lasted a second before I turned off my Kimber brain and stepped into the character's shoes instead, where the words were waiting for me on the tip of my tongue. "We need to finish our conversation."

"I think we already said everything there is to say."

The scene flowed smoothly, Dale getting more and more animated with each line, and I did my best to match him not only word-for-word but with the same energy level too, keeping my response proportionate to his. His acting really impressed me, and when we finished, I felt more excited than ever about the possibility of getting this part. I would love to be able to work with him.

The men at the table remained stone-faced as they asked me a few questions about my experience and availability before thanking me for coming in. They gave no indication of how well I had done, but I hadn't expected them to. Getting any kind of notes after an audition was the exception rather than the rule. Most of the time, I heard a simple yes or no answer through my agent.

Dale stayed behind in the room as I gathered my things and left, eager to get back to Henry and Nick and tell them all about it. However, halfway back to the waiting room, I remembered that I should probably use the washroom before I got on the bus back home. I thought I had seen one right next to the audition room, so I doubled back to head there now.

Only when I got back to the door of the room I'd just exited did I realize I hadn't fully closed it behind me, and nothing stopped the voices inside from carrying out to me.

"She's good," said a voice that had to belong to Dale. He had a very distinctive sound. "Better than the one this morning."

My heart soared as I quickly looked behind me, making sure no one could see me eavesdropping. Though I knew I shouldn't, I couldn't resist the chance to hear the reply.

"I agree," one of the other men said. "She's got real potential. And at least we know we don't have to worry about the problem we had with Amanda."

A round of laughter echoed around the room as my stomach sank, and I quickly hurried into the washroom, my cheeks flushing in embarrassment. It couldn't be more clear what they meant. Amanda had lost the role because she had done an adult film, but they wouldn't have to worry about that with me, because who in their right mind would ever want to see me having sex?

Obviously they didn't see anything desirable about me at all.

They might not have used those words but they meant it, and the presumption both mortified and infuriated me. The temptation rose up inside me to march back in there right now and announce that my two incredibly sexy lovers were at home waiting for me, but I still valued my career a little more than that.

In the end, I simply had to suck it up and head out, smiling at the assistant as I said goodbye, putting on my happy-go-lucky face that told the world that nothing bothered me.

For that role, at least, I already had plenty of experience.

~Nick~

To my relief, I woke up the next morning feeling fantastic. Not only did I not feel bad anymore, I couldn't even see my low in the rearview mirror. I felt completely invincible and on top of the world. Today, everything would go right.

After my workout, I grabbed a quick breakfast in the kitchen where I saw the flowers I'd bought for Kimber the night before, displayed in a small vase. Henry must have done that last night since Kimber wouldn't have known where to find one. Those kinds of thoughtful gestures on his part always made me smile.

Thinking back on my conversation with Kimber from the night before, my anger had dissipated, but I also knew now that she had been overreacting. Nothing was wrong with me. How could there be when I felt this good?

I felt far too good to hold a grudge, so I left her a note on the whiteboard wishing her luck at her audition before heading out to work.

Just as I expected, everything at the office went perfectly too. I had several client meetings, including a couple I had rescheduled from yesterday since I hadn't felt up to seeing them then. Today, they found me charming and confident, if I did say so myself, and they all left completely convinced that they'd invested their money with the right company and with the right man for the job. My manager even stopped by to compliment me after one of our top clients got in touch with him directly to say how positive he felt after meeting with me today.

During the time between meetings, I reviewed movements in the markets from the past few days, and I spotted a potential mover in a company that had publicly launched a couple of weeks ago with little fanfare. It just seemed to jump out to me, in the way things did on days like this, like it had a big flashing neon arrow that I couldn't understand how anyone else missed.

I moved quickly, buying up a couple of million in shares, and that move attracted attention from others who followed the market just as closely as I did. Within hours, others across the continent were following suit, and by the end of the day, the value had nearly tripled.

The people at that company were having a very good day, and so were my clients and my company too.

That just proved my point: I could handle the bad days, just as I always had.

I kept my phone nearby, waiting for Kimber's update after her audition, but when it came, it confused me. Although she didn't say anything negative, I could detect a distinct lack of excitement.

It went well. Now we wait. See you both soon.

That came through about an hour before I left work for the day, so if she had just left the audition now, I should beat her home. Wanting to do something nice for her, I called my personal shopper once again, apologizing for the last-minute request, and asked her to find something special for Kimber to wear to my work event tonight. Hopefully, she wouldn't mind. Henry loved when I bought him clothes I wanted to see him in, and I loved making him happy.

The garment bag awaited me in the lobby of our building when I arrived, and I took it up to the condo, feeling almost giddy with excitement. I couldn't wait to see the look on Mr Montgomery's face, and all the other board members too, when I showed up with Kimber on my arm. I suspected several of the others felt the same way as him, he'd just acted as the spokesperson when he came to see me the other day.

As I expected, Kimber hadn't arrived yet, so I busied myself picking out my own clothes for the evening. I could wear the suit I had on now, but I'd rather wear something that better complemented Kimber's dress. My heart raced in anticipation as I got things ready, leaving me far too hyped up to take my power nap.

The door opened about fifteen minutes after I got home, and I pulled Kimber into my arms before she even stepped fully inside the apartment, giving her a deep kiss. "How did it go, really?" I murmured after I pulled away, leaving her panting in surprise and, hopefully, a bit of desire too.

"Hi, Nick," she replied with a laugh, her blue eyes sparkling. "I guess I don't need to ask how your day went."

"I had a great day," I confirmed. "But I want to hear about yours."

I led her into the bedroom where we both took a seat on the bed as I waited for her to speak.

"It went well, as I said." She looked around the room as she spoke rather than at me, her eyes landing on the suit I'd just laid out. "Is that what you're wearing tonight?"

"Don't change the subject," I chided her firmly. "What does 'well' mean? I don't know how these things usually go. Tell me everything."

She acquiesced, telling me about the audition in detail, and I had to agree that it all sounded positive. So what was I missing? Clearly, she had left something out, something that tempered her enthusiasm.

"And then what?" I prompted when it seemed she had finished.

Kimber grimaced before finally looking me straight in the eye. "How can you read me so well after only knowing me for a week?"

"The same way you can read me, I guess. We've got a connection, Kimber."

I hadn't thought of it in those terms before, but as the words came out of my mouth, I realized just how true they were. There were very few people I clicked with as quickly as I had with her, with Henry being the obvious exception.

It seemed to please her that I thought so, and she nodded thoughtfully. "Yeah, I think we do."

She leaned over to kiss me, but I knew a deflection when I saw one, and she couldn't distract me that easily. "So? What happened?"

With a sigh, she finally admitted to me what she'd overheard after leaving the audition, and my blood boiled on her behalf.

"They *all* laughed? Even that other actor?"

She shrugged. "I'm not sure since I couldn't see them, but they must have all been thinking it."

I could have asked why she didn't say anything, but it would be the same reason I hadn't said anything when that ass Montgomery told me about the board's considerations, and the same reason Henry hadn't told his parents about us yet. Sometimes, not making a fuss seemed easier, but it didn't make it right. I intended to do my best to rock the boat tonight, and I thought Kimber should too, but first, I wanted to make sure she wouldn't let those assholes mess with her self-confidence.

"You know they're wrong, right? There are plenty of men who find women sexy for a lot of reasons besides their dress size."

She gave me a look full of tenderness even as she disagreed. "They're not entirely wrong, though. Whether it's right or not, people out there do think that way, a lot of them, and ignoring it won't make it go away. I'd have a far better chance of making it as an actress if I looked different. That's a fact."

"They don't speak for all viewers, though," I pointed out. "They're the gatekeepers, which sucks, but to say that people wouldn't want to watch you, or don't find you sexy? That's flat-out false, and I can prove it."

Taking her hand, I placed it over my suit pants, letting her feel just how stiff the mere thought of her made me.

Heat flashed in Kimber's eyes as her hand rested against me. "You and Henry are definitely the exception rather than the rule."

"I don't believe that. We're just regular guys, Kimber. Regular guys who think you're sexy as all hell."

My hand went between her legs as I kissed her again, and her fingers pressed against me even more firmly. We were both getting turned on now, and I had no complaints.

"Aren't you supposed to be sleeping?" she asked, as though she'd just realized that.

"I think as long as I'm in bed, it counts," I argued, pulling her down with me as I kissed her again. "Besides, we need to get changed for tonight. That starts with taking our clothes off, right?"

She couldn't argue with that, and soon, between kisses and groping and licking and sucking, we were both completely naked. I hadn't been entirely sure if this would be strange without Henry here, but it felt natural, just as natural as being with him on our own.

Kimber's thoughts must be following a similar line as she looked up at me with those big blue eyes, both hesitant and impatient. "Should we wait for Henry to come home?"

He would be arriving soon but we didn't need to wait. "He can join us when he gets here, but I want you now, Kimber. You want me too, don't you?"

My fingers plunged deep into her warm, wet pussy as I asked the question, and her body answered me loud and clear before her mouth could form the words.

"Fuck, you're so big," she muttered as she wrapped her hand around me, as far as she could.

"And yet you take me so well." I'd thought about that time inside her several times since it happened, and I'd also been thinking about what she said about wanting to try some double penetration. "And I bet you'd take me just as well here."

With my fingers still coated in her wetness, I moved further back, running my finger gently around her other hole.

"Can I try with my fingers?" With just a tiny bit of trepidation in her eyes, she nodded, so moving slowly and steadily, giving her plenty of time to adjust, I pushed my finger in up to the second knuckle. "How's that?"

"A little weird," she admitted. "But it doesn't hurt."

"Good. Then let's try something else." I pulled out and went to grab the lube from my bedside table instead. When I'd put a generous amount on my fingers, I laid down on the bed. "Get on top of me, in reverse."

Willingly, she climbed up onto the bed, facing away from me as she got into position, her legs beneath my thighs while she lowered herself onto my hard cock. As she leaned forward onto her hands, I had a perfect view of her ass, far softer than Henry's, and I ran my hands across it in appreciation.

"Perfect. Now, you just worry about you – ride me, rub your clit, do whatever you need to feel good. If I make you uncomfortable at any time, just stop."

"Okay." Her breath came out a little short as she raised her hips up and then lowered them back onto me, swallowing my cock inside her once again. For a moment, I simply watched, enjoying the combined sight and feel as I disappeared inside her, over and over again, and then I took my lubed-up fingers and began to gently prod at her hole once again.

To her credit, Kimber kept going, not stopping or slowing her pace. She continued to rise and fall on me, my cock burying deep into her pussy each time, and after rubbing along the surface of her ass a few more times, the next time she sank down on me, I pressed my finger into her ass fully.

"Urgmph." The sound she made wasn't quite a word, but not a cry of pain either. This time she did stop, resting for a moment with both my finger and my cock inside her, getting used to the feel. "Is that... just one?"

"One finger, yeah. Keep riding me, Kimber. I'll hold my finger still, you can take it at your own pace."

With that encouragement, she did just as I asked, lifting herself off me, and then lowering herself back down, both holes taking me in at the same time. Fuck, she was sexy.

"Anyone who doesn't want to see this is a fucking idiot," I growled as she continued to move. "You're amazing, Kimber."

The praise made her clench around me, in both places, and I groaned in appreciation.

Just then, we both heard the door close, and Kimber tensed again. "You're sure this is okay?" she whispered to me, and I knew just what she meant. She still worried Henry would be upset that we were doing this without him, but I knew better.

"Positive," I promised her before calling out to him. "Henry, I'm awake. We're both in here and we'd love for you to join us."

Seconds later, he appeared at the door, a smile on his face that quickly turned into a look of wonder as he took in the scene in front of him. "Well, hello. This is so much better than what I expected."

I grinned over at him. "Kimber's just about to make me come. Do you want to watch?"

"Fuck, yes!" His eager response made both of us laugh, Kimber's body vibrating on top of me as the laugh rippled through her.

"You see?" I told her as Henry quickly shed his coat and took a seat on the edge of the bed next to us. "He wants to watch you, and so do I. Now, give us a show, Kimber. Ride me until I can't take it anymore."

With that encouragement, she carried on, her body moving quicker, stroking me faster and stronger. Henry's eyes widened ever further as he realized I had my finger up her ass too, and his hand quickly moved to his own cock, stroking himself through his pants as he watched us.

Kimber's breathing became heavier as she got closer to her peak, just like me. Catching Henry's eye, I nodded my head towards Kimber and he immediately caught my meaning. Shuffling closer, he reached down between her legs to rub her clit as she continued to move on me, and that seemed to do the trick. Shuddering into her orgasm, she sank down onto me hard one last time, and the feel of her body gripping me in the rhythm of her pleasure tipped me over as I emptied myself deep into her.

After a moment, Henry helped her off of me, and she lay down next to me, still panting. "I really need to work out more if we're going to keep doing that," she groaned, making us both laugh. "I need a rest, but Henry still needs some help."

She reached down to run her fingers across his cock which strained against the front of his pants.

"What do you have in mind?" I asked curiously.

Kimber looked over at me with a cheeky smile. "I think it's my turn to watch. I'd love to see the two of you together, what you do when I'm not here."

"Henry?" Though I fully anticipated his approval, I asked for it anyway, and he eagerly gave it, nodding enthusiastically. "Get naked, then. You're the odd one out here."

As all three of us laughed, I couldn't remember the last time I'd felt this good. This day just kept getting better and better.

~Kimber~

I asked to watch Henry and Nick for a couple of reasons, the first being that they truly had exhausted me. If my reward involved having longer, more energetic sex, I might need to start exercising more frequently going forward.

The other reason was even simpler: I really loved to see the two of them together. The love and passion they had for each other turned me on, I couldn't deny it, and though they'd done things together when all three of us were involved, I hadn't seen them be really intimate with just each other. By watching them, I hoped to not only bring all three of us closer together, but maybe pick up some new ideas on how to please them too.

As Henry quickly shed his clothes, I looked over at Nick's softening cock curiously. "I'm sorry if this sounds ignorant," I apologized in advance. "But so far, I've only seen you fuck Henry. Do you guys do it both ways?"

Thankfully, the question didn't offend Nick at all. "We do, yes. It's different between different gay couples. Some like to switch, like we do, and others have more defined roles. It's whatever works for them."

"Nick's a lot rougher with me than I am with him," Henry added, helping himself to some of the lube from the bottle that Nick had left on the bed earlier, rubbing it all over his already completely firm cock. "But I like it."

Given what I knew of them both, that made perfect sense. I still had more questions, but I held them back for now as Henry joined us back on the bed, kneeling between Nick's legs. Leaning down over Nick, Henry kissed him firmly while his hand, still coated in lube as much as his cock, went down between Nick's legs.

Nick's groan let me know that Henry's fingers felt good, and Nick pulled him closer, one hand on the back of Henry's head and the other on his shoulder as their tongues tangled.

Henry had spoken about Nick's roughness, but there was nothing particularly tender about the way he leaned back, grabbed Nick's hips and tilted them upwards, spreading his legs wider. With no further foreplay, he lined up his cock with Nick's ass and pushed deep inside, both of them letting out groans of satisfaction as he bottomed out.

I almost whimpered too, finding myself both turned on again and fascinated. They were both a lot more gentle with me.

Once inside, Henry leaned down again, kissing Nick once more as his hips moved against him. Their firm chests were pressed tight together, Nick's limp cock between them, as they both grunted and grabbed at each other, hands roaming and hips slamming.

I had never seen anything hotter.

The thrumming in my own body started up again as I watched them, and my own hand drifted downwards, moving across my still sensitive clit in rhythm with Henry's thrusts.

Leaning back onto his knees, Henry hooked his arms under Nick's thighs, raising his hips even higher as he pumped into him harder. Meanwhile, Nick looked over at me, his eyes hazed with pleasure, and when he saw my hand between my legs, he growled at me in that incredibly sexy way of his. "Get over here."

I shuffled a little closer and his hand pushed mine away, taking its place, fucking me with his fingers as Henry continued to fuck him with his cock. Having been invited in, I leaned over and kissed Nick, running my own hand down to his cock and trailing my fingers lightly across its softness.

"You guys look amazing," Henry grunted, his hips slamming into Nick with even more urgency. "I love this, all of it."

I did too, and from Nick's grin, it seemed he agreed.

Unbelievably, I felt myself getting close again already, but not as close as Henry. "Shit, Nick," he cried out as he pushed into him one last time, and I could tell from both their reactions that he had finished.

For just a moment, I wondered if that would be the end of it, but it seemed neither of them intended to leave me hanging. With his cock still in Nick's ass, Henry leaned over and added his clean fingers to Nick's that were already inside me. Having them both there provided just the push I needed, and my peak followed soon after, my whole body surrendering to the onslaught of pleasure that they provided together.

Gradually, we all disentangled ourselves, and Henry got back to his feet with a grin. "I could definitely get used to coming home to this."

Nick smiled back, looking utterly satisfied. "Except we're all dirty now, and Kimber and I still have to go out tonight."

"Shower?" Henry suggested, and laughing, we all got up and headed together into the large walk-in shower that easily held all three of us.

As we took turns washing and rubbing each other, Henry asked about my audition. Nick insisted I tell him everything, and the situation upset

Henry just as much as Nick, though he showed it in a less forceful way. "Do you even want to work with people like that?" he asked in concern.

"They're all like that," I pointed out. "If I avoided every fat-phobic person in television, I'd never work again."

When we were all clean, we returned to the bedroom and Nick directed me to a garment bag draped over one of the chairs. I had completely missed it earlier with all the distractions he'd provided.

"What's this?"

"It's for you to wear tonight, if you like it."

Henry looked just as curious as I felt. "Let's see it."

Unzipping the bag, I let out a gasp of surprise. The beautiful, slinky, sparkly silver dress wouldn't look out of place on any red carpet. I'd never owned anything like it before. There were even three matching pairs of shoes at the bottom of the bag.

"I don't know your shoe size," Nick admitted when I picked up one of the pairs and looked over at him curiously. "Hopefully one of them will fit."

I returned to the bathroom to get dressed and do my hair and makeup, and when I stopped to look at the final product, I had to admit, it looked pretty damn good. The dress flattered my shape, hiding my lumpier parts while drawing subtle attention to my chest and hips. It went down to my knees, and the strappy low heels that came with it were the perfect mix of fashionable and comfortable. I definitely needed to meet Nick's personal shopper sometime and learn her secrets.

When I got back out into the bedroom, Henry and Nick were waiting. Henry had put some comfortable clothes on, while Nick had dressed in the suit I'd seen laid out earlier, with a silver tie that matched my dress exactly. Their eyes both lit up as they caught sight of me.

"Wow." Henry's immediate and sincere response made me blush. "Kimber, you look incredible."

"It's perfect," Nick agreed. "All eyes will be on you tonight."

They both meant it completely, I had no doubt. "Thank you, but I think more than a few eyes will be on you, looking like that."

Henry nodded in agreement as he looked back at Nick. "I have never felt as lucky as I do right now, knowing you're both coming home to me. Can I take a picture?"

Nick rolled his eyes, but he posed gamely next to me, his arm around my waist. When Henry showed it to me, Nick wearing his usual sexy smirk and me beaming, I couldn't remember ever seeing myself looking happier.

"Have a great time," Henry said, giving us both a kiss. "And Nick, try not to cause too much of a scene, okay?"

"No promises," Nick replied cheerily as he swept me out the door.

A taxi waited for us downstairs so I didn't have to walk too far in my shoes, and soon we were pulling up outside a very elegant restaurant in Coal Harbour. Nick gave his name at the door and the hostess ushered us into a room filled with other men in expensive-looking suits like Nick's and other women all dressed to the nines. Waiters dressed all in black circled with trays of wine and champagne as Nick's colleagues and their partners stood around in small groups. Feeling I fit in with my sparkly dress and with Nick by my side, I chatted comfortably with everyone that Nick introduced me to, using only my name without specifying any relationship between us.

Eventually, an older man came over to us with an elegant older woman on his arm, his eyes examining me shrewdly as he approached. "Good evening, Lewis."

"Mr Montgomery," Nick greeted him, and though he kept his tone pleasant, I could see the way his jaw tightened. "Mrs Montgomery, it's a pleasure to see you. I'd like you to meet Kimber, my girlfriend."

Even though I knew that he intended to introduce me that way tonight, I hadn't heard the words from his lips before, and my cheeks warmed with pleasure at the sound of it.

Mr Montgomery, however, looked less than pleased. "Girlfriend?" he repeated in surprise, looking me up and down before turning back to Nick. "Is this some kind of joke?"

"Harold!" His wife, to her credit, looked aghast at his rudeness before offering me an apologetic smile. "He didn't mean anything against you, dear."

I hadn't thought he had until she said so, but she'd just made it clear that they *did* find the idea of someone like me with Nick laughable. She just thought it would be rude to say it out loud.

However, her husband had meant something else entirely. "What happened to the man you were seeing?" he asked Nick, leaning closer so he wouldn't be overheard, his voice full of disapproval.

"I'm seeing Kimber now," Nick replied, skirting around the truth as his arm tightened around me. "That's not a problem, is it?"

The man's lips tightened. "Of course it's a problem! I told you why the board is considering you."

"And I don't think it should matter," Nick countered firmly. "My personal life doesn't affect my work in any way. I made the company another million dollars today, at least. That's what should matter, not who I'm sharing my bed with."

Mr Montgomery shook his head. "If you're trying to make some kind of point here, you've chosen the wrong way to do it. There are others up for consideration..."

"Others who have performed as well as I have?" Nick shot back. "I don't think so."

"Others who don't try to make me look foolish," Mr Montgomery hissed back. "I stuck my neck out for you, Lewis."

Nick just shook his head. "No, you stuck your neck out for yourself. You wanted me because it would make you look good."

"Is there a problem here, gentleman?" Their voices had been growing louder, and it had obviously attracted the attention of two other, older men, who joined us now, their partners also giving me rather curious looks.

Mr Montgomery turned to them, clearly expecting them to take his side. "Lewis says he's now dating this... woman."

The other men both stared at me too, and even at my auditions, I had never felt under quite as much scrutiny as I did right now.

"I thought you were... you know..." one of the men said, and I could feel Nick's eyes roll as much as see them.

"Gay? It's not a dirty word."

Nick's back was fully up now, and I remembered Henry's warning about not causing too much of a scene. Should I try to stop him? How would I even do that, and did I really want to, when I completely agreed with him?

"I'm bisexual, actually, not that it's *any* of your business. I've dated men and women, and right now I'm dating both. It doesn't change a damn thing about how I do my job."

"That's harder to sell," the second man said to the others, as if Nick couldn't hear him despite standing right there. "We want our executives to look stable, not like they can't make up their minds."

Nick's expression grew dangerously dark. "You want someone decisive? Then you can find yourself another token gay man to parade around to show how fucking inclusive you are, because it won't be me. I quit."

An audible gasp filled the air from several people nearby, all of whom had obviously been listening in, and my stomach sank.

"Nick, are you sure?" Making such a huge decision in the heat of the moment could be a recipe for regret.

"I'm positive," he assured me. "Come on, Kimber. Let's go home."

Taking my hand, he led me from the room, leaving a buzz of chatter and speculation in his wake.

Chapter Thirteen

~Henry~

In my t-shirt and sweatpants, my laptop on my lap and the TV on in the background as I read over some files for work tomorrow, I had well and truly settled in for the night, but all that changed as soon as I read Kimber's text.

Nick just quit his job. We're in Jack Poole Plaza, I think he needs you.

"Shit, shit, shit." Muttering to myself, I quickly put the laptop down, turned the TV off, grabbed socks, shoes and a jacket, stumbling over my own feet, and ran out the door as fast as I could possibly go, my heart racing.

Nick's impulsiveness could be one of his best qualities, but also one of his worst. He went with his gut more often than not, and more often than not, it served him well. But when it gave him the wrong advice, things could go south quickly, and this time, he might have pushed too far. Clearly, Kimber thought so too or she wouldn't have asked me to come.

It would normally be about a twenty-minute walk from our building to the plaza on the waterfront, but since I jogged over, I made it in just over ten. The four-legged Olympic cauldron, lit up in bright blue lights at the entrance to the plaza, shone as spectacularly as always, but I barely saw it as I scanned the open space for the two people I wanted to see. Luckily, Kimber's dress sparkled beneath the street lamps, so I quickly spotted them down at the far end of the open space, close to the water's edge. Kimber sat at the top of the steps that led down to the sea wall while Nick paced next to her, speaking animatedly.

My heart continued to pound as I made my way over to them, more out of nerves than because of the run over here. I had no idea what kind of mood I'd find him in, but it quickly became apparent that he was still in high spirits, his laughter ringing out over the space between us.

"They're going to have to explain to their best clients why I'm not there anymore," he told Kimber as I walked up. "I wonder what kind of lie they'll come up with. It's always fun to see what kind of bullshit they try to pass off as perfume..."

He trailed off as he caught sight of me and his brow furrowed in surprise and confusion. Kimber must not have told him she asked me to come.

"Henry? What are you doing here?"

"I heard you guys left the party early," I said, keeping my voice light until I had a better idea exactly what happened. "I didn't want to miss out."

For just a moment, his eyes moved suspiciously between me and Kimber. He knew that she must have said something to me, but a moment later, he relaxed, seeming to accept my being here as a positive development. "Good. You *should* be here. We're celebrating."

Kimber and I locked eyes for a second, and though she gave me a smile, I could see the concern in her expression. Nick's adrenaline still held the reins; if regret planned on making an appearance, it hadn't arrived yet.

"What are we celebrating, Nick?" I asked.

"The fact that I'm not answering to those blowhards anymore. I quit and I'm glad. I don't need them and I never did."

I couldn't argue with that. Nick had never *needed* to work. He could live comfortably on the money he had from his parents, so his six-figure salary merely served as a bonus. He had invested it so well that he never had to work another day in his life. But while he didn't *need* the money, he loved his job. He worked hard, did it well, and it gave him a sense of purpose and a feeling of self-worth that mattered to him, no matter what he tried to convince himself now.

"You went out in a blaze of glory, huh?" I asked, trying to figure out how public this resignation had been. Could he take it back if he changed his mind?"Something like that." Nick came over and threw his arm around me, looking down at Kimber with an excited smile. "Let's do something crazy. What do you guys feel like? A helicopter ride? We could go up Grouse Mountain."

My gaze flitted over to the mountain across the water. The lights of the lodge at the top sparkled against the clear, cloudless night sky. "That sounds amazing, but I think you have to book that kind of thing ahead of time. You can't just get a helicopter at short notice... and no, Nick, I don't mean that as a challenge."I quickly added the last part since he'd been known to prove to me that things I said were impossible were actually do-able.

Thankfully, tonight, he just laughed. "Alright, fine. How about a boat, then? There must be somewhere we can get a boat and sail around the city."

"That sounds amazing." Kimber smiled up at him, sounding genuinely interested. "But that's going to take a little while, and even if you don't have to work tomorrow, Henry and I do. Maybe we could do it this weekend? Then you've got time to plan something really spectacular."

That seemed to satisfy Nick. I could practically see the wheels in his head turning. "I'm going to find something none of us have done before, something we'll remember forever."

I had no doubt he would. When he set his mind to something, he never failed. "Everything we do together is memorable, Nick."

When I leaned over and kissed him, he pulled me closer, hanging on just a little tighter than usual, like he needed something to anchor him down. I could feel his arms trembling.

"Why don't we go home?" Kimber suggested, getting to her feet. As she took a step towards us, I noticed her wincing. Her shoes must not be completely comfortable for walking very far, which probably explained why she had been sitting down in the first place. "There must be ways we could celebrate there too," she suggested. When Nick's eyebrows shot up, Kimber rolled her eyes. "That's not what I meant."

"Oh, I think it is," Nick retorted, winking at her with his irresistible charm. "You just don't want to admit it."

"Okay, come on, Casanova," I said, laughing at them both. "Let's go home and you can argue about it there."

We hailed a taxi out on the street so Kimber's feet wouldn't suffer and she mouthed a grateful 'thank you' at me as I held the door open for her. When we were all safely back in the apartment and Kimber had kicked her shoes off, Nick popped open a bottle of champagne.

"To a future free of bullshit," he toasted, holding up his glass, his eyes still bright. "Being proud of who I am, and answering to no one."

"To the future," Kimber agreed, much more vaguely, and I held up my glass too as we all took a drink. Kimber and I both sipped ours, while Nick practically drained his whole glass in one gulp.

"So what do you think you might want to do now?" I asked tentatively as he refilled his glass. "Are you going to look for a new job?"

"No need," he assured me. "As soon as it gets out that I'm a free agent, I'll have people knocking on my door. There's going to be a waiting period, of course, it's in my contract. Maybe we could go on vacation somewhere? A month on a tropical island somewhere, just the three of us?"

He made it sound so appealing, and so simple, even though reality disagreed. "As much as I would love that, I've got that big arbitration coming up next week, and Kimber's waiting to hear on that part she tried out for today. We might need a bit more notice before taking off for a month."

His second glass of champagne disappeared almost as quickly as the first. "You don't need to work either, Henry. Or you, Kimber. I could take care of all of us. I can look after everything."

"Nick." Kimber's soft but firm tone made him pay attention as she went over and took the empty glass from his hand. "That's not your responsibility. You don't have to always be the one in control. Henry and I can look after you too sometimes."

"I don't need anyone to look after me." His eyes flashed with anger and defiance, and for a moment, fear ran through me; not fear *of* him, but *for* him. I'd never seen him look so close to losing control before. "I've been doing it my whole life and I do a fucking good job of it. My parents never gave a shit and they still don't. I took the only good thing they gave me, their money, and I made this whole life for myself."

He gestured wildly around the apartment as Kimber quickly ducked out of the way to avoid being accidentally hit by his swinging arm.

"I worked my way up that company for eight years, giving them every-thing they ever asked for, and now they want to pretend that they're doing me a favour by giving me the position that I earned fair and square, because I tick some box they want filled? They're the ones who need me. I don't need anything from anyone."

"Nick..." My attempt to calm him down only got that far before he rounded on me too, pain etched on his face as he grimaced.

"No. Don't look at me like that, Henry. Did she say something to you? Did you tell him there's something wrong with me?"

He turned back to Kimber with the last question, which confused me. What was he talking about? But even though I had no idea, Kimber seemed to. She shook her head as she tried not to flinch, holding his gaze as well as she could. "I didn't have to, Nick. He loves you. He can see you're struggling. The only person you're fooling is yourself."

That stopped him in his tracks and he looked between the two of us, his eyes full of confusion, disbelief, regret, and hurt. For a long moment, no one said anything. I barely even breathed. Tension thickened the air around us, thick enough to cut through and no one wanted to make the first slice in case they hit the wrong nerve. My eyes darted between Kimber and Nick, Kimber still watching him carefully as Nick looked at the floor, the muscles in his jaw working as he debated what to do next.

When he finally looked back up, tears had gathered in his eyes, and my stomach dropped. In all the time we'd been together, I'd never seen him like this. Nick had seen me cry several times, over things that were worth it and stupid things that weren't, but I had never seen him that way. He looked incredibly young, and vulnerable, and lost as he stared over at me, his eyes searching my face desperately.

"Please, don't leave me."

Those were about the last words I expected to come out of his mouth, and for a moment, I simply blinked at him, trying to process what he meant. He couldn't really think that would ever happen, could he?

As soon as it sank in that he did, I stepped forward and wrapped my arms around him, pulling him close to me. He began to shake as the adrenaline left his body, crashing down after the high he'd been on, and he clung onto me as I whispered into his ear.

"I'm not going anywhere, Nick. We'll figure this out, I promise. I'm right here, and I'm not going anywhere."

He said nothing as he trembled against me, and I stretched out my arm to Kimber. Instantly, she took her place beside us, her arms around us both too. It felt lighter somehow with her there to take on some of the weight. Together, we could hold him up easier than I could alone.

"We'll figure this out," I repeated, holding them both tight. Nick had always been the strong one, the one I looked up to and the one who supported me. Now, I finally had the chance to give him some of my strength too, and I wouldn't let him down.

~Nick~

When the sun hit my face through the window the next morning, panic immediately raced through me. I must have overslept and now I would be late for work.

I had already sat up and thrown the covers back before I remembered that I had no job to be late for. I still needed to give a formal letter of resignation, but I wouldn't have to work out my notice period. In our industry, as soon as you gave your notice, they wanted you out of the office immediately. In one trade, I could lose millions, and no one wanted to take the risk that a disgruntled former employee would do just that, or that I might try to find a way to sneak confidential client information out with me.

Trust hardly formed the cornerstone of my employment, not when the amounts of money we were talking about were so big. Therefore, nobody would be expecting me to show up today, so I could relax for now, at least.

Relief replaced my panic. Staying home sounded perfect since a dull ache had taken up residence in the back of my head, partly from the drinking last night both at the party and once we got home, but much more so from the emotional strain of the evening. As it all came back to me, I lay back down on my pillow and squeezed my eyes closed as I covered them with my hand, fighting against all the feelings those memories stirred in me.

Shame came first, my knee-jerk response. I had scared both Henry and Kimber, I could see it in their eyes. The way that Henry in particular looked at me, the concern written across his handsome face, hit me like a punch to the gut. He'd never looked at me like that before, like he thought I didn't have things under control. I *always* had things under control. That formed the basis of our whole relationship dynamic. He complained sometimes about me keeping things too close to my chest, but he never thought I couldn't handle it.

That look broke me, sweeping my feet out from under me and making me lose what little grip I had left on the whole situation. I lashed out at Kimber again, accusing her of saying something to influence Henry's feelings for me, even though I knew deep in my heart she never would. And when she answered me, simply and calmly, that she hadn't had to say a thing, I heard the truth in her words immediately. My own actions had given me away; I had no one to blame but myself.

I'd kept it all bottled in for so long that it finally burst, and now, shoving it back in again felt impossible.

"Hey."

My eyes shot open again as I looked over to the doorway in surprise. Henry stood there in his cotton t-shirt and pajama pants, holding a cup of take-out coffee in one hand and a small brown paper bag in another.

"Perfect timing, I just came to check if you were up. Kimber just dropped this coffee off for you from Rocco's, it's still warm."

In confusion, I looked over at the clock by the bedside table, which read 8:57. "Shouldn't you be at work?"

"I took the day off," he explained, as if he did it all the time, though in all the months we'd been together, he'd never taken a day off at short notice before. Henry planned everything in advance. "I'd rather spend the day with you."

Not giving me a chance to protest, he came over and sat down on the bed next to me, handing me the coffee as I propped myself up and placing the bag down between us.

"That's a millionaire's shortbread, apparently. Kimber brought that too, she made it at the shop this morning. She said it made her think of you."

The gentle second-hand teasing made me smile. I had certainly done my best to try to throw my wealth around last night in an effort to make it seem like I still had things under control. She had every right to think of me as a total ass now, but she simply teased me in baking form instead.

"You said she just brought this over?" The day's events still weren't entirely making sense to me as I took a sip of the strong, black coffee which, at that moment, seemed like the best thing I had ever tasted.

Henry nodded. "She texted me to see how you were doing, and when I said you weren't up yet, she ran it over for when you did wake up. She would have stayed home today too but Rocco would have struggled to find a last-minute replacement and she didn't want to leave him in the lurch."

That sounded about right. Her thoughtfulness extended to everyone around her, though I still had my doubts whether I deserved that kind of treatment.

Tentatively, I tried to share those fears with Henry. "After last night, I'm surprised she wants anything to do with me."

Henry immediately reached out and took my hand. "We both meant what we said last night, Nick. We're not here because you're flawless and have it all figured out. We're here because we care about you, in good times and bad. You know that, right?"

I tried to accept that, even if it didn't completely make sense to me. "You've had a lot more good times than she has though," I pointed out. "I wouldn't blame her for backing out now. She's only just met me and I've completely lost my shit."

"She's not going anywhere," he assured me. "And neither am I. So what's your plan, Nick? I know you always have one."

He did know me. My forward-thinking helped to maintain that feeling of control I craved, even when that control was only an illusion. "Well, first, I need to formally resign, but that shouldn't take long."

I opened the paper bag as I spoke and pulled out the square of shortbread covered in a layer of caramel and another of chocolate. As I took a bite, I couldn't stop the groan of enjoyment that came out as the sweet richness of it filled my mouth.

Henry's eyes watched me so longingly that I couldn't keep it to myself. "Do you want some too?"

I held the square out to him and he leaned forward to take a bite, his reaction just as strong as mine. "Oh, God. We are going to have to ban her from baking like that in here or else we'll have to double our gym time too."

As I took another sip of the coffee and he finished munching on his mouthful of shortbread, he gave me a scrutinizing look.

"So, you don't regret quitting?"

I shook my head firmly. "No. Could I have handled it better? Probably, but I'm still glad I did it. I didn't suffer from temporary insanity or anything, if that's what you're worried about."

He smiled at my phrasing, but I could tell he had been wondering. "Okay, so you're going to quit, and then what?"

I had been thinking about that long into the night. After our conversation, Henry insisted we go to bed, and this time I took the middle spot, spooning up against Kimber while Henry held onto me from behind. It felt safe and secure in a way I'd never really felt before.

But even after they both went to sleep, I lay away thinking over everything that had happened, not just that night but over the weeks and months and years before then. If I wanted to be truly honest with myself, I had to admit my mood swings were getting worse, and something Kimber said just before she fell asleep kept coming back to me.

"Nobody would be ashamed of getting cancer," she mumbled to me sleepily. "They would just go to the doctor and get treated. This is the same thing. If you don't feel well, you can get help to feel better."

The longer I thought about it, the more I realized she had a point. People dealing with cancer weren't seen as being weak; on the contrary, they were fighters. If something really had been wired wrong in my brain, something that went beyond the regular emotional fluctuations that everyone has, then dealing with it properly would be the braver thing to do.

Hiding it hadn't done me any good so far, so maybe I needed to try something else.

I summed that up for Henry now, as bluntly as I could. "I think I should see a psychiatrist."

He simply nodded, his smile warm and supportive. "I thought you might say that. I hope it's okay that I've already made you an appointment for this afternoon."

"What?" How the hell did he manage that?

"You don't have to keep it," he quickly assured me, looking suddenly worried that he'd offended me. "I just know you like to get to the point, without having to wait, so I set it up. We can cancel if you're not ready."

"No, it's fine, I definitely want to do it today, I just... how did you do that so fast?"

Most doctor's offices would only just be opening now, and very few took last-minute appointments for anything non-urgent.

"I called in some favours," he told me mysteriously, obviously getting some enjoyment out of being the one to pull the strings for a change. "You're not the only one who knows how to get things done."

"I know that." He amazed me more every day. "Let's go enjoy our day then."

He brought me my laptop so I could quickly draft my formal letter of resignation and then we showered together, taking our time as we stroked and fingered each other, making each other come before we were finished. We went out for lunch and then headed over to the psychiatrist's office where Henry sat down in the waiting room to wait for me.

"You've got this," he told me, giving my hand a squeeze when they called my name.

The petite Asian doctor spoke to me plainly and directly. After asking me some questions about my moods and the way I felt during my down days, and a few questions about my mother's mood swings too, she gave me her blunt assessment.

"It sounds like you have symptoms of bipolar disorder, and likely something we refer to as rapid cycling, where your moods change much faster than they do in the more classical presentation. It can get harder and harder to find your equilibrium the quicker you cycle. It's caused by a chemical imbalance in the brain and there's nothing you did to make it happen. It often runs in families, so it's very possible your mother has it too. I'd be happy to speak to her if she would like."

That seemed unlikely, since I didn't even know exactly which continent to find her on right now, but I'd mention it the next time I spoke to her. "How do I fix it?" I asked instead. I needed to focus on something I could actually do, some way to feel in control again.

She shook her head sympathetically. "There's no cure, and it's going to be a bit of trial and error. There are some mood stabilizers we can try to start out with. For some people they work great, for others, they make them feel a bit strange, so if that's the case for you, then we try something else. We'll also help to figure out what triggers these episodes for you and how to recognize them before they start, so you can adjust your medication accordingly. This is a lifelong condition, Mr Lewis, but if we work together, along with the other people in your life who care about you, there's no reason it has to define you."

She gave me a handful of pamphlets to read through and we made an appointment for me to come back and discuss the first treatment early next week. As I stood up to leave, she asked me to say hi to Henry on her behalf.

"How do you know Henry?" I asked in surprise.

"His parents and my parents are good friends," she explained. "I've known him forever."

Well, that explained the last-minute appointment.

Henry sat scrolling through his phone when I got back to the waiting room, but he jumped to his feet as soon as he saw me. "How did it go?"

"It's alright." I wouldn't lie and say things were fine, but it felt manageable. Not too overwhelming. I could learn to handle this, especially with Henry and Kimber on my side. Just like Henry said last night, we could figure it out together. "I'll tell you and Kimber all about it later. Are you ready to go home?"

He took my hand and gave me a quick kiss before we headed out together to enjoy the rest of our day off.

Chapter Fourteen

~Kimber~

Every time my phone buzzed in my pocket during the work day, I struggled not to pull it out and check it immediately. I usually left my phone in my coat while I worked for just that reason, so I wouldn't be distracted, but today, not only might my agent be in touch about the role I tried out for, but regular texts came in from Henry too, letting me know how things were going with Nick, and I couldn't stand the idea of going hours between updates.

This time when I checked, Henry's message let me know they were at the doctor's office and Nick had just gone in to speak with the psychiatrist. It seemed that Nick had taken everything in stride after last night, deciding that action served him better than inaction. When he set his mind to something, he did it, and thankfully he seemed to have accepted now that talking to someone would be the right way to go.

Even so, anxiety still plagued me about my own involvement in the whole thing. None of this would have happened without me. If I hadn't shown up in their lives, Nick would have simply taken Henry to that work party and there would have been no scene and no resignation. He might not have said anything to Henry about the struggles he faced either. Everything would still be as it had been the week before, and though personally, I thought everything being in the open between them made a positive change, I couldn't be sure that Nick agreed.

Did he regret quitting his job? When he had time to think everything over, would he resent the role I'd played? Would he decide I'd brought more trouble than good into his life?

That fear made up part of the reason I'd come to work today, besides the fact that I didn't want to leave Rocco scrambling to cover for me. I wanted Henry and Nick to have this time to reflect on everything and have some time to themselves. If they were going to choose to move on without me, I would rather know it now, before I fell even deeper than I already had. As much as it would hurt, I would survive, but if the bonds connecting us grew any stronger, I wasn't sure I'd be able to let them go. It might rip me open too wide.

As the door of the coffee shop opened again, I shoved my phone back in my pocket and looked up with my usual smile, only to freeze in surprise at the sight of the person who had just walked in. A few of the other customers noticed him too and immediately started whispering excitedly amongst themselves.

"Hey, Kimber."

It took me a second more to fully register that Dale Winters, TV star, stood in front of me *and* that he had just greeted me by name. His thick, short, dark, perfectly-styled hair and his green eyes were just as stunning as they looked on the TV screen. Although I had seen him in person yesterday, I'd been so focused on what I needed to do that I hadn't really had time to take in anything about him. Seeing him now, I had to admit he was a really ridiculously good-looking man, and I knew a thing or two about the subject.

"Um, hi, Dale." We hadn't called each other by name when we met at the audition. He hadn't really said anything to me then apart from the lines we read. What on earth brought him here now? "Would you like some coffee?"

He smiled, and I could practically hear the girls swooning around us. "I'd love some coffee, but I'd also like to talk to you if you've got a minute?"

I glanced back at Rocco, who stood just behind me, listening not-so-casually to the whole conversation. He obviously recognized Dale too, and from the look he threw in my direction, found him just as attractive as any of the teenage girls did.

"Go ahead," he told me quickly. "I'll bring something over for both of you."

My stomach fluttering with nerves, I walked out from behind the counter and led Dale to a somewhat secluded table in the corner. Since total privacy wouldn't be possible, this would have to do.

Doing my best to ignore all the jealous stares being sent in my direction, I leaned forward across the table so I could keep my voice quiet enough so we weren't overheard. "This is a big surprise."

He smiled again, running a hand through his impossibly perfect hair. "I hope it's okay that I tracked you down."

"It's fine," I assured him quickly. "But how did you find me?"

"I've got contacts. My friend Paul is friends with Daisy who knows Jane Edwards, who's a friend of yours."

I should have guessed, even if I wouldn't have known the particular chain of people. Most actors in the city were at least aware of the others who went up for the same kinds of roles that they did. The fact that Jane knew where I worked surprised me, but that didn't really matter in the grand scheme of things. I moved on to the question that interested me far more: "*Why* did you find me?"

Now that my surprise had faded, the idea of him laughing with the others after my audition yesterday stung me all over again, making me wary about what, exactly, he wanted from me.

He leaned closer too. "I wanted to talk to you about your audition yesterday. I think you've got a good chance of getting the part, but I just wanted to give you a word of warning, from one actor to another."

"Warning?" I repeated curiously, just as Rocco came over with our cups of coffee. He set them down, giving Dale a smile and me a wink before he returned to the counter.

When Rocco had retreated out of earshot, Dale leaned in again. "This show, while it's great, has some pretty restrictive clauses in the contract. That's how they were able to let Amanda go once word got out about her 'other projects'. You basically have to sign a morality agreement, meaning you won't do anything they would consider unbecoming to the reputation of the show."

My stomach immediately sank as I realized just what they would mean for me. A lot of people would consider the situation between Henry and Nick and I as immoral. If I got the part, would I have to try to hide my relationship? Or worse, end it?

Was any job worth that much to me?

"Now, I'm not saying you've got some secret kinky life," Dale added, giving me a wry smile. "But I think most of us have things we'd rather keep private. As much as I like doing the show, it's been... stifling."

My eyebrows raised in surprise. What kind of things did Dale Winters want to do that he felt he couldn't under the terms of his contract? Unfortunately, we definitely didn't know each other well enough for me to ask, so my curiosity would have to remain unsatisfied.

"And if I can be perfectly frank with you, Kimber, the showrunner, Kevin, is a bit of an ass. He made some comments after your audition yesterday that were completely uncalled for. When I called him out on it, he claimed to be joking, but that's what he's like. Everyone I talked to said you're really sweet, and I don't want you to have to deal with crap like that."

He had stood up for me yesterday? I must have left before I heard that part, and it surprised me how much it meant to know that he had.

Taking a sip of my coffee, I tried to put together everything he'd just shared. "So, you don't think I should take the part even if it's offered to me?"

"I can't tell you what to do," he qualified quickly. "And I'd love to work with you, so please don't think this is some kind of underhanded way to put you off. I just kind of wish someone had sat me down and told me to really think it through before I signed, and I don't want you to make the same mistake."

He sounded so sincere that I couldn't help feeling a bit sorry for him, as ridiculous as that sounded. This show had made him a household name, but it sounded like it might not be as good as the hype made it out to be.

"Isn't there any way you could get out of it if you really wanted to?"

He gave me a rueful shrug. "There's always a way, but then I get myself a reputation for being difficult and unreliable, and who wants to hire me then? Maybe if I had something amazing to step into next, I could consider it, but right now I don't, so I'm kind of stuck. You know how it is, it's never just about how good you are."

I definitely knew that for a fact. "I really appreciate this, Dale. I haven't been offered the part yet, but if I am, I'll read everything over very carefully."

"Good." His smile appeared to be entirely genuine. "So, tell me more about you, Kimber. How'd you end up here?"

We talked until our drinks were gone and then a bit longer, until I really had to get back to work. For someone so famous, he couldn't be nicer or more down-to-earth. Now, I wanted to work with him more than ever, but also took what he said seriously. As he stopped to sign a few autographs and take some selfies with the other customers in the shop before leaving, I went back behind the counter to where Rocco waited for me eagerly.

"Is this a third man for you now, Kimber?" he teased me. "You need to leave some for the rest of us."

"It's nothing like that," I assured him, though I knew he was joking. "I auditioned with him yesterday, and he just gave me a lot to think about."

"Like what?" Rocco's question carried only support and sympathy, as always.

I did my best to put it into words. "Well, ever since I moved here, I thought getting my break on TV meant everything to me, but now that I might be about to get it, I don't know if it's worth it."

Obviously, I left out a few details, but that had never stopped him from offering advice before, and it didn't stop him now. "All I know, bella, is that I've never seen you as happy as you've been this week. There is more to life than work, and sometimes, when we decide what's important to us, the rest falls into place. We just have to stop fighting it."

That sounded like a man speaking from experience, and I looked over at him curiously. "Did something happen with you?"

He leaned a little closer to me, his eyes twinkling. "Let's just say you inspired me, Kimber. There is someone I have been interested in for a while but I hadn't done anything about it. I convinced myself he couldn't feel the same. But seeing you so happy with that man you were so sure you couldn't get, I decided the risk might be worth it, so I told him. We have seen each other every day since."

My squeal echoed around the shop so loudly that several of the customers looked over at us. "That's amazing, Rocky! I'm so happy for you."

"Me too." He really did look delighted. "And the best part? He's a doctor, and he already 'examined' my mama and told her the only way for her to get better is to go out of the house for walks every day and learn English down at the seniors' centre. She is already making some new friends."

We laughed together over the irony of that. Things really were falling into place for him, just like he said.

Maybe, if I could be totally honest about what I really wanted, the same could happen for me too.

~Henry~

Kimber's smile when Nick and I walked into the coffee shop at the end of her shift would brighten up anyone's day, and it especially warmed my heart to see the way Nick smiled back at her. They hadn't seen each other yet today, and despite all the uncertainty that remained, that one moment of real and unfiltered affection gave me faith that things would eventually work out.

As long as we had each other, we could deal with anything.

"I hope you don't mind us coming by," I said to her as Nick and I walked up to the counter. "Nick wants to take us for dinner."

"Dinner sounds wonderful," she said, her sunny smile looking completely genuine. "Give me just a minute."

As she went into the back room to get her things, I turned to Nick. "Are you going to tell me yet where we're going?"

After we left the psychiatrist's office, Nick had spent some time on his phone before telling me he wanted to treat Kimber and I to something special tonight to make up for last night. Although I assured him we weren't expecting anything, he insisted, and since it seemed to make him happy, I didn't argue too much. But even once I agreed, he wouldn't drop any clues at all about what he had planned.

"You'll find out soon enough," he claimed, his eyes darting to the man behind the counter, and he leaned in a little closer to me. "Why is that guy staring at us?"

"That's Kimber's boss," I whispered back to him before offering a greeting. "Good afternoon, Rocco."

"Henry," he replied, giving me a smile. "And this must be Nick."

"Nice to meet you." Nick held out his hand for Rocco to shake. "I'll take it as a compliment that you've heard of me. Henry's doing his best to get me hooked on your coffee, and other things here too."

Though he could have been talking about the baking, he clearly meant something else entirely, especially as his eyes went to the kitchen door where Kimber had just gone.

Rocco understood what he meant too. "I only have the best and the sweetest in my shop," he said, giving us both a wink. "I'm sure you agree."

"We definitely do." Apparently, Kimber had filled Rocco in on the situation between us, and that idea filled me with pride. I wanted everyone to know how lucky I felt, how lucky we all were, just as I intended to tell my parents this weekend.

Leaving the shop, we walked over to Canada Place and along the waterfront as Kimber told us funny stories about her day. We were getting farther and farther away from any restaurants and our destination baffled me until I saw the helipad in front of us.

"You didn't."

Nick's eyes twinkled as he grinned over at me. "Of course I did. I said I would."

Kimber hadn't spotted it yet, and she looked between the two of us in confusion. "What?"

I pointed to the helicopter just coming into view, and her mouth fell open almost comically. "Wait, for real? We're going in a helicopter?"

"We've got a reservation at The Observatory up on Grouse Mountain," Nick explained, gesturing to the mountain in the distance. "I hope you're not afraid of heights."

"Now you ask?" she demanded, and we all laughed. "This is so exciting, Nick! I've never been in a helicopter before."

He couldn't look more pleased at her enthusiasm, and with smiles on all our faces, we made our way over to the small booth at the edge of the helipad where Nick gave the employee his contact information. The guy made friendly small talk as he checked everything over, but soon, his smile faltered as he looked over the three of us.

"Um, Mr Lewis? Did you read all the conditions when you booked?"

Confusion flashed across Nick's face for just a second. "I think so. Why?"

"Well, um, there's a..." the guy trailed off, looking more uncomfortable by the second. "There's a combined weight limit for the passengers?"

He said it like a question, but his eyes went to Kimber, making the implication clear, and Nick's face immediately darkened. "It said you could take up to four people."

"Yes, but there's still a weight limit, no matter how many people it is. It's for safety, sir.""What's the limit?" he demanded.

The man grimaced as his eyes flitted to Kimber again, almost against his will. "550 pounds, total."I quickly did the math and realized we were well over that amount. Nick and I were both almost 200 pounds each.

"Nick, it's okay." Though Kimber smiled at us both, I could see the colour in her cheeks and the tightness of her lips, betraying her embarrassment even as she pretended not to be bothered. "I love the idea, but we don't need to do anything so fancy. We can go somewhere else, or we can just eat at your place. I'd be just as happy with that."

"No," he flat-out refused. "We're doing this. There has to be a way."

He really didn't need this right now. He'd been holding everything together so well all day, and he wanted to give us a treat as his way of demonstrating that even after everything that had happened, he still had it together. Having someone tell him he couldn't do it would not help at all.

"There are other ways up Grouse," I suggested, trying to find a compromise that would spare Kimber's feelings and let Nick keep his pride too. "We can just take a taxi over and take the Skyride. Or a limo, if you insist it has to be special."

That made him smile, at least, as he turned the idea over in his head. "Alright, here's what we're going to do. Henry and Kimber, you go in the helicopter and I'll meet you over there."

"Nick, no," Kimber quickly protested. "This is your treat. You two should go, and I can take the taxi. Or you can just go without me, I don't mind having a quiet night in."

"No," Nick and I exclaimed at the same time. I looked over at him and nodded to give him the go-ahead, which he quickly did. "Kimber, this is just as much your date as it is ours. Everything is equal here between us all, right?"

Although she nodded, a hint of doubt still lurked in the back of her eyes, so I put my two cents in too. "There's something we want to talk to you about. It would be hard to do that if you weren't there."

Nick and I had discussed the conversation we wanted to have earlier today. Though we hadn't specifically said we were talking about it tonight, if the moment felt right, we might as well.

"Okay, then I'll take the taxi," she offered again, but Nick wouldn't hear of it.

"You just said this is my treat, and I want to treat the two of you. Go up together and I'll meet you there. You never know, I might just beat you."

Giving us both a firm nod, Nick walked away before either of us could say anything else, and I gave Kimber a shrug. "Guess we're going for a ride?"

"Everything with the two of you is a ride," she teased, doing her best to recapture some of her earlier enthusiasm despite her discomfort. "Doesn't look like we have much choice though. Nick doesn't take no for an answer."

"Not when he really wants something," I agreed.

Hopefully that foreshadowed how things would go later tonight. When Nick and I explained to Kimber what we had discussed earlier, I really hoped her answer would be yes.

~Kimber~

I did my best to keep a smile on my face as the helicopter pilot gave Henry and me the run-down on what we needed to know for the flight. The flight would go overtop of Grouse first, heading further into the mountains before circling back to land us on top of the mountain next to the five-star Observatory restaurant with its incredible view over Vancouver, or so I'd heard.

I'd never done anything like this and normally I would have been thrilled, but I couldn't entirely get rid of the lump in my throat as Henry and I got on board and buckled in. I felt terrible that Nick couldn't be there with us when this had all been his idea. If they had tried to do this with a smaller woman, there would have been no problem. If they had done it on their own, it would have been even easier.

The inconvenience made an unexpected and unwelcome reminder that having me along made things more difficult for them. Although in the grand scheme of things, the minor setback hardly mattered, it also served as a warning that the world was made for couples, not sets of three. Were we just fooling ourselves that this could really be something serious? If we kept running up against obstacles like this, how long would it be before the inconveniences piled up into something insurmountable? Eventually, they were going to have to choose between having fun and being realistic.

Sooner or later, I would have to make the same choice too.

"Is everything okay?" Henry's voice echoed in my ear through the headsets we were both wearing, and when I turned to look at him, concern clouded his sweet brown eyes.

My nod didn't seem to do much to convince him, so I added a qualifier. "I just wish Nick had let me go instead of him."

Henry gave me a sympathetic smile. "That wouldn't have happened, no matter what. He could never enjoy himself if he thought you were unhappy."

Nick and I seemed to have that in common, then.

Henry's smile turned indulgent as he realized how unsatisfied I still felt. "Honestly, don't worry about him. The way to make him happy will be to have fun and tell him afterwards how much you enjoyed it. All he wants is to make us happy."

The helicopter lifted into the air as I thought over what Henry just said, and I couldn't really argue with it. Nick had put me first in lots of little ways ever since we met. Even if he didn't show it in the more overtly sentimental ways that Henry did, he had a thoughtful, caring nature that showed itself in the little things as well as the grand gestures.

I had no doubts about whether he was a good guy; I knew the answer to that. The real question remained whether we were good for each other.

As the city grew smaller beneath us and we headed over to North Vancouver and higher into the air, climbing the side of the mountains that towered just above the city, the breathtaking view managed to distract me. The soaring pine trees looked tiny from our vantage point, and Henry excitedly pointed out a mountain stream winding its way down through the forest. In the winter, these mountains were covered in snow and a popular skiing and snowshoeing destination, but at this time of year, they were popular with hikers who visited the distinctive peaks that we headed towards now: Crown Mountain and the Lions.

The spectacular vistas made it easier to put everything else out of my mind, and I quickly pulled out my phone to snap some pictures. My family back home would be amazed at this, such a contrast to the flat part of the country where they lived, and by the time we finally touched down on Grouse Mountain, my earlier disappointment had mostly disappeared. Henry and I took a moment to admire the view out over the city before heading to The Observatory, where the hostess quickly ushered us inside as soon as Henry gave Nick's name.

And to my shock, when we reached the table, the man himself already sat there next to the window, looking up at us both with his character-istic smirk as we approached. "What took you so long?"

Henry and I exchanged stunned looks. "How did you get here so fast?" I demanded, which made Nick smile.

"I have my ways," he replied enigmatically, which made it clear he had no intention of telling us what they were. "Take a seat. I've already ordered some wine."

I shot Henry one more confused look, and he simply shrugged before holding my seat out for me, ever the gentleman.

"Did you enjoy the ride?" Nick asked, and here I could fully follow Henry's advice, showing my appreciation.

"I'll never forget it," I told him sincerely. "Here, I took some pictures."

He eagerly took my phone to flip through them, and then insisted on taking one of me and Henry at the table, sending it to himself before handing the phone back to me. We talked over the incredible-looking menu before ordering our meal and then sat back with our wine.

We hadn't been out in public all together before and it felt surprisingly normal, though of course no one knew anything about the relationship between the three of us. We could simply be a group of friends or colleagues. No one knew the truth besides us.

I asked Nick about his meeting with the psychiatrist and he answered me openly and honestly. The provisional diagnosis held no surprise for me at all; I'd expected as much, and it heartened me to see Nick taking it so well, though I knew from the experience with my cousin that there would still be ups and downs along the way. At least he wouldn't feel like he had to deal with it alone anymore.

"I don't know if I would have faced it anytime soon without you pushing me to think about it," he said starkly, and my stomach sank as he put voice to the exact thing I'd been afraid of. "And I'd probably still have my job too."

"Nick, I'm sorry..."

He didn't let me finish. "I'm not saying it's a bad thing, Kimber. In fact, I think it's just what I needed. Sometimes we get stuck in a mindset or a situation that we don't even realize we're stuck in, until something new comes along to shake things up."

"So, you're not mad about the way you quit?" I asked tentatively.

"The *way* I quit?" Nick repeated. "I've had finer moments, to be fair. But I'm not at all upset about the fact that I quit. That company didn't deserve me."

That sounded exactly like the confident, self-assured Nick I had come to know, and Henry's nod of approval confirmed that he thought so too.

"So will you look for a new job? Or are you going to take some time off?"

Nick gave me a smile from behind his wine glass as he took another drink. "Well, actually, that depends on you."

"Me?" I looked over at Henry again, wondering if he had any idea what Nick meant, and the way he avoided my gaze suggested he did. They were up to something, it seemed.

"Well, I've had an idea," Nick explained. "I thought about everything you said about how difficult it's been for you to get work and how unrepresentative TV is in general, simply because those in power have a ridiculous idea about what the public wants to see."

I could only nod, not having a clue where he might be going with this.

"So then I thought: why don't we start our own production company and make some shows with people who look like real people? We could cast whoever the hell we want."

My lips parted in surprise as my eyes went once again to Henry, who smiled at me encouragingly. "It's... uh, it's a lovely idea, Nick, but producing a TV show is very expensive."

"I have money," he said with a shrug. "I could still run a small boutique investment firm on the side, to help fund it. Henry could handle the legal side of things, and you could pick the shows you want to make. And star in them too, if you want to."

The scale of his ambition truly floored me. "You want to start your own production company to try to make me a star?"

"You *are* a star," he corrected me. "I just want everyone else to see it too."

I really couldn't wrap my mind around this. "Nick, this is too much. Why would you do that? There are a million other things you could spend your money on."

"There are," he agreed. "But there's nothing I want to do more."

"Why? You don't know anything about TV production." I still had to be missing something.

This time, Nick and Henry exchanged looks, and Henry answered me, giving me his soft, sweet, tender smile. "Because we love you, Kimber. Isn't it obvious?"

Chapter Fifteen

~Nick~

It had taken a while to get my heart rate back to normal after Henry and Kimber arrived, but I managed it. For most of the meal, I felt comfortable and at least. Now, however, it pounded hard again as we waited for Kimber to say something to Henry's declaration.

Earlier today, when he pointed out to me that we hadn't told her straight-out how we felt about her yet, I looked at him in surprise. "What do you mean? We asked her to move in with us and said we wanted a relationship. That seems pretty clear to me."

"Those are practical things, not emotional ones," he pointed out. "I think maybe that's why she hasn't agreed yet, because we haven't told her *why* we want her."

That kind of thing fell far more into his comfort zone than mine. "What do you suggest?"

He shrugged. "Well, I don't want to speak for us both, but I know how I feel. I'm in love with her, Nick. It's different to the way I love you, but it's the same too, and I want her to know that she's got my heart just as much as you do. We're all equal not just in terms of living together and sleeping together, but emotionally too."

Those words had never come easily to me. I'd told Henry very early on that I took our relationship seriously and that I wanted him to move in with me, and I had long ago accepted that I wanted to spend the rest of my life with him. But he had a point: those were practical considerations. Actually talking about love, even after being in love with him for months now, still tripped me up.

I could give the usual excuses: my own parents never spoke about love, to each other or to me. The word had never been uttered in our house, and maybe that explained why I found it awkward. Maybe my job and the industry I spent my time in focused on facts and figures rather than emotions, so I'd carried that over to the rest of my life. Whatever the reason, I found it a lot easier to demonstrate my feelings through extravagant gestures like arranging a helicopter trip to a mountaintop than I did to say that one little four-letter word.

Did I love Kimber? Defining my feelings had never been my strong suit but I knew that I felt happier with her around. She made me laugh, she made me feel special and important, and she turned me on. I could see a future with her, the same way I could with Henry. If that wasn't love, then I really didn't know what was.

But what if she didn't feel the same way? She had known Henry a lot longer than she'd known me, and she'd just found out that I had mental health problems that were not going away anytime soon. If she decided she'd rather not get involved any deeper than she already had, I would completely understand.

"The only way to find out is to ask her," Henry pointed out, taking a line from my own book. No point in wondering when a simple question could provide the answer.

So, I made the arrangements for tonight, with the helicopter and the fancy meal, hoping to find a moment to put those feelings into words. It would have been perfect, if the stupid weight limit rule for the helicopter hadn't thrown a wrench in the works. Others might have accepted defeat, but that had never been my style.

As soon as I knew Henry and Kimber couldn't see me anymore from the helipad, I broke into a run, pulling my phone from my pocket. "I need a motorcycle waiting for me at Lonsdale Quay," I told the concierge service that I used for all my unusual requests. They were the same service who had hooked me up with my personal shopper, and for a price, they would do almost anything I asked. "I'm taking the Sea Bus now and I need to be at the Grouse Mountain Skyride as soon as possible."

I ran onto the boat at Waterfront station with minutes to spare before departure, keeping my eyes fixed to the window to watch for the helicopter taking off. They would have to do a safety briefing before take-off, so that should give me a little extra time. We were almost pulling into the dock at North Vancouver before I saw them lift up into the air.

I still had a chance of making it. They were going to do a quick sightseeing tour around the North Shore mountains before landing on Grouse, so as soon as we docked, I raced off the boat and onto the waiting motorcycle taxi. I'd asked for the bike so that we could weave in and out of any stalled traffic, and I promised the driver a bonus if he got me to the mountain in time for the next departure of the gondola.

Once again, I ran onto the waiting transportation just moments before it departed. The ride up to the mountaintop took twelve minutes, and my fingers drummed impatiently against the rail of the gondola the whole time. The stunning view usually made the ride go quickly, but today, it all passed in a blur. All I cared about was getting to the top, and just as we were approaching the landing platform, the helicopter came in to land.

As soon as the Skyride door opened, I bolted for the restaurant, running at an all-out sprint. When I got to the door, I could see Henry and Kimber looking out over the city at the lookout point, and I managed to sneak in without them seeing me. The hostess showed me to the table and I managed to wipe the perspiration from my forehead and pick up my glass of wine, leaning back with it just as Kimber and Henry showed up. Outwardly, it looked as though I'd been waiting there for ages, even though my heart still raced violently within my chest.

All the effort proved worth it just to see the looks of surprise on their faces, the disbelief that I had managed to beat them there, and it helped to ease over the earlier awkwardness of the evening. Kimber showed me the photos she'd taken, and as we ate and drank, any disappointment from before seemed to be forgotten on all sides.

And now, I had shared my idea with Kimber about my new business venture, and Henry had told her that we loved her, and we were both eagerly awaiting her reply.

"You love me?" she echoed, looking between the two of us in utter amazement, and my chest tightened a little. Why should that be such a surprise to her? I thought we had been doing a pretty good job of showing her, even if we hadn't said the words, but it seems Henry had been right. She really didn't know.

"Of course we do," Henry quickly replied. "Kimber, I had feelings for you even before all of this started, though I did my best to hide them, even from myself. And Nick, well, he..."

He would have answered for me, but I cut him off. In this case, I needed to say the words myself, even if they weren't perfect. "Nick doesn't always do the best job of sharing his feelings," I finished for him. "But what I feel for you, for the three of us together, it's more than friendship and it's more than lust. I guess we have to call it love."

"I know it's fast," Henry added when Kimber still didn't say anything. "And we don't want to put you on the spot if you're not sure yet, but it's important to me that you know. I don't want you to think any of this is just some passing fancy that we're going to move on from in a week or two. Asking you to move in with us, the idea of Nick starting this business, we're serious about all of it. We're sure about it because of how we feel."

She still remained silent, and my stomach started to sink while Henry's lips tightened. Maybe this really had been too soon. Maybe she thought we were both out of our minds, not just me.

"I've never been in love before," she answered finally, looking hesitantly from Henry to me and back again. "But I've also never felt the way I do with the two of you before. It's what I imagined love would be like, but even better."

"Better how?" I asked curiously.

"Better because it's both of you. Because you love each other too, and that just makes it even more complete somehow."

I knew exactly what she meant, and from his smile, it seemed Henry did too. Seeing Henry and Kimber together made me happy in a way I never anticipated. It didn't detract from my own happiness in any way; it only enhanced it.

"I love you, Henry," she said, taking his hand and smiling at him with so much affection, he couldn't possibly doubt the truth of what she said. When she reached out for me with her other hand, I quickly took it, squeezing it firmly. "And I love you, Nick. And I don't have a clue how this is going to work in the real world, but right now, I really don't care. I want to move in with you, and I want to start a TV production company, and I want to do it all. If we're crazy, then we'll all be crazy together."

I couldn't have put it any better myself, and as I took Henry's hand in my other one, completing the circle, I had never felt as much at peace as I did right now.

"In that case, I think it's time to get off this mountain and back home where we belong."

~Kimber~

Nick's suggestion that we head home immediately set my body on fire once again. It couldn't be clearer what he meant: he wanted the three of us in bed together, and right now, I wanted that too, more than anything.

They loved me. They were actually in love with me, both of them, and of course I loved them too. I'd be fooling myself if I pretended otherwise. I loved them separately and I loved them even more together. Nothing would ever make me as happy as hearing those words from them, so even if Nick's grandiose ideas fell flat and I missed my chance at a career on the screen by turning down the opportunity currently in front of me, I really didn't care.

Other people sat at home and watched great love stories on TV. I had the chance to live one, with two men who *loved* me, and I wouldn't pass that up for anything.

I ducked out to the washroom while Nick settled the bill, and as I headed back to the table, the woman who'd been serving us pulled me aside.

"I never do this," she assured me. "But those guys you're with are both amazing. Are they single?"

The question almost made me laugh. If I looked more like her, thin and confident that any man would find her attractive, she would have never asked me something like that. She must have looked at me and decided neither of the men with me could possibly be interested in me, and that explained why she felt comfortable enough to ask that kind of question. She probably didn't even realize the assumptions behind her question, assumptions that were ingrained throughout society in the way people viewed someone who looked like me.

"Actually, I'm in a relationship with them," I told her sweetly, giving her my best fake smile.

"Oh." The look of surprise on her face confirmed my suspicions: she hadn't expected that at all. "Which one?"

"Both."

Her mouth dropped open as I breezed past, trying not to grin. Henry and Nick were both getting to their feet, unaware of the conversation that had just taken place, but Henry put his arm around me as we moved towards the door, and Nick held my other hand, reinforcing what I'd just said, and when I threw one last look back over my shoulder on the way out, I could see her whispering furiously with one of the other waitresses, both of them glancing over in our direction.

That felt way too good.

Nick had already decided we would all go home together via the Skyride, and when we got to the bottom of the hill, we found a limousine waiting.

"Seriously?" Henry groaned, rolling his eyes.

"You're the one who suggested it," Nick reminded him, giving me a wink. "After you, Kimber."

It only took a matter of seconds in the back of the car before we were all kissing and touching each other, our mutual desire growing stronger by the second, so that by the time we were dropped off back at the apartment downtown, I was practically dripping in anticipation. I had never wanted them as badly as I did right now, and considering how much I wanted them most of the time, I could hardly stand the wait.

We didn't even make it to the bedroom. As soon as we were through the front door, they pressed me between them. Nick's hands were on my hips, his hard cock grinding against me from behind as he kissed Henry over my shoulder. Henry's fingers ran through my hair as I rubbed mine down the front of his pants, feeling his erection just as strong and hard as Nick's behind me.

"I want to be inside you," Nick murmured into my ear. "I want us both to be."

My thighs clenched tight together as the steady pulsing between my legs grew even stronger. "I thought... I thought we needed to work up to that," I managed to stutter. I wanted to, I'd already made that clear, but I could still remember how much it hurt the last time I tried anal penetration. Nick's finger had been alright the other day, but having either of their much larger cocks in there would be very different.

"I'm not talking about your ass," Nick replied, grabbing onto it now firmly to illustrate his point. "We can start with something else."

Though his meaning eluded me, I trusted him enough to find out what he had in mind as he stepped away from me and whispered something to Henry. They both began shedding their clothes, and I hurried to keep up until all three of us were standing there naked, just inside the entranceway.

"The living room should work," Nick instructed, taking my hand and leading me the short distance down the hall. Once there, he let go of me again, and to my surprise, they both laid down on the couch, on their backs, facing in opposite directions. Their legs went over and under each other so that their groins were right up against each other, and the sight of those two impressive cocks side-by-side, different from each other but equally enticing, made my mouth water.

I still had some confusion about exactly what Nick had in mind, but I *did* know what I wanted to do right now, so I immediately went over and dropped to my knees beside the couch and took them each in one of my hands. The contact made them both groan, and when I rubbed their cocks against each other, the groan grew even louder.

"Fuck, that's sexy," Nick muttered, and Henry quickly nodded in agreement.

Stroking Nick with one hand, I took Henry into my mouth, bobbing up and down on his cock a few times, making it nice and wet, and then I switched places. My hand ran along Henry's cock firmly as I sucked Nick, and when I glanced up at either of them, they were both watching me intently, seeming to enjoy the sight just as much as the sensation of my actions.

Now that they were both wet, I rubbed them harder against each other, their skin sliding smoothly together, alternating with a few strong pumps from me in between.

"That feels so good," Henry groaned, and Nick readily agreed.

"Try taking us both in your mouth," he suggested. "I want to see if you can."

That would be a challenge, but I was up to giving it a try. Bringing their cocks together again, I swirled my tongue around Nick's head and then Henry's, doing a figure-eight shape around the two of them, and then, pressing them firmly together, I wrapped my lips around them both at the same time.

I couldn't take them in very far, but it didn't seem to matter. They both swore in pleasure as I sucked what I could, until Nick sat up, gently pushing me back.

"You're amazing," he said, his eyes full of appreciation. "And if you can do that, you can definitely take us both other ways too."

He pulled me to my feet, his fingers sliding between my legs, and a jolt of surprise and excitement went through me as I finally realized what he intended to do. He wanted me to take *both* of them in my vagina, at the same time? Was that really possible? I felt full enough with just one of them in me, what would it feel like with two?

It looked like I wouldn't have to wonder for long as Nick got up and helped me up onto the couch so that I straddled Henry's firm stomach. Nick kissed me as I sank down onto Henry's stiff cock, which already filled me just fine all on its own. With Nick's hands on my hips for support, I rode up and down Henry's cock a few times, until Nick gently pushed me down until I lay down on Henry, my chest pressed against his.

"How is he going to do this?" I whispered to Henry, who simply chuckled.

"I have no idea, but we'll let him figure that out. You just stay focused on me."

His hands cupped my face, pulling me down to kiss him, and successfully distracting me from whatever Nick planned to do behind us. I could feel Nick's hands running across my ass and down to where Henry's cock was already buried in me, until finally, the tip of Nick's cock began pushing into me, stretching my inner walls wider than they had ever been before.

"Tell me if you need me to stop," Nick commanded from behind me, his voice tightly controlled, just like his body.

I nodded, but I never needed to. It didn't hurt at all. It felt different, and a little strange, and so very full that I could hardly breathe, but not painful at all.

"How does it feel for you?" I managed to ask Henry, who had his eyes closed beneath me.

"It's incredible," he gasped, sounding short of breath. "It's so tight, but in the best way."

The *best* way. We could definitely agree on that.

Nick moved slowly at first, making sure we were all comfortable, but once I had adjusted to the feel of it, he began to go faster. Henry's hips thrust up beneath me too, their cocks moving in alternating directions, in and out, and at different rhythms, as they stroked each other as well as me.

All the emotion that had been building up in me all night, the excitement of them telling me they loved me and of me confessing it back to them in turn, followed by the proof – if I needed it – of just how much they desired me too, it all culminated in this, with both of them inside me at the same time, together.

This was sex, without a doubt, but it felt like more than that too. The three of us were joined together, physically and emotionally, in a way that felt important and permanent. And as we brought each other higher and higher, kissing and touching and fucking each other until we all found our fulfilment, I finally accepted, fully, that we were no longer the two of them and me.

Now, we were truly a set of three.

Chapter Sixteen

~Henry~

Getting ready for my mother's birthday party on Saturday, I couldn't remember ever being so happy. I used to think that happiness involved an absence of things to worry about, but it turned out not to be much of a factor. I still had problems: helping Nick find his new normal would take some time, the company that Nick planned on starting would be a lot of work, and before any of that, I still had to get through today's party with my parents.

But none of that seemed important compared to the two people getting ready next to me. After our amazing evening on Thursday, Nick insisted that Kimber and I both go to work on Friday. When we got home, not only did Nick have an incredible meal waiting, he'd already got the ball rolling on starting his TV production company and eagerly filled us in on all his ideas about what to do next.

When he committed to something, he went all in, and it only made me feel more special that I was one of those things he'd committed to.

After talking over Nick's plans, we all went over to Kimber's apartment to help her pack up more of her things, and then we came home and spent the night in our bedroom, having a long, lazy, lustful evening. I assumed we were eventually going to run out of new things to try, but it didn't seem likely to happen anytime soon, not to mention there were some things that we had already tried that I definitely wanted to do again.

"How are you feeling about today?" Kimber murmured as she came over to check my progress. She must have noticed that I had changed my shirt three times already. What should a person wear to announce to their parents that they have a boyfriend and a girlfriend?

"I'm doing okay," I told her honestly. "I know it doesn't look like it, but I'm actually feeling pretty confident. After watching you two both face your fears this week and be so honest and open about everything, it's my turn to step up too. I don't have any doubts that this is what I want, so there's no reason I should hide it."

Her smile shone with both pride and support. "We'll be right beside you the whole time."

"We will," Nick agreed from the other side of the room. "But don't wear that shirt."

"Nick!" Kimber shot him a disapproving look as I quickly changed again.

An hour later, we arrived at the Chinese Cultural Centre. As soon as we walked in the door, the loud chatter in Mandarin floated out to us, and my nerves finally kicked in. All along, I had been convinced it would be better to do this in front of a crowd, but now, suddenly, doubts came flooding in. Maybe I should have spoken to them in private instead, but now that I'd built up to this day so much, the idea of waiting any longer held no appeal.

"It's going to be fine." Kimber squeezed my hand tightly on one side of me, while Nick clapped his hand on my shoulder.

"If you'd taught me some Mandarin, I could make the announcement myself."

"You were the one who gave up," I shot back, making him smile.

"That's the spirit you need. Just keep that attitude and you'll be fine," he promised me.

He had managed to briefly take my mind off my fear, which he'd clearly been trying to do. Taking a deep breath, I walked into the room with Kimber on one side of me and Nick on the other.

The buzz of conversation in the room immediately quieted as people got a look at us. I could hear some of the whispered comments in Mandarin, wondering who these people were and why I'd brought them there.

"Hello, Henry." My father came over and greeted me in English, clearly out of deference to my guests as he nodded to them politely. "Your mother is excited to see you."

Excited wouldn't be a word I typically used for my mother, but when I looked over to where she stood with her friends, she did indeed have a look of anticipation on her face. I followed my father over to her, with Kimber and Nick still close beside me.

"Happy birthday, Mama." I spoke to her in Mandarin as I gave her a hug.

"Thank you for coming, Ka Yiu," she answered me, using my Chinese name. "I know you are busy."

"Not too busy for you," I assured her. "I have a present for you, but first, Mama, Baba, I'd like to introduce you to some people who are very important to me."

I turned back to Kimber and Nick, who were both smiling politely, though they obviously weren't following along with the conversation. I switched to English now so that they could understand me.

"This is Nick Lewis, and Kimber Page. Nick, Kimber, my parents."

They all exchanged handshakes before my mom looked up at me curiously and asked a question in her accented English. "So, which one are you dating?"

Nick let out a quick laugh before he could stop himself as I stared at my mother in shock. I'd never expected her to ask that kind of question. "What do you mean?"

She switched back to Mandarin to explain herself fully. "Well, Mrs Huang saw you and the girl at her restaurant, looking very cozy, but Dr

Yang's parents told me you were at her office with this man, holding hands. That's why I'm asking, which one are you dating?"

My mouth hung open in surprise as I processed all that. I knew my mother and her friends liked to gossip, but I really hadn't anticipated her being quite so up to date on my activities.

And what surprised me most was that she simply asked the question curiously, with no suggestion that it would bother her to find out that Nick and I were, in fact, dating.

I decided to address that part first to make sure I hadn't missed anything. "You wouldn't mind if Nick and I were together?"

She shook her head firmly. "Not if you are happy. Do you know Mrs Smith at the garden centre? Her son is married to a man and they have two little boys. They make her very happy."

I didn't know anyone from any garden centre, and I began to get the strange feeling that I didn't know my mother very well either. "So, you don't care, as long as I give you grandchildren?"

She and her friends all laughed, making me aware of just how many people were listening to this entire conversation. "That would be a bonus, Ka Yiu, but I just want you to be happy. You are always so serious."

Me? She and my father were the serious ones. I only behaved seriously with them because of how they were.

Or maybe... maybe they just acted that way because they thought I expected it, the same as I kept myself more reserved around them?

Maybe none of us actually knew each other very well at all.

Well, if nothing else, I had a chance now to let them into my life more than I ever had before. With one more deep breath, I spoke the words out loud. "Actually, Mama, I am dating both of them. We are all in love with each other. I know it's a little unusual, but if you want me to be happy, you can be satisfied now. I am very happy, and I hope you can understand that."

She definitely hadn't expected that. Her eyes widened as her friends all exchanged stunned looks too.

And then, to my great shock, she turned to her friends with a wide smile. "Did you hear that? Ka Yiu is so special, he has both men and women in love with him."

Her friends began to chatter excitedly amongst each other, no doubt thrilled to have something new to shock their other friends with. I suspected this revelation would be a topic of conversation in every corner of Chinatown for some time to come.

Turning back to us, my mom surprised Nick by opening her arms to him, asking for a hug. He hadn't understood any of that conversation, but he happily went along with it, leaning down to embrace her small frame. Next she moved to Kimber, who looked equally bemused but just as happy to return her hug.

"She is a good, strong woman," my mom told me in approval. "She can have many babies for you."

"Mama!" Thankfully, she said that in Mandarin too so I wouldn't have to apologize to Kimber for it. But now that it had been said out loud, I couldn't pretend that I didn't find the idea a little bit appealing too.

I could see my whole future with the two amazing people next to me, and as we joined the rest of the party, eating the amazing food and chatting with all my mother's friends, it seemed more real than ever before.

My days of hiding were over. My secrets had all been revealed, and though not every day would go as well as this one had, moments like these would make the harder ones worthwhile.

~Nick~

The mood on the walk back to our condo felt joyous; no other word did it justice. Henry had never expected that reaction from his parents. His mother not only embraced his bisexuality, but our whole relationship. His father seemed a little more reserved, but he shook my hand and Kimber's too, and we were all invited to have dinner with them the next Monday night, on Henry's usual day. Now, it would be a true family dinner.

Sometimes, things blew up in your face, and sometimes, they went better than you could dare to hope.

In a way, that explained what happened with this whole relationship. When I suggested inviting a woman into our bedroom, I really hadn't expected it to be more than a night or two of passion. What we got in Kimber, and in the new dynamic that we three had together, surpassed even my wildest imaginings.

My good mood carried over once we got home, so I decided to call my parents and share the news about my relationship status and my career change. It felt like a good day for getting things out in the open. Putting the phone on speaker so that Henry and Kimber could hear the whole thing, I called my father first, and then my mom. I expected no real reaction from them to either piece of news, and in that, they didn't disappoint. My father simply advised me to protect my own assets so that neither Henry nor Kimber had any claim on them, and my mother made a backhanded comment about how I never could make up my mind about anything.

"At least when you were gay, you'd made some kind of decision," she sniffed. "Now you're backtracking on that too."

Henry's nostrils flared when I hung up, his blood boiling on my behalf, but I shrugged it off. "She's projecting her own insecurities onto me. It's how she's always been. I don't need her approval, I simply wanted to tell them, and now I have."

Though Henry still looked unhappy, he did his best to move on. "Are you going to tell your parents too?" he asked Kimber.

She bit her lip nervously as she thought it over. "I guess I'm going to have to eventually. Maybe it's better to just get it over with."

With both of us encouraging her, she placed the call on my phone, still on speaker so we were all part of it.

When she told her parents she had some big news, they immediately jumped to the wrong conclusion.

"I'm sorry it didn't work out for you, but it's better that you make this choice now while you're still young enough to start something else," her dad said, as Henry and I exchanged confused glances. What the hell did that mean?

"Have you already booked your flight?" her mom asked.

Kimber rolled her eyes so hard, she nearly fell off the couch. "I'm not moving home. Did it ever occur to you I might be calling with good news? Maybe I got a big part."

A slightly too-long pause made it clear they never considered that. "Did you get a big part?" her mom finally asked.

"Well, no," Kimber admitted. "I am up for one, but that's not why I'm calling anyway. I wanted to tell you that I'm in love."

"Oh." Her mom sounded even more surprised now than when she thought Kimber might have an acting job. "And he, uh, he feels the same way?"

Seriously? Until now, I couldn't quite understand how Kimber didn't fully appreciate her own amazingness, but after only a minute speaking with her parents, the more surprising thing was that she had any self-confidence at all.

"He does," Kimber answered firmly, her parent's disbelief seeming to give her more confidence rather than less. "And so does the other one."

"What?" This time her father's confusion made sense, and made me smile too.

"I'm in love with two different men," Kimber explained, smiling over at us as she spoke. "And they're in love with each other too. I'm moving in with them, and I'm really happy about it. They're amazing people. I think you'll really like them."

The silence that followed this pronouncement lasted a lot longer. "Is this some kind of joke?" her dad finally asked. "It's not funny, Kimber."

"It's *not* funny," she agreed. "And it's not a joke. I know it's unusual, but it's for real, and I couldn't be happier. I love them both and they love me too. We're all in this relationship together."

"You can't honestly think that's okay." Her mother stated it firmly, like a fact. "I know morals are looser out there, but it's wrong, Kimber. These men are obviously preying on a naive girl like you, and even if it's flattering, it's still wrong."

Henry reached out a hand to calm me, knowing my breaking point wasn't far away, but I tried my best to control my temper and let Kimber handle this. "It's just love, Mom. How can love be wrong? If you knew them, you wouldn't think that."

"It sure as hell is wrong," her father replied angrily. "The law says it's wrong. You can only marry one person, for a good reason."

"Which is what?" Kimber shot back. "Laws can be wrong too. That's why they're able to be changed. And no, I can't marry them, but I don't need to. I know that they love me anyway."

"What about a family?" her mother added, not seeming at all convinced by Kimber's explanation. "Don't you want to have a normal life?"

I couldn't listen to another word. "Normal is overrated," I blurted out, and Kimber looked over at me in surprise. I raised my eyebrows at her, asking her silently if she wanted me to back off, but she only smiled at me instead, giving me her approval. "I love your daughter and so does my boyfriend, and we're going to give her a life that's a hell of a lot better than normal. Maybe there won't be a piece of paper that says she's ours, but in every way that counts, she will be. We'll love and support her, and hopefully we can have a family all together. I'd love for her to have my children or my boyfriend's. It wouldn't matter. They'll be loved as much as any children, and even more, since they'll have three parents that love them rather than just two."

Another stunned silence stretched out on the other end, followed by the unmistakable sound of the phone disconnecting.

They hung up on us.

Henry immediately went to put his arms around Kimber, but she didn't look upset. Instead, her eyes were shining over at me as she leaned into Henry's embrace. "Do you really mean that, Nick? You want us to have a family together?"

"Of course." I may not have said the words out loud before, but I thought my actions made it clear. "I want it all with you two. We can't be legally married, but we could have a hell of a party anyway. Anyone who's cool enough to appreciate it can come along, and anyone who's not, well, it's their loss."

I was done living my life for anyone else. Leaving my job had given me a new freedom, and now, I wanted to embrace all that life had to offer, the good and the bad, the easy and the hard.

Henry kissed Kimber gently as he agreed with me. "I want that too, Kimber. And not just so that my mother can have her grandchildren to show off."

That made us all laugh, but I couldn't help asking a rather obvious question. "And she won't care if they're technically my children rather than yours?"

"How would she know?" Kimber asked innocently, and Henry and I exchanged amused glances until she figured it out a moment later. "Oh, right. The whole Chinese thing."

That set us all laughing again as Henry and I started teasing each other over which of us would manage to knock Kimber up first once we were ready to start trying.

"Maybe we need to get some practice in, just in case," I suggested, giving Kimber a wink. "I think it's my turn."

"How is it your turn?" Henry protested as we moved to the bedroom, the air between us growing more heated by the second with the excitement of the possibilities that awaited us there.

"My turn to be in the middle," I clarified. "That's something we haven't done yet."

They couldn't argue with me on that, and as soon as we were all naked, I set the scene, as usual.

"Henry, on the bed, on your back."

He quickly complied, grabbing the lube and rubbing it over his long, hard cock. Just the sight of it filled me with anticipation as I climbed up on him in reverse, lowering myself down until I sat directly on top of him, his cock firmly buried in my ass.

"Suck me first," I instructed Kimber, who raised her eyebrows at me, and I grudgingly added an extra word. "Please."

"So you do know how to say that word," she teased me as she climbed onto the bed too, on her hands and knees beside me.

As she took my throbbing cock into her mouth, Henry's hands gripped my hips, lifting me up enough that he could thrust up into me. That incredible feeling of fullness, at the same time that Kimber sucked and stroked me, topped almost anything I'd ever felt before. Her hand went down to my balls, and then lower to Henry's too, alternating between the two as her head continued to bob, taking me deeper and deeper down her throat.

"Shit," I groaned after not much more than a couple of minutes of that. "That's too good, and I don't want to come in your mouth. Get on top of me instead."

Kimber looked at the configuration in front of her a little nervously. "Are you sure? Henry's going to get squished on the bottom."

Henry and I both laughed. "How many times do I have to tell you?" I asked her. "You can't hurt us, Kimber. We're strong enough to take anything that comes our way."

I meant more than just sex, and from the smile in her eyes, I knew she knew it too.

Holding my hands, she got to her feet and straddled me, sinking down onto my cock from above just as Henry was buried in me from below.

"Fuck, yes."

Now I knew what perfection felt like. Complete and utter perfection.

She leaned on me, my hands helping to support her as I thrust up into her, all while Henry thrust into me. Deeper and faster, the boundaries between our bodies becoming more blurred by the second, we kept going until we were all satisfied and exhausted, collapsing together onto the bed, naked and sweaty and fully sated.

Sex had never been better. My *life* had never been better.

If this was wrong, who would ever want to be right?

Epilogue

Two years later

~Kimber~

"That's a wrap, everyone! Great work!"

Cheers and applause met the assistant director's announcement, and I grinned as Dale pulled the white, oval mask off his face and gave me a warm hug. We'd just finished shooting the last scene of the first season of our new drama, and not a moment too soon. The costumes were already starting to get very tight on me.

"This is going to be a hit, Kimber," Dale promised, keeping his arm around me as he turned to face our two executive producers who were making their way over to us. "Everyone's going to want a piece of her soon, guys. I hope you're ready to share."

"We do enough sharing already," Nick retorted, giving me a not-at-all-subtle wink. "They can have her on the screen. The rest of the time, she's ours."

"That scene looked amazing," Henry told us enthusiastically. "Even though I've seen the script for season two, I still held my breath when Orra asked Cassiel for his help."

"Let's hope everyone else appreciates that cliffhanger too," I said with a laugh. "Now, if you'll all excuse me for a second, I really need to pee."

The worst thing about being seven months pregnant was the extra weight on my bladder. It felt like I had to run to the washroom between every take.

"Do you need me to come with you?" Henry had become so protective of me lately, he hated to let me out of his sight.

"To the bathroom? I think I can manage," I teased him. "I'll be right back."

Reluctantly, he stayed put as Dale and Nick continued to talk over the upcoming promotional schedule. Although filming had finished now, a lot of work remained to be done before the show premiered. Nick had sold the rights to one of the big streaming services, and it would be the first real money-maker for his production company.

Having Dale on board had definitely helped to sell the show. Two years ago, when I got offered the part on the show I'd auditioned for, I did as he suggested and reviewed the contract carefully with Henry, my personal lawyer. As Dale had warned, that ridiculous morality clause would almost certainly cause me problems, and I quickly decided I didn't want to work for anyone who thought the love that Henry, Nick and I shared was something shameful. I turned down the role, to my agent's shock, and I set about finding a new show for Nick to produce instead.

It took a while, but finally I found the perfect show – a fantasy story based on a little-known book series. The books never specifically mentioned the female character's size, so I got in touch with the author to ask if she'd mind a fuller-figured woman playing the lead, and she had no problem with it. Nick was entirely on board, of course, and quickly secured the rights. And when I approached Dale to ask if he would be interested in playing the male lead, with no 'morality clause' in sight, he jumped at the chance, even though he had to keep his face hidden beneath the character's mask for most of the show. He said he enjoyed the opportunity to act with everyone judging him solely on his appearance.

With our script and main cast set, we still had to hire the rest of the creative team, audition actors for all the other roles, get the studio space and create the costumes and sets, all before we could even begin shooting. The learning curve had been steep, but Nick and Henry were meticulous, making sure they had the best people on board and trusting them to do their jobs properly. Nick even hired his former assistant, Erin, to help keep him organized, and she had already been a lifesaver multiple times.

We also hired Rocco's business to provide all the on-set catering. His new boyfriend had been looking for a career change and loved to cook, so between the two of them, they had food, baking and coffee covered. They still ran his shop but they were branching out into other ventures too and it gave me great joy to be able to recommend them to other people in the industry.

They were also getting married this summer, where I'd be the maid of honour. I couldn't wait.

With all the work that had gone into it, I truly hoped the show would be a success, but even if it flopped, it wouldn't be the end of the world. We had all enjoyed the process and the time spent working together, and everything about the business would be temporarily moved to the back burner once the baby arrived anyway.

Pretending to be someone else still brought me a lot of joy, but these days, none of it compared to my real life.

~Henry~

Two months later

Nick and I were working in our home office, reviewing contracts for a new show we'd just optioned, when Kimber appeared in the doorway.

"Okay guys, don't freak out..."

She didn't need to say another word. "Is it time?" I asked eagerly, jumping to my feet. She had just gone to have a rest a few minutes ago, promising us she felt fine, but at five days overdue, we were all on edge.

"The wet spot I just left on the bed would suggest yes," she told us sheepishly. "We'll need to get the comforter dry-cleaned."

Neither of us could care less about that right now. I grabbed Nick's hand anxiously as a rush of adrenaline kicked in.

"It's go-time," he said, nodding at me firmly. "We've got this."

Kimber rolled her eyes at us both. "*You've* got this? How about me?"

"We've got you too," Nick assured her. "Come on, let's go."

We made it to St Paul's Hospital in no time at all, where we were quickly ushered into a delivery suite. We'd been here for a tour a couple of weeks earlier, so things were at least a little familiar, but everything also felt completely new right now. My heart raced with nerves and excitement, and I didn't even have to do anything.

We were still fussing over getting Kimber settled in her bed when the labour and delivery nurse came in and introduced herself as Aubrey. "Which of you is the father?" she asked with a warm smile.

Nick and I exchanged glances. "Both of us," we replied in unison.

"Oh, congratulations," she exclaimed, still smiling as she turned to Kimber. "So you're the surrogate?"

Kimber shook her head. "No, it's my baby too. We're all in this together."

Aubrey's eyes widened, but her smile never faltered. "Well, sounds like this is a pretty lucky baby, then. Let's get ready to meet him or her, okay?"

Nick sat on Kimber's right side while I took her left just as my phone buzzed with a text from my mom, checking for updates.

I'll let you know when I have news, I quickly replied. *Until then, I'm turning my phone off.*

I wouldn't get any peace otherwise. She had been messaging me almost hourly since Kimber's due date passed. The constant interruptions almost made me miss the days when I only talked to my parents once a week, but not quite. Now, they were a huge part of our lives, fully adopting both Nick and Kimber into our family and into their local community too. The three of us were fixtures at events in Chinatown, and if anyone ever dared to make a snide comment about our relationship, my mom would shut them down in an instant.

"I only have one child, but I have a daughter-in-law and a son-in-law to help look after me when I get old," she would say. "What do you have?"

Nick's parents were as absent as always, and Kimber's family still struggled to come to terms with the whole situation. Her sister had been out to visit us, but I still hadn't met Kimber's parents. It was a shame, but as Nick pointed out, the loss was theirs. We had each other, and I would take that end of the deal any day.

As Kimber's contractions started to get stronger, excitement and guilt warred inside me. I couldn't wait to meet our baby, but I also felt bad that Kimber had to go through this pain on her own when we had all participated in the much more fun first step of this process.

"How bad is it?" I asked after Nick and I helped her to breathe through another contraction.

"Compared to when you guys made me do the Grouse Grind?" she asked with a grimace. "This is nothing."

Nick and I grinned at each other over her head. The pain hadn't dampened her sense of humour, and the memory she brought up made us both smile. Nick had sworn to Kimber that climbing Grouse Mountain on foot wouldn't be that much worse than going up it in the helicopter. He promised she could definitely handle it.

She told him afterwards, as she panted her way to the last of the 2,830 steps, that he'd never lied to her before then.

Before long, things really started to pick up steam and the doctor came in. She must have been briefed by the nurse because there were no questions about why the two of us were there, she just got right to the business of delivering the baby. When the first cries pierced the air, my heart had never felt so full.

"Congratulations," the nurse said, giving us all a big smile as she placed the baby on Kimber's chest. "And say hello to your daughter."

~Nick~

There were a few times in my life when it felt like time just stopped. Everything around me faded into the background, my vision narrowing onto that moment as it etched itself into my heart and memory.

The day I met Henry in Stanley Park immediately sprang to mind. I saw the seals first, playing in the harbour, and stopped to take a look. A moment later, I saw the gorgeous man standing there looking at them too, a look of innocent delight on his face, and I knew right then that I'd found something special.

It happened again when Kimber came out of our bathroom wearing the lingerie I'd bought her, that first week we were getting to know each other. Maybe she wasn't everyone's stereotypical idea of beautiful, but at that moment, I had never seen anything as sexy as her accepting just how much Henry and I both wanted her and giving herself over to us completely.

And now, I had to add the moment that the little bundle of limbs on Kimber's chest looked up at me, her eyes slightly unfocused. Instantly, I knew that as good as my life had been until now, it had just gotten immeasurably better.

I still had good days and bad days, but the medication I took helped me to even them out a bit more. Now, when the bad days came, I didn't hide. I let Henry and Kimber know and they helped me through it. Even when I couldn't keep control and lashed out sometimes, they never took it personally or made me feel bad about it afterwards. Managing my illness would remain a work in progress, one that we were all in together, just like we were now in our new little family.

The dark hair on our daughter's head looked like Henry's, but her eyes were blue, like mine and like Kimber's. Was she biologically my daughter? At this moment, I couldn't tell, and I truly didn't care. She was mine and Henry's and Kimber's. She wouldn't exist without all three of us, and the three of us would give her everything she could ever need. We would never be distant like my parents, judgemental like Kimber's parents, or closed off like Henry's parents had been for so long.

Whatever life held for the little girl in front of us, we would be there for her the whole way.

Our set of three was now a pack of four, and that influenced the name we'd chosen for our new addition if we had a girl: the Roman numerals for the number four, IV.

Or Ivy, the spelling Kimber wanted to go with despite my best tongue-in-cheek efforts to convince her otherwise.

She would be Ivy Lewis-Zhang in full, the surname we'd all decided to adopt. Kimber would be credited that way when her new series debuted in the fall, and I couldn't wait for the whole world to fall in love with her just as Henry and I had. We had no plans to hide our relationship from anyone. Some people wouldn't like it, but maybe it would help to normalize it for the people out there who were lucky enough to find the kind of love we had, but weren't able to live as openly as we did.

But for just this moment, as we all embraced around our beautiful new baby girl, I didn't mind keeping it between us for just a little while longer.

The rest of the world could wait.

~~THE END~~

More From the Author

Standalones
Leading Lady
A Set of Three
Charity Case
Hired Lover

Contemporary Romance – New Adult/Clean
It Figures duet
It Figures
Figuring It Out

Historical Romance – 18+
Lady in Waiting Series
Lady in Waiting
King in Training
Princess in Hiding

Paranormal Romance – 18+

Standalone
Out of My Depth

Cold Lake Pack Series
The Curse and the Prophecy
The Spell and the Legacy
The Dream and the Destiny

Mismatched Mates Series
Mismatched Mates
Misguided Motives
Mistaken Meanings

Serena's Story
The Alpha's Second Chance
The Returned Mate
The Vampire's Consort

Sacrifice Series
Blood Donor
Life Giver

Paranormal Romance – New Adult/Clean
The Alpha's Prey

Keep in Touch

Daily updates from my works-in-progress, bonus chapters and more can be found on my Ream account, Chilli & Chocolate, along with Emma Lee-Johnson:
https://reamstories.com/chilliandchocolate

You can find and follow me on Facebook at:
facebook.com/melodytyden

Join the Facebook group Melody's Romance Corner for fun games, interaction with the author and exclusive news and excerpts.

You can also sign up to my newsletter at www.melodytyden.com for all the latest news.